Praise for Snow Falling

"Jane Villanueva's words jump off the page and make it impossible to put the book down."

—**AMANDA ELAINE**, author of *Love Under the Bridge*
(Winner of the 2007 Romance Book of the Year) and
The Christmas Cookie: Sprinkled with Love

"From the moment I met her, I knew Jane would be a success. Her captivating, melodic, emotional writing can make even the most cynical person believe in romance."

—**MARLENE DONALDSON**, author of *ReVulva: Locked and Loaded*

"Prepare to be swept off your feet by this beautiful story about love, heartbreak, betrayal, and the power of passion. Villanueva's debut is a true standout."

—**DEIRDRE SHAW**, author of *Love or Something Like It*

Snow Falling

Jane Gloriana Villanueva

Inspired by the Following Episodes of
the Series *JANE THE VIRGIN*®

"Chapter One," Pilot
Teleplay by *Jennie Snyder Urman*

"Chapter Fifty-Seven," Episode 313
Written by *Madeline Hendricks*

Lorden + Gregor Publishing
Adams Media
New York London Toronto Sydney New Delhi

Adams Media

An Imprint of Simon & Schuster, Inc.

57 Littlefield Street

Avon, Massachusetts 02322

First Adams Media trade paperback edition November 2017.

ADAMS MEDIA and colophon are trademarks of Simon and Schuster.

For information about special discounts for bulk purchases, please contact Simon & Schuster Special Sales at 1-866-506-1949 or business@simonandschuster.com.

The Simon & Schuster Speakers Bureau can bring authors to your live event. For more information or to book an event contact the Simon & Schuster Speakers Bureau at 1-866-248-3049 or visit our website at www.simonspeakers.com.

Interior design by Colleen Cunningham

Manufactured in the United States of America

10 9 8 7 6 5 4 3 2 1

Library of Congress Cataloging-in-Publication Data has been applied for.

ISBN 978-1-5072-0662-1
ISBN 978-1-5072-0663-8 (ebook)

———— TO ————

MICHAEL CORDERO, JR.

You live in my heart forever

Prologue

Knowing what would happen—the heartbreak, the tears, the love, the hope, the betrayal, the heartbreak (yes, it was always the heartbreak)—would she do it over? And she knew the answer was yes because of how it all ended.

But I'm getting ahead of myself…

On the night that Josephine Galena Valencia turned twenty-one years old, a miracle happened.

MIAMI, 1900

The rasp of Josephine's pencil on the page of the pristine journal her mother had gifted her that very day was loud in the still of a sultry Miami night.

Pictures played across her mind as she tried valiantly to capture the right words to describe them. She leaned close to the oil lantern beside her, pouring her imagination out onto the pages, wanting to immortalize the images quickly before they flickered out and faded away. Excitement welled up within Josephine, and the ideas percolated until they were bubbling so quickly, they were like water ready to boil. As the story spilled over onto the page, she finally felt like she was moving one step closer to her dream of becoming a writer. That hope had lingered in her heart and the idea had clung in the back of her mind ever since her *abuela* had read that first fairy tale to her as a child.

Today she had turned twenty-one years old, and despite the happy celebration she'd shared with her mother and *abuela* and her friends from the hotel where she worked, Josephine couldn't help but feel that the day had been incomplete. Although her *abuela* and mother always warned Josephine that she let her imagination (and her temper) get away from her too often, she couldn't shake the idea that something had been missing. Something that would have made the day just absolutely perfect. Maybe the father she'd never known. Or even her long-gone *abuelo. Something…something magical,* she thought as she scratched out another word on the rough paper.

There was only dim light on the veranda from the lantern she had set on the table beside the rocking chair as she eagerly poured out the story from her heart. With each completed page, pride and satisfaction fed the determination growing inside her to reach for her dreams.

Josephine was so engrossed in her task that it took her a moment to notice the harsh scrape of a footstep on the wooden porch and the shadow now looming over her.

Fear suddenly gripped her as she noticed the large man's shoe barely a foot away from the chair where she was huddled. Heart beating at a frantic pace, she mustered the courage to look up at the face of the man towering above her.

Dark blond wisps of hair escaped the confines of a straw boater that cast shadows on his features until she raised the lantern to chase away the darkness. Smiling blue eyes as bright as a summer sky held no malice, only concern. A sharp, straight nose led to full lips and a strong jawline with a hint of light evening stubble.

"It's a little late to be outside, miss. There have been some problems in town lately, and I've been sent round to make sure everything is secure," he said and drew away the lapel of his mud-brown suit to reveal the shiny silver badge on his chest.

Pinkerton National Detective Agency was engraved on the shield along with a small star. A little quiver of fear returned to her heart. Josephine had heard stories—not all positive—about the Pinkertons and how they'd busted unions in other cities. The owner of the Regal Sol had supposedly hired them to protect the hotel and the nearby cottages where many of the employees lived, but who knew what his real motives had been.

"It's my birthday," she stammered, suddenly self-conscious since she was clad only in her nightshirt and robe. She drew the lapels of the robe together and hugged the journal to her chest. Her *abuela* would never approve of Josephine being so immodestly clothed in front of a gentleman.

The young man jammed his hands in his pockets and rocked back on his heels as he examined her, and she hoped he couldn't see that she was clearly a little flustered by his presence. Nervously she pulled back long tendrils of dark, curly hair that had slipped loose of the Gibson girl bun at the top of her head. At his prolonged perusal, heat spread up her neck and to her cheeks, and Josephine prayed she was not blushing, although she knew she was.

"Happy birthday, Miss…"

He paused, prompting her, and she hesitantly replied, "Josephine." After a pregnant pause, she shifted the journal to one hand and stuck out the other as she stood. "Josephine Galena Valencia. I'm one of the—"

"Concierges at the hotel. Yes, I noticed you there before," he said, and she lost some of her embarrassment as his face now pinkened with his revelation. Quickly, he took her hand and said, "I work there too."

When his fingers enclosed hers, Josephine felt a small frisson of heat, and when she looked down, sparks of light seemed to be dancing along their intermingled skin. Her pulse quickened. Suddenly, she wanted to know more about this endearingly awkward lawman. "And your name, sir, is…"

"Martin. Cadden. Detective Cadden," he said and then looked away, gesturing with his head in the direction of the darkness on the street. "As I said before, we've had some issues in town. You need to be careful out here, a beautiful girl like you."

He shut his eyes tight and grimaced, but then a lopsided grin spread across his features and the joy of it spread to a place inside her. He gestured to the journal held tight against her breasts. "What were you doing out here all alone in the dark?"

Hesitant to reveal her secret wish to be a writer, she reached for the copy of the Jane Austen novel she'd also received that day as a gift and said, "Just scribbling in my diary and reading."

He smiled, his genial face alight. "I enjoy a good dime novel now and then."

He might not have known it, but Detective Martin Cadden had uttered exactly the right words. "Oh, I love to read, especially romantic novels like Jane Austen. Have you read her?"

Martin's smile broadened, though he shook his head slightly.

"The nuns at the convent where I go to school said they've never seen anyone before who likes to read as much as I do. I only have a few more correspondence classes to finish, and Sister Elizabeth said she'd help me get a job as a tutor."

Martin looked at her questioningly, almost as if he was deciding something. He took a step closer and sank down on the edge of the table, his eyes fixed on Josephine. "What is it that you love about those stories?"

"That idea that two people are destined to be together," she answered. Their gazes met and held. Tiny flutters, like the beating of a butterfly's wings, resonated within Josephine's chest. Perhaps this was it, the elusive *something* she had been anticipating all day. "That feeling they have when their eyes meet, and they think, *I knew it was you. I just knew.*"

She waited for his censure, but instead Martin smiled once more, took off his boater, and sat down on the rocking chair beside her. "Please, tell me more, Miss Valencia."

And she did, for what might have been hours as they sat and talked comfortably like old friends, trading tales of their favorite stories and some of their hopes for the future. The night grew ever darker until the flame in the lantern suddenly sputtered out entirely, leaving them bathed only in moonlight.

She stared into the handsome detective's bright eyes, her breath held. The moment stretched on, shimmering with potential like the stars in the night sky, until she quietly, and with some disappointment, murmured, "Well, it's getting late, Detective, and I have work in the morning." She could have spent the entire night talking with him, and maybe even more than talking, if she dared.

"Of course. I'd feel better walking you to the door and making sure you're safe," he said, the very model of proper behavior as counter to Josephine's rather improper thoughts, and held out his hand in the direction of the cottage's entrance.

Ahem, we should note at this time that the entrance to the cottage was barely a few feet away, and Josephine could have made the journey quite safely all on her own...but alas, then the miracle would not have happened.

Josephine inclined her head in agreement and took a step, but tripped on one of the loose wooden floorboards of the veranda. Strong arms kept her from falling and drew her close against a lean body and the hard butt of the pistol in the holster he wore beneath his suit.

Heat spread everywhere from that simple touch, and, beneath her nightshirt, her skin tingled. She peered up and met that caring gaze that was looking at her as if she were special. *So special...* But suddenly, a big, fat white flake landed on Martin's shoulder. Then a flurry of flakes drifted down like snow falling as the plaster ceiling above them finally succumbed to the Florida humidity and peeled loose.

Josephine laughed in delight. "I've never seen real snow but I've always thought it was so romantic," she said wistfully.

Tenderly, Martin reached up and brushed a flake from the loosened curl at her temple. "And maybe even magical?" He applied gentle pressure at her waist to urge her upward.

"Maybe even miraculous," she said as she rose on her tiptoes.

Unbeknownst to the young lovers so completely enthralled with each other, the flame in the small oil lantern flickered to glorious life once more, as he covered her lips with his.

And as romantic and magical as snow might be, it couldn't stand a chance against the heat of that kiss on a sultry Miami night. For this was the night that Josephine Galena Valencia's life would change forever.

Chapter One

Two Years Later

Josephine Galena Valencia always did things the right way and in the right order. At the ripe old age of twenty-three Josephine had finalized her master plan, and nothing was going to keep her from accomplishing it: find a job as a tutor, finish a novel, and marry Martin. Or so she thought…

Passing through the Regal Sol Hotel's luxurious lobby, Josephine smiled in satisfaction. The hotel had opened just three years earlier and had quickly become Miami's premiere lodging for the nation's rich and famous. Since she had secured a position as a concierge there, she'd hobnobbed with the likes of the Astors, Andrew Carnegie, various US senators and European royalty, and even the big man of Miami himself, Henry Flagler, the owner of the nearby Royal Palm Hotel and one of the city's founders. That is, if you consider making sure that such luminaries had transportation from the rail station and choice spots for the nightly lounge show as "hobnobbing."

Her long skirt and petticoat swayed around her legs as she pushed through the door into the immense dining room, where nearly two hundred guests were enjoying an extravagant four-course meal. The expensive fragrance of the ladies' perfumes battled with the scents from the floral arrangements scattered along the edges of the space and on the tabletops. The murmur of conversation sounded almost like the susurrus of the nearby Miami River, broken only by the clatter and clank of cutlery against fine porcelain.

Silver centerpieces gleamed on tabletops, but paled in comparison to the glint of gold and sparkle of jewels draped on ears and necks, or gracing the wrists of the hotel patrons. Perfectly groomed ladies swathed in rich silks and brocades sat alongside dashing gentlemen in elegant evening dress.

Such amazing opulence, Josephine thought as she sashayed through the dining room, smiling at the various patrons and stopping to chat with one couple for whom she'd arranged a romantic yacht cruise along the Miami River. Before long her cheeks ached from the smile she kept firmly in place, and even with the breeze sweeping in from the open-air entrances around the room, a line of sweat trickled down her neck and beneath the high collar of her prim, white cotton shirt.

Josephine was counting the minutes until the end of dessert, when the guests would hurry out to the hotel's lounge for the nightly entertainment. Once the dining service ended, she could slip away to spend some precious time with Martin before having to turn in for the night.

Martin. Even after two years of courting, her heart sped up a little at the thought of seeing him. Of maybe sneaking away with him to…

But she was getting ahead of herself again, which sometimes happened when she thought of Martin.

As a passing waiter placed the last dish of tutti-frutti ice cream in front of Mrs. Smith, of the Boston Smiths, Josephine hurried outside to one of the back paths to avoid the crush of guests that would shortly be heading to the rotunda that doubled as a lounge at night.

And there he was. Martin was waiting for her, leaning against a column at the edge of the passage. Unlike the guests dining in their evening wear, Martin still wore his daytime charcoal-gray sack suit over a pressed white shirt. Despite the slightly boxy cut of the suit, the single-breasted vest beneath hugged the lean lines of his body.

His gaze locked with hers for only a second until, with a gentlemanly dip of his head, he said, "Miss Valencia. So nice to see you. I trust that you are well."

"I am, Detective Cadden. Thank you for asking. And you?" she asked and accepted the arm he gallantly offered.

He darted his gaze around and led her to a darkened spot beneath a poinciana tree just off the path. As he turned to her, crystal blue eyes dancing with humor and happiness, she smiled and leaned into him. Rising up, she whispered playfully into his ear, "Is it time for a proper welcome now, Martin?"

His hard, hot kiss was answer enough as he drew her deeper into the shadows for privacy. As the kiss grew more and more heated, Josephine's head swam and her body ached for his touch. When he reached up and cupped her breast, little sparks heated her skin, but she broke away from him.

"We must stop, Martin. You know I want to wait until we're married," she said and slapped a hand over her mouth as the words slipped free.

"Married?" he repeated and guided her from the intimacy of the dark bower and back onto the path. Placing a hand at the small of her back, he led her in the direction of the cottages, obviously intending to walk her home. They were silent during the short stroll, the impact of that one small word hanging over them until they reached the cottage and entered. Josephine fretted. She had said too much. She thought, as she often had during recent months, that perhaps Martin still needed more time to decide if marriage was in their future.

"*Abuela? Mami?*" she called out just to confirm Alberta and Zara weren't home. Her grandmother had been asked to work an extra shift at the hotel and her mother was performing at a saloon in North Miami.

When it appeared they were alone, Martin tried to draw her close, but she shied away from him again. "Martin, please. You make it so hard to wait, but you know why I must. What we have is so special. I think it's worth waiting for." *And I don't want to get carried away and be left alone like my mother,* she thought, not that she would ever confess that to Martin or anyone else except possibly God. Her *abuela* always said that Josephine could say anything to God and He would understand.

"I think it's worth waiting for too, Josephine. I want it to be special for you," Martin said, his words hesitant. "We have both been so busy with work, and I know you're still hoping to get a position as a tutor—"

"I just have another couple of classes," she said, disheartened as she thought of the correspondence lessons sitting on her desk upstairs.

"It's not an easy thing, but you've accomplished so much in two years. Don't get discouraged," he said, stroking her upswept hair and the loose tendrils trailing down her neck.

"I suppose," she agreed, but that did little to assuage her disappointment that she hadn't accomplished her one real desire: to write a novel. She knew Martin was just being practical, as always, but secretly she wished she could share her real desire with him and have him understand.

He must have seen the shadow that crossed her face, because he took hold of her hand and urged her to face him. "I do want us to be together," he repeated. "Do you doubt that?"

She shook her head. "No, I don't, only…it's been two years, Martin." She blushed, adding shyly, "I had thought that maybe by now we'd be talking about marriage."

He smiled that lopsided grin she'd grown to love so much.

"You know that I love you, don't you?" he said, with a look in his eyes that took Josephine's breath away. The blue, as bright as ever, seemed to shimmer and gleam with a light that warmed her heart and chased away her doubts with its strength.

"I love you too," she said, then watched with stunned surprise as he reached into his pocket and brought out a small box.

"Then it seems like it might finally be the right time to ask—"

She gasped in shock. Josephine had dreamed about this moment so many times before, but she hadn't expected it to happen like this. She felt surprisingly unprepared. "Martin, what are you doing?"

"I'm proposing, my dear girl."

Almost on instinct, she protested, "But our plans… We haven't…" She trailed off, having trouble finding the words, and he held up a hand to stop her.

"It doesn't matter, darling. You will. We will. Together. I don't want to wait any longer to make you mine." He blushed. "And not because I want to do things with you that are inappropriate for an unmarried lady. I want to spend my life with you, Josephine. And raise children with you. And well, yes, do inappropriate things with you." His smile turned slightly devilish and he bent down on one knee, opening the box. "So, Josephine Galena Valencia, will you do me the honor of marrying me?"

Another gasp escaped her lips at the knowledge that it was finally happening. The rest of her life was finally beginning. "Oh yes, Martin, yes! I'd be honored to be your wife." Her hand shook as Martin slipped the simple gold band with a small but brilliantly glittering stone onto her finger. The metal warmed her, and for a second it seemed as if sparks glanced off it, awakening fire in the stone.

Then Martin drew her into his strong arms. He kissed her until she was almost breathless. Her heart raced madly beneath her breast, and behind her closed eyelids, she saw fireworks.

Martin laid his hands on her, tracing the shape of her curves and drawing her ever closer. Josephine hoped that neither her *abuela* nor *mami* would be home anytime soon so she and Martin could celebrate in ways that were inappropriate, but not that inappropriate. At least not yet.

As Martin and Josephine rejoiced, it seemed to Josephine that it was just a matter of time before the other parts of her plan fell into place. But of course, the road of love is never quite so smooth. In fact, for Josephine Galena Valencia, the journey on that road was about to hit quite a number of bumps.

✳

Martin stood with his boss in the Pinkerton office as Mayor Reilly paced before them. The man's agitation was apparent as he stroked his thick moustache and complained about the city's problems with their neighbor to the north.

"There isn't a day that goes by that Doc isn't called to North Miami to patch up someone who's gotten shot or been knifed," the mayor railed and shot a pained look at his marshal as the man fidgeted beside him.

"I'm sorry, Mr. Mayor, but even with an assistant, we're so busy checking licenses, sidewalks, and street lamps, and now you want me to be the fire chief too. There's only so much a man can do," the marshal replied, but stopped his excuses at a steely glare from the mayor.

"Which is why you're here, detectives." The mayor crossed his arms. "We need the Pinkertons to find out who's supplying these North Miami dens of iniquity with their liquor and prostitutes, and we need you to keep that filth from moving downward into our area. Miami prides itself on being a moral and chaste town."

Martin shared a look with his boss, who said, "We'd be delighted to assist you and investigate, sir. Detective Cadden is one of our best, and I have no doubt he can get to the source of the problems."

Mayor Reilly nodded and gestured to his marshal. "We have some information for you on the murders that have occurred in the area lately." Chaste and moral as it may have been thanks to the restrictions one of the city's founders, Mrs. Julia Tuttle, had placed on landholders, in recent months Miami had been the center of a small crime wave. In the nearly six years since Mrs. Tuttle had finally convinced Henry Flagler to expand his railway line to the city, the town seemed as if it had doubled in size. And now that growth showed no signs of stopping, as people came in search of their fortunes in the burgeoning Magic City. Unfortunately, as of late, more and more of those enterprising individuals were being kidnapped and killed. "We believe some of them may be connected to whoever is bringing in the contraband."

The marshal handed Martin a folder containing a stack of grainy photographs as well as the list of names and dates for the deceased. As he peered at the photos and the dates, he could already see a pattern. "It seems like the murders first started while the railways and hotels were being built five or six years ago, and then there's a gap before they begin again. Do you have any thoughts about why that might be?"

The mayor and marshal shared an uneasy glance. With a cough, the mayor said, "You are sharp, Detective Cadden. We suspect it's someone connected to one of the hotels. Maybe someone with a large yacht that can transport liquor into one of the marinas."

A yacht at either the Royal Palm or Regal Sol, the only two hotels with marinas on the river, means the criminals have both money and social connections, Martin thought. "If that's what our investigations reveal, it may be hard to prosecute them," he said.

"We understand. We'll deal with that when you find the person or persons responsible," Mayor Reilly replied.

Martin was happy that the mayor had said "when" and not "if."

"You won't be disappointed, Mayor," Martin said and hoped that were true. But if there really was a criminal enterprise using the Regal Sol as a base of operations, Josephine might unknowingly be in the middle of a possibly dangerous situation. He'd have to be extra careful to make sure she wasn't drawn into the investigation and that nothing he said or did compromised the task he'd been asked to complete.

This was a very big case he'd been entrusted with, and solving the case could help Martin secure his position with the agency and allow him to provide a very comfortable future for himself and Josephine. She wouldn't have to work so hard, and maybe she could finally finish her classes and land a job as a tutor. He smiled at the thought as the men said their goodbyes and he left to return to the Regal Sol.

The diamond glittered in the light from the electric sconce as Josephine held out her hand so her best friend Liana could see the engagement ring.

Liana grasped her hand and gushed, "It's so lovely, Josephine. I'm so happy for you and Martin. He's one of the good ones."

"He is one of the good ones," she repeated as they strolled through the hotel gardens on their way to work. Dozens of guests sat in rocking chairs on the nearby veranda, enjoying the early morning sun and views of Biscayne Bay.

Martin was patient. Kind. Responsible. Gentlemanly. Yes, very gentlemanly and patient (*always* patient, maybe even *too* patient).

"Have you set a date yet?" Liana asked.

"Not yet, but I don't think we want to wait too long." *Especially not another two years,* she thought, because she could not be *that* patient.

At the entrance to the hotel the uniformed bellman opened the door and smiled. "Good morning, Miss Valencia. Miss Duarte," he said and dipped his head in greeting.

"Good morning, Mr. James," Josephine replied.

Liana saucily winked at the handsome young man. "Good morning, Matthew."

"You are so forward, Liana," Josephine said with a shake of her head. Her friend's one hope was that she would meet someone who would take her somewhere far more glamorous than Miami, so she kept her flirting skills honed for that moment.

"Practicing just in case I run into Rake Solvino. Rumor has it he's come back," Liana whispered and scanned the lobby for any sign of the Regal Sol's mysterious owner and wealthy railroad tycoon—not to mention reputed robber baron. It had been years since the man had taken part in extending the railroad down to Miami and built the Regal Sol. If the gossip was true, which it almost never was, both the railroad and hotel were an attempt to launder ill-gotten gains into more respectable businesses.

"Do you even know what he looks like?" Josephine asked.

With a shrug, Liana said, "Francesca saw him arrive. She says he's tall, dark, and handsome. A rake true to his name." She sighed, and Josephine rolled her eyes. She loved her friend dearly, but sometimes she could be entirely too much.

"Hmm. Well, I must be off," she said, hugging her friend and hurrying to the concierge desk to start her shift. But as she arrived, it was obvious that her supervisor was in an agitated state, rare for her normally unflappable boss.

"Is something wrong, Mr. Adams?"

The man dabbed at the sweat on his upper lip with his handkerchief and then mopped away even more perspiration from his brow. "I've just heard that we'll have a very important guest arriving later today: Mr. Deering."

When the name clearly didn't ring a bell with her, he added impatiently, "From International Harvester." That did register; Josephine recognized the name of the well-known manufacturing conglomerate. "Quite a coup that he chose us, but he won't be arriving until very late tonight and I have no one to cover the desk in case he needs anything."

"I can do it," she volunteered. The extra money in her paycheck would be welcome to start some savings for her wedding to Martin.

"You're willing to do an extra shift? I'd do it myself, but I've just worked a double, since Richard failed to show up yesterday afternoon." He tut-tutted disapprovingly.

Josephine took up her spot behind the desk, and as she organized the pamphlets for the guests, she said, "Oh dear. Is he sick?"

"I don't know. He just didn't come in for his shift. Thank you so much for helping out, Josephine. I truly appreciate it." He dashed off, leaving Josephine to man the desk.

Luckily, except for the late arrival of their very important guest, it was a quiet day. She booked a fishing expedition for a lovely gentleman from New York and trips into the Everglades for a number of other guests who wanted to go birding and possibly see some alligators or a panther.

Liana helped her out by bringing her some small sandwiches from the high tea service and covering for her to take a short break. By evening, however, Josephine's stomach was growling. When a buzz began from the few guests in the lobby as a nattily dressed elderly gentleman with a short white beard entered, she gathered that it was none other than their very important person. The hotel manager rushed over to greet him and in short order, Mr. Deering and his family were on their way to a room.

She gestured to the night manager, who hurried over. "Is everything all right, Miss Valencia?"

"It is, Mr. Jackson, but if Mr. Deering doesn't require my services, I was hoping to take a short dinner break."

The older man nodded and smiled. "You may. We appreciate you stepping up to help us out. It's unlike Mr. Slayton to be so irresponsible. The kitchen is already closed, but I'm sure you can find something to eat."

With a nod, she hurried off and into the empty kitchen. A loaf of bread that had been freshly baked that morning sat on a countertop. Scrounging through the icebox, she found a block of Cheddar and a crock of butter and knew exactly what she would make.

As she laid out the items on the counter, the squeak of a door opening and the sound of footsteps drew her attention to the kitchen entrance. The shadow of a man, a big man, filled the entryway for a second before he walked in, but remained at the dark end of the room.

"Who is it?" Josephine asked, still unable to see his face in the shadows. Decidedly uneasy at being alone with a total stranger—especially since there had been some strange incidents around the hotel lately—she picked up the knife she had intended to use on the cheese.

The man strode into the room, and much to her surprise, a soft golden halo like that of an angel seemed to dance around the edges of his silhouette. It glimmered warmly as he approached, until he stepped into the circle cast by the hotel's new-fangled electric lighting, and the brighter illumination cast his features in sharp relief.

There was nothing angelic about him.

The man was tall, dark, and handsome. Way too handsome. *Way too dangerous,* she corrected herself as she took in the sight of him. Dark stubble across a strong jaw called attention to full lips set in a scowl. His shirt was unbuttoned to midchest, revealing a hint of lean, smooth muscle beneath. Pinstriped pants hugged a slim waist and hips, and powerful thighs. Thick brown hair waved around his face, billowing as if touched by a breeze.

He could be the embodiment of the swashbuckling pirate hero in one of the books Josephine longed to write someday. Only he was no pirate. She knew exactly whom he was: the Regal Sol's mysterious owner, Rake Solvino.

And, much to her surprise, the man with whom Josephine Galena Valencia had shared her very first kiss.

Well...I did not see that coming. Perhaps this was actually the night Josephine Galena Valencia's life would change forever? Let's read on and see, shall we?

Chapter Two

Josephine remembered meeting Rake years before, when she was working at the saloon near her house for the summer. She was cleaning up the saloon after hours when he appeared, seemingly out of nowhere. He was charming, and she was impressed, and before she knew it, they were eating together and talking for hours in the empty saloon. After discussing her fears and her dreams, Rake smiled at her and told her to be brave. Then they kissed.

Josephine knew in her heart that this was the last thing she should be doing...the absolute last thing.

As she stood completely thunderstruck in the kitchen of the Regal Sol, the indelible memory played across Josephine's mind like one of Mr. Edison's fancy new moving pictures:

Mopping spilled beer from one of the scarred wooden tables in the Golden Horseshoe saloon, sixteen-year-old Josephine Galena Valencia watched as her mother, Zara, flirted with the band conductor. Zara leaned up on tiptoes and whispered something to the man that had him blushing and nodding furiously. With a sexy smile, her mother whirled and the skirt of her costume danced in a circle around her legs. The cotton fabric caressed her curves from her waist up to the sweetheart neckline that revealed enough to be enticing while still being somewhat modest. Until her mother tugged at the waist and shifted the fabric down just another inch.

Ay, Mami, Josephine thought, heat rising to her cheeks as she finished cleaning and hurried to the back room of the North Miami saloon.

Even though Josephine was young, the bar's owner let her clean and do odd chores so she could help earn money for her family and buy the journals where she penned her stories. Normally, Josephine kept away from the patrons, who were usually inebriated and often too free with their hands. Zara had made sure that no one touched Josephine, and for the most part, the patrons kept to themselves.

In the back, Josephine returned to cleaning and putting away the assorted dishes and glasses that had been used that night. If she finished her chores fast enough, she had a journal and pencil in her bag so that she could sit and work on her new story. It was an exciting tale of two lovers pulled apart by war and their struggles to be reunited. She had already written the part with the magical first meeting and the heartbreaking separation. Just a little more and she'd be able to give them their miracle.

When she put away the last clean glass, she sat down at the small table in the back room and pulled out her journal and a pencil. She closed her eyes and imagined the scene she was about to write, and in the distance Zara's lovely voice serenading the audience accompanied her thoughts. Shortly after, loud applause confirmed the patrons had appreciated the song as well.

The heroine stood at the front of the saloon, singing about the pain of lost love. She searched the crowd for him, but he wasn't there. He hadn't been there in months since his squad had been called to the front lines to try to defend the city.

And so she sang, trying to make believe all was right in her world when nothing could be further from the truth. As she finished and walked off the stage, one of the patrons grabbed at her and snared her skirts with a filthy hand.

"Come here, girl," he said and hauled her onto his lap. He smelled of stale alcohol and onions. Groping her, he earned a sharp elbow that forced the air from his lungs and allowed her to escape.

The man rose, fury in his rheumy gaze. Hands outstretched, he tried to grasp her again, but then a body stepped between the two of them, protecting her. With a flurry of punches, the drunk was soon flat on his back.

Her protector turned and she gasped. A blood-stained bandage marred his forehead, and days of stubble darkened his cheeks, but she would have recognized him anywhere.

He had finally come back for her.

Smiling, Josephine put pencil to paper to capture the scene when she suddenly realized that a man was standing before her, staring down at her.

She shot out of her chair and away from him as a moment of panic gripped her. It slipped away quickly when she saw that the smile he blessed her with was friendly and so dazzling it was like starbursts exploding. He was no more than a decade older than she was and quite handsome in a dark, mysterious way, much like the hero in the scene she had just visualized.

Arms akimbo, he said, "Who might you be? You're too young and innocent to be in a place like this."

"Josephine Galena Valencia." Pride and defiance slipped into her voice. "My mother, Zara Galena Valencia, sings here, and Mr. King lets me clean up to earn a little extra cash."

With a little harrumph, he sauntered to the table where her open journal and pencil rested. "Doesn't look like cleaning to me."

He turned the journal around to read it and she rushed over and snatched it out of his hand. "Did you want something, sir? Should I get Mr. King?"

Shaking his head, he said, "My business with King is concluded tonight, but I'm hungry. If you wouldn't mind cooking, I'd be willing to pay you for it."

Since he'd asked politely rather than commanded, and she could use the cash, Josephine nodded and went to work on a meal. "It won't take long."

She hurried to the icebox, where she found a slightly stale loaf of bread, cheese, and butter, and quickly prepared sandwiches to grill for both of them since she was actually quite hungry. She could feel his gaze on her as she worked and it discomfited her, making her feel like she was on display.

Glancing at him over her shoulder as she flipped the sandwich, she said, "Don't you have anything else to do?"

With a wry grin, he crossed his arms along his chest. "No."

Ignoring him, she finished and plated the sandwiches. There was half a bottle of milk in the icebox also, and after a whiff to make sure it wasn't sour, she poured it to accompany their meal.

When she returned to the table with the sandwiches, they sat and ate, but not in silence, much as she might have hoped. He was quite engaging, complimenting her on the sandwiches and her mother's singing, which filtered in from the saloon. As they neared the end of the meal, he gestured to her journal again and said, "So what were you doing before I arrived?"

"I was writing while I waited for someone to bring me more glasses to wash."

"Writing? A letter?" He reached for the journal again and she swatted his hand away, earning the challenging arch of one raven-dark brow. Not that she found it intimidating surprisingly. If anything, he was intriguing her in ways that she should not be thinking about. Her *abuela* had warned her about men like this.

"It's nothing," she answered, closing the book and sliding it closer toward her on the table.

"Oh, then you won't mind if I take a look," he said, as long, quick fingers snagged a corner of the journal and tugged it back toward him.

"No!" Josephine said, temper rising at his boldness. She slammed her hand down flat on the journal to stop him, afraid that his reading it would reveal too much about her. Aware she'd forgotten all manners and decorum (and lost her temper), she forced herself to relax and shrugged, even as she gently pulled the journal back and hugged it close. "It's just silly scribbling, that's all." She'd gotten caught writing in class one day when she was supposed to be solving mathematic equations, and when the sister looked at it, that's what she'd said.

"And do you do this 'silly scribbling' anywhere else?"

"Sometimes when I'm supposed to be taking classes at the convent," she confessed.

He wrinkled his nose as if smelling something foul. "The convent? It would be a shame for a girl like you to become a nun."

Was he flirting with her? she wondered as her heart beat a faster staccato. "No, not a nun. A tutor."

"A tutor?" He wrinkled his nose again. "You don't strike me as the kind to be happy with such an ordinary life."

Intrigued that he saw something in her that others didn't, she said, "So what do you think I should do?"

He gestured to the journal she still hugged to her chest. "Seems to me that whatever is in there is important to you."

Josephine paused. She'd never shared her fondest dream with anyone before, not even her mother or *abuela*. But there was something… something in the way this man's eyes sparkled, the way this stranger's whole attention was fixed on her like she was the most interesting girl in the world.

"Maybe it is. I like to write," she said, and at his questioning gaze, she reluctantly continued. "Stories. Maybe even a book someday."

He grinned and leaned closer across the width of the table. Reaching out, he skimmed a finger along the edge of the journal and her heart skipped at his nearness. "Only maybe?" he said.

"Well, that depends. Am I being practical or brave?"

"Practical," he said, smiling.

"A tutor."

Then he leaned even closer, and his perfect smile widened and gleamed brightly. "Brave."

She took a deep breath. "I'm a writer." The words tumbled from Josephine's lips, sounding more like a question than an answer, and she laughed nervously. "I've never told anyone that before."

"I'm honored to be the first, then," he said, still staring at her with that impossibly warm expression. She could get lost in those eyes.

A beat stretched between them, long and full of promise. Then Josephine finally pulled back, shaking her head. "But I have to be practical, because being a writer is not an easy thing."

He reached out again and twirled a piece of her hair around his finger. With a gentle tug, he drew her near, closed the distance between them, and whispered in her ear, "Don't be practical, Josephine."

Before she could protest or draw away, he skimmed a kiss along her cheek and said, "Be brave."

He shifted those last final inches and kissed her, which was absolutely the last thing she had expected. *And absolutely the last thing I should be doing,* she thought as she returned the kiss.

In the kitchen at the Regal Sol, Josephine stared at Rake Solvino as he stood in the dim light. She didn't think it possible, but he was even more handsome than he'd been when she'd first seen him years earlier. Shortly after their kiss, one of the waiters had entered the saloon's kitchen and she hadn't even gotten a chance to ask his name. She'd had no idea who he was, the interesting man who had dared her to follow her dream.

Until now.

He peered at her, his countenance inscrutable, and Josephine wondered if he had found her as memorable. He jammed his hands on his hips and said, "I've seen you before."

You kissed me before, she thought, feeling satisfaction that he might remember their brief encounter, but then he quickly added, "You're one of the hotel concierges, aren't you?"

In her mind's eye, dozens of fine crystal glasses hit the floor, shattering into millions of pieces, just like her illusions.

Crestfallen, she said, "I am. The night manager gave me a break so I could get something to eat. Would you like a sandwich?"

He paused for a moment.

"It wouldn't take long. I was just about to make myself something."

He seemed about to relent and sit down, but then shook his head. "Next time, perhaps. I was actually just on my way out."

Out? At this hour? she thought, but before she could respond, he exited as stealthily as he had entered and it felt as if all light had left the room.

Feeling silly that she had expected something different, that he might actually remember her, she quickly made herself a grilled cheese sandwich. But unexpected disappointment lingered, making her favorite food utterly tasteless for the first time ever.

Unbeknownst to our dear Josephine, that first bump in the road was rapidly approaching as Rake Solvino hurried out of the hotel and down to his yacht in the marina, all the while wondering why the pretty concierge girl looked so familiar.

The bartender from the Golden Horseshoe glanced around nervously and backed deeper into the narrow alley as Martin and his new partner, Detective Nita Alvarez, peppered him with questions.

"You said the man who came in to offer you the contraband liquor was Richard Slayton?" Nita said.

The bartender nodded. "I'm pretty sure that's him. I think he works in one of those fancy hotels."

Martin's adrenaline revved up as he recognized the name. If Slayton was dealing contraband liquor in a dry town like Miami, what else had the hotel concierge been up to? Could Slayton somehow be connected to the recent murders? And if he wasn't involved in the illegal goings on, where was he now? "When was the last time you saw Slayton?" he asked. According to Martin's investigations, Slayton had been missing for days and no one seemed to know where the man had gone.

The bartender shrugged. "It's been a while."

Nita looked over at Martin and tilted her head toward the man, prodding him to press for more. She always seemed to be pressing, but then again, as only the second woman to become a Pinkerton, she might feel that she had something to prove.

"You say that you saw Slayton with someone just before he came into the saloon the other day. Can you describe that other man?" he said.

With another shrug and shake of his head, the man said, "Can't say. He kept to the shadows so I couldn't see his face."

His gut told him the man was being truthful, so he didn't hound him. He handed the man his card and some monetary enticement. "If you hear or see anything else, you know where to come."

He pivoted on his heel and headed out of the alley, Nita matching him stride for stride. She was a tall woman with a walk and attitude that said she could take care of herself. "You seemed very interested once he mentioned Slayton. You know that name?"

Martin nodded. "He's one of the clerks at the Regal Sol. Josephine had to stay late because he didn't show up for his shift earlier this week."

Her eyes widened. "You think he could be our man?"

Martin thought about it for a moment, then shook his head. "Not likely. He never struck me as much of a leader. If he's selling alcohol or dealing in other contraband, he's doing it on someone else's orders." He sighed in frustration. "How is it that no one seems to have seen this mysterious crime boss?"

"*El hombre sin sombra.* There was talk about a crime boss with that name when I was with the Palm Beach office," Nita said.

"*Sin sombra,*" Martin said, mangling the pronunciation and obviously confused.

She explained. "The man with no shadow. You're going to have to learn some Spanish if you're marrying Josephine."

"*Sin sombra*," he repeated more clearly and smiled. "I like it."

"And Josephine. I guess you like *her* a lot?" Nita said, a hint of hesitation in her tone.

He nodded as they walked to the next saloon to continue their investigation, his heart swelling with delight at the mere mention of his beloved. "Josephine is like no one else I've ever known. She's smart and independent. Caring. When I'm with her everything just feels... right." He was smiling, but then heaved a sigh. "I hope we can finish up this case before we get married."

"Why is that?" Nita wondered aloud.

"Because I worry that by working at the hotel, she may be in danger the closer we get to this Sin Sombra character. As much as I want to catch him, I can't let my work put her in jeopardy."

Nita looked annoyed at that. "Maybe you've chosen the wrong line of work, Martin. Danger is the nature of our business. If you let emotion interfere, it just makes our job even more dangerous."

Martin hated that on some level, Nita's words hit too close to home. He couldn't let emotion interfere, but he also couldn't let his job touch his personal life. It was a tightrope that he would have to walk carefully because falling could cost him the most important thing in his life: Josephine.

Josephine walked around her family's small kitchen table, laying down cutlery, plates, and glasses while her mother and *abuela* prepared dinner. She loved that they were able to dine together every other Sunday because the hotel owner insisted on the workers being able to spend time with their families on the Lord's Day and made sure everyone received some time to do so with a rotating schedule. Perhaps Rake Solvino wasn't as bad or unscrupulous as some of the rumors said. It also made her wonder if either her mother, who sang at the hotel lounge when she wasn't at the saloon, or her grandmother had heard any gossip about him.

"I ran into the owner of the hotel the other night," she said and walked toward where her mother was cooking *arepas* in a skillet while her grandmother put the finishing touches on a big pot of *pabellón criollo* that she had started earlier in the day. The savory shredded beef in tomato sauce would be even tastier once they stuffed it into the fresh *arepas*.

"He's finally come back," Zara said and flipped one of the *arepas*.

Her *abuela* glanced over her shoulder. "I hear he's quite a handsome man."

"I didn't really get a good look at him," Josephine said with a shrug.

Suddenly, her conscience pricked at her for the mistruth. *That must be the devil's pitchfork*, her *abuela* would have said. Growing up, whenever Josephine had behaved badly, Alberta would say the devil must have made her do it, while good deeds meant a guardian angel was steering her path. In this moment, she imagined them both perching on her shoulders. On the right, her angel tsk-tsked and shook her head at the lie. Not to be left out, her devil arrived a moment later to stab her angel with a pitchfork and say, "It's for you to know and them to find out."

She hoped that her sharp-eyed grandmother would not detect her subterfuge. But as her *abuela's* gaze narrowed and fixed on her, she realized she had failed. Little angel Josephine whispered in her ear, "You can never fool your *abuela*."

With a wistful sigh, Zara said, "Well, I saw him in the lounge with some of the other railroad barons. He's quite good-looking. I wouldn't mind getting to know him better."

Her little devil danced with amusement and said, "Now that's a woman who goes after what she wants," while she and her grandmother both chided her mother simultaneously.

"*Mami*," Josephine warned.

"*Mi'ja*," her *abuela* chastised.

Zara barked out a laugh. "Well, he is handsome, and what concern is it of yours, my dear Josephine? You have your Martin after all."

"And a kinder, gentler, sweeter, more patient man you will not find," her *abuela* said, almost as if to remind Josephine. "Except maybe your sainted *abuelo*," she tacked on, looking heavenward as she made the sign of the cross.

"I know that, *Abuela*. It's not that I'm interested in Mr. Solvino—"

Her little devil stabbed her with the pitchfork while her concerned angel lifted her hands in prayer for Josephine's lying soul.

"Although it certainly sounds that way," her mother singsonged playfully, raising an eyebrow.

"It's just that I met him once before," she confessed, and in the blink of an eye, the warring representatives of good and evil evaporated, but not before her angel gave a satisfied laugh.

Both her mother and grandmother whirled to face her and her grandmother said, "You did?"

"When?" her mother added.

Heat rose to her cheeks at their prolonged scrutiny and that very noticeable flush only escalated their interest.

"Josephine?" her mother urged, her voice rising in question.

"A long time ago at the Golden Horseshoe. He came into the back one day, and I made him some food. I didn't know who he was, and he didn't tell me." Trying to draw the conversation away from their meeting, she said, "And now he's back. So why did he go away? And why come back now?"

With a *tsk*, her grandmother shook her head and said, "What does it matter? You have your wonderful Martin, and that's all that's important."

As her gaze collided with her mother's, Josephine could see that Zara sensed there was more to her story. But the smell of burning *arepas* demanded her mother's attention, and for that, Josephine was grateful.

For, in her heart of hearts, she knew her abuela's words were wise and true: men like Rake Solvino were best forgotten. But as the days passed by, Josephine could not seem to forget the enigmatic man who'd once dared her to dream big.

Or perhaps it was just that she couldn't forgive him for forgetting their epic first kiss...

Chapter Three

As he walked into the Regal Sol, Martin slid the note that Josephine had left behind for him last night in their secret drawer at the concierge desk back into his pocket. He'd been so busy trying to track down a new lead yesterday that he hadn't been able to meet her to walk her home the night before. So he'd swung by the desk and left her a note, picking up the one she'd written for him. He'd reread it several times already this morning.

Martin smiled as he recalled her vibrant description of the arrival of another prominent guest who, in her words, "waddled like a penguin and had bushy muttonchops that extended so far below his jaw that they looked like walrus tusks." His fiancée had an imagination like no other. It was one of the things he loved most about her.

Chuckling, he headed over to the concierge desk to see his beloved before he had to go back to work again tonight. Maybe he'd even ask her about Slayton's mysterious disappearance. Adams had told him the man still hadn't turned up. As much as Martin hated to involve Josephine, he hoped she could give him a little more information about her fellow clerk.

She was at the desk, smiling at one of the hotel guests, and he held back, not wanting to interrupt her. When she finished getting the necessary details to book rail tickets for the man and his wife, the guest walked away and she shot a covert glance in his direction.

Martin walked over and dipped his head. "Miss Valencia. Are you ready to go home?"

She gave him a tight smile. "Unfortunately, I have to work just a little longer until Mr. Adams arrives. One of my colleagues didn't come into work. Again."

It had to be Slayton. But he was hesitant to ask, knowing that once he did so, Josephine might easily catch on that there were problems at the hotel.

"Are you okay, Martin?" Josephine asked, narrowing her gaze to examine him the way a schoolteacher might a guilty student.

"It's nothing. It's just this investigation that's taking so much time away from seeing you."

Tension crept into her features as she saw past his ruse. "It's more than that, isn't it?"

With a shrug, he said, "I can't say, Josephine. You know I can't talk about the investigation."

"Which may or may not involve someone I work with," she challenged.

Josephine was too clever by half, and Martin didn't like secrets. He wished he could simply tell her everything, but he couldn't put her in harm's way. So he changed the subject slightly. "I'd feel better if you didn't have to work late tonight. Can't someone else watch the desk?"

"I can take care of myself, Detective Cadden. You don't need to protect me," she replied and tilted her delightful little chin up a defiant inch.

He chucked her under the chin playfully, trying to ease the tension. "I know you can. But I also hope that if there was anything… odd happening around here, you'd be sure to come to me."

To his alarm, she glanced away uneasily and if anything, got even more withdrawn. "There's nothing odd happening. Everything is just as it has been," she replied and fiddled with some papers on the top of her desk.

Except for a desk clerk who'd possibly gone missing. "You would tell me truly if there were?"

Her head snapped up and she met his gaze full on. He hadn't realized brown eyes could get so chilly.

"Just as you'd tell me?" she countered. "After all, a husband and wife are supposed to trust each other with everything, aren't they?"

"Yes, they are," he said, perhaps a beat too late.

For the first time in the two years that Martin had known Josephine, it occurred to him that maybe he didn't really know her as well as he'd thought.

Rake spread out the assorted papers his accountant had just brought him, reviewing the numbers in the journals with growing distress. He should have paid more attention to the reports he had been getting the last few years about both the railroad and the hotel. Unfortunately, he'd been too busy recovering from a tropical fever and trying to shut down the other not-so-upstanding businesses that had provided a good deal of the capital for his expansion into the legal businesses.

"Are you sure that we have no other way to cut our operating costs at the hotel?" Rake pressed while flipping through the pages of the ledger in disgust.

The accountant shook his head. "I'm sorry, Mr. Solvino. We've taken on a great deal of extra staff in order to compete with Mr. Flagler's Royal Palm and entice those wealthier patrons to choose us instead. It has worked to some extent, but the costs of running some of the areas, like the marina—"

"The marina stays," he said curtly. "Please prepare a list of other areas and staff that we can trim by the morning. I'll review it then and decide what action to take."

"Certainly, Mr. Solvino. I'll have the report for you first thing," the man said, bowing and scurrying out of Rake's office to work on his assigned task.

Rake ran his gaze across the papers again, searching the figures to make his own determinations. His father had always told him that a real leader knew every aspect of his empire down to the lowliest foot soldier. Of course, his father had also told him that he didn't think Rake had what it took to be a leader.

So he'd saved the small allowance his father had given him over the years to create the seed fund for his first business, a legitimate fruit import/export company. Unfortunately, after several freezes in upper Florida that had damaged the citrus crops, he'd had to find a way to keep the business going—both for himself and the many employees who depended on him for their livelihoods. It had been an easy thing to start slipping moonshine in with his deliveries to make the extra money. From there he'd expanded into moving contraband rum from Cuba to sell to those who wanted to avoid the government's hefty liquor taxes. Rake knew his actions were not exactly virtuous, but he'd rationalized it by reminding himself that Mrs. Tuttle had already granted permission to the Royal Palm and the Regal Sol to sell alcohol, so it was only a matter of time before the rest of Miami would likely follow suit. After all, could he help it if the good people of North Miami liked their rum and medicinal tonics? Besides, the smaller establishments he was selling to would make more money and be able to pay their employees more, and, as he'd learned from his father, all was fair in the business world if it made you money.

When news had come of Flagler's plan to extend the railroad to the very tip of Florida, Rake knew it was his chance to become a legitimate businessman and guarantee positions for those who had been loyal to him. He had jumped into the venture, using almost all his savings and the income from his less respectable enterprises to build the Regal Sol. He hoped the hotel's success would once and forever prove that he could make it on his own and one day run the lucrative Solvino business empire. He was his father's son in more ways than one, which was why they'd earned the distasteful title of robber barons. Rake would never steal from the people, and the government coffers would hardly feel the impact of a few illicit sales.

Returning to the ledgers, he didn't need his accountant to tell him that the marina was a huge drain on the monies brought in by the hotel and his share of the railroad profits. While it was expensive to keep the area functional due to the dredging and digging necessitated by the silt and mud that constantly flowed down from the Everglades, he needed the marina to bring in the money to keep the hotel afloat until it could truly stand on its own. With the rail lines closely guarded by Pinkertons, the hotel's location on the unregulated Miami River provided the only way to support his other operations.

Of course, business was slow right now since Slayton had disappeared with some of his best booze. Some theft was expected in this kind of operation, but Rake hadn't thought Slayton would be the type. But laying off staff and trimming other operating expenses could help out the hotel's bottom line, and Slayton would be the first to go. If he ever turned up again, that is. Closing the books, Rake returned to his desk, lit a cigar, and walked to the wall of windows that overlooked the large park that separated the Regal Sol from the Royal Palm. Dozens of well-heeled patrons strolled through the gardens, enjoying yet another sunny Miami day. Almost as many employees in the blue and white colors of the Regal Sol scurried here and there, busily at work.

Like the young woman at the concierge desk who had been on his mind ever since their meeting in the kitchen a few days earlier.

She had been pretty in that untouched, innocent way that normally had him running in the other direction. He had no need of crying, guilt-ridden virgins in his bed, or worse, behind his concierge desk, no matter how appealing their charms.

Still, he couldn't help but catalog those charms again now. Intelligent brown eyes had seemed to see right through him, recognizing there was more than what was on the surface. Thick, nearly black hair had been pinned ruthlessly in a bun, but the wildly curling tendrils that had escaped to frame her heart-shaped face and long, elegant neck said that maybe she wasn't quite so prim and proper.

Plus, she had courage and spunk. Even though she had been fearful when he'd surprised her in the kitchen, he hadn't failed to miss how she'd surreptitiously reached for that knife for defense. He suspected that even if he'd had ulterior motives, she wouldn't have hesitated to use that knife.

An intriguing young woman, indeed, and maybe that was the sole reason she had taken such hold in his mind. Perhaps she seemed familiar only because he had seen her before at the concierge desk, despite the lingering feeling that he knew her from somewhere else. At least that's what Rake told himself as he went back to poring over the books, hoping all the while that one particularly intriguing young woman would not be on his accountant's list in the morning.

What? Josephine might be fired! Now friends, please consider that our dear Josephine had not only never called in sick in all the years that she had worked at the hotel, but that everyone at the Regal Sol knew that if you ever needed any help or needed the seemingly impossible done, you went to Josephine. Besides, how will we ever see what will happen with the notorious Rake and our spunky and pure Josephine if he fires her?

Josephine had arrived at the hotel early the next day, fully intending to tell Martin about the strange happenings around the Regal Sol that were weighing on her mind. Martin had left a note in their secret spot last night explaining that while he'd be busy with his investigation for most of the day, he would drop by for a few minutes at the start of her shift.

But as she went to enter the lobby, she suddenly got cold feet and decided that a stroll through the park nestled between the two hotels was just what she needed. A little extra time would help her figure out what to tell Martin about Rake's odd nighttime outing and how to inquire if her missing colleague was part of his investigation.

Of course, if Slayton was the subject of the investigation there was little she could do to help Martin. She knew virtually nothing about the man other than that he had been punctual, efficient, and responsible before a few days ago. Maybe a bit of a loner too. He never talked much to his coworkers, and she never remembered seeing anyone come by to chat with him on days when they were both manning the desk.

Unlike Josephine or Mr. Adams, Slayton did not display personal items anywhere. Her supervisor kept a picture of his family tucked in one corner of the desk when he was on duty. And in the secret drawer where she and Martin passed notes, there was a rare Viennese snow globe that Martin had purchased for her during a visit to a Pinkerton office in New York City. He had said that he couldn't pass it up because it would always remind them of their first meeting.

So what could she really tell Martin about him? Or about Rake Solvino, for that matter? The hotel's darkly handsome owner was a mystery as well. Josephine pondered these thoughts as she meandered around the lush gardens, not really paying much attention to the manicured lawn and flower beds bursting with tropical colors. Then at the far edge of the park where a line of tall royal palms marked the start of the grounds for Flagler's hotel, she suddenly paused as she caught sight of someone who looked remarkably like Martin.

But it couldn't be him, she thought and ducked behind the immense trunk of one of the palms to peer around the edge unseen. Especially since this man was with a woman, his forehead intimately tucked against her hair, his arms snug around her waist as she leaned her head against his chest.

No, it couldn't be him. Except... *Except* that the man had Martin's slightly wavy blond hair. And he was the right height and build. And that mud-brown sack suit looked quite familiar...even down to the slightly worn right elbow. A tight knot formed in Josephine's stomach as the man then raised his face to gaze down at the woman.

Josephine's breath left her as if someone had punched her in the gut. When she finally recovered from the blow, she turned and leaned back against the trunk, wondering how this was possible. Angel Josephine appeared in an instant and whispered, "Oh my" in her ear, while the devil had a string of choice words about what to do. All of the suggestions involved violence. While Josephine was sorely tempted to listen to that voice as her temper roused, she instead heeded the angel who sounded remarkably like her *abuela* as she urged trust and calm.

Calm, Josephine told herself, remembering the mental trick her *abuela* had taught her to think about her favorite things that began with the letters of the word in an effort to cool her sometimes too-quick temper. *C-A-L-M.* Cheese, *Abuela*, Lists, and…Martin. She stifled a sob, valiantly trying to hold the tears in as she marched back to the Regal Sol to start her shift and await her fiancé's arrival.

It seemed like hours until Martin strolled through the lobby even though it had barely been half an hour.

Calm and trust. C-A-L-M, she repeated to herself as he approached and as her devil reemerged, telling her to toss the treasured snow globe straight at his cheating head.

When he reached the desk, he smiled at her, but it didn't quite reach up into his eyes. She'd always thought Martin's eyes were as beautiful and bright as a summer sky, but today their crystal blue seemed icy and reserved.

"Miss Valencia. How are you this fine morning?" he said, the warmth of his voice dispelling some of that imagined ice.

But the devil inside her couldn't resist saying, "Is it a fine morning, Detective Cadden? I imagine that you have been quite busy with your…work."

He peered at her intently, obviously sensing her pique. "I was at… work and looking forward to seeing you very much," he replied, with confusion in his tone.

Well, he certainly hadn't been looking forward to her enough to pass up a rendezvous with another woman! She wanted to spit the accusatory words at him, but bit them back.

C-A-L-M. She was at work and could not afford to make a scene. Shuffling some papers around on her desk, she said, "Unfortunately, I have a great deal to do this morning."

He grasped her hand to still the nervous motion. "Tell me what's wrong, Josephine."

She looked around, drew her hand away, and whispered, "Detective Cadden. This is my place of employment and not the right time to discuss this."

Shock registered on his features at her words and tone. "*This* being…?"

"Us, Martin," she said louder than she intended. She looked around and cleared her throat, lowering her voice. "Maybe later we—"

"I have to work later, Josephine. But *this*," he began and gestured to the two of them with a finger. "*This* is important to me."

She tilted her chin up stubbornly and said, "It's important to me as well."

He acknowledged her statement with a slow dip of his head. "I'll try to come by later," he said, but didn't wait for her response before he pivoted and hurried away.

She watched him push through the lobby doors and as they closed behind him they transformed into jail cell bars that shut with a loud, metallic clang.

Jail cell bars, my friends. Things are looking very bad. Our kind, caring, responsible—and normally very honest—Detective Martin had suddenly become a man with secrets. A man who could break Josephine's heart!

Despite her best efforts, Josephine couldn't get the image of Martin and that woman out of her mind all day. He had come by at mid-afternoon, but she had been on her break and missed him. According to the note he'd left her, apparently, he would not be able to meet with her that night. Again.

Josephine folded and unfolded the note, literally reading between the lines of every word Martin had written.

I'm sorry I didn't have more time to speak with you this morning, but I had things I had to do for work.

Like having an assignation with a mysterious woman? she thought.

There are things I long to tell you, but cannot, my darling.

Like why you were holding her in your arms beneath the palms?

If I could, I would share what is happening in the investigation, but to do so could put you in danger, and I could not live with myself if anything happened to you. I want to be sure that you are always safe.

But I don't need you to protect me, Martin, she wanted to shout out, and in a fit of pique, she tore the note into tiny pieces and let them drift down like snowflakes into the kitchen wastebasket.

She had only a short break to make herself a bite to eat before returning to finish her shift. She could not spend the whole time agonizing over Martin and his deception. Hurrying to the icebox, she removed all the makings for one of her favorite grilled cheese sandwiches. As she turned to go to the counter, she noticed the shadow of a man in the doorway, but had no fear this time.

Like clouds parting to reveal the sun, Rake Solvino stepped from the shadows and into the kitchen, smiling that devilish, dimpled grin.

"We must stop meeting like this," he teased.

"That might be difficult since this is your hotel," she shot right back, dragging a chuckle from him.

"It certainly might since I do live here. Unfortunately, I don't cook and the restaurant is closed. Would you take pity on me and make me something to eat?" he said and held his hands together as if begging.

He might technically be her boss, but there was something in his playful attitude that said he wasn't thinking of her as an employee at that moment. "All right, but beggars can't be choosers. You'll have to settle for one of my very special grilled cheese sandwiches."

He grinned and flares of light burst from that smile to light up the room and cause parts of her to tingle. "Somehow I don't feel as if I'd be settling," he said and sat at one of the stools by the work counter.

"I guess you'll see," she replied saucily, sensing a growing connection between them. She worked quickly, her movements sure after so many years of preparing the sandwiches her mother had first taught her to make when she was a child. They contained three different types of cheese, which is what made them so tasty. While they cooked, she set two places for them on the counter.

When the sandwiches had reached the perfect state of golden-brown bread and cheesy meltiness, she scooped them onto plates and went to the fridge for milk. She grabbed a bottle and returned to the counter where Rake waited, and as she set the meal before him, he sat up straighter and peered at her.

"I remember now. You were the girl at the Golden Horseshoe. The writer. Did you ever finish your novel?"

For a moment, her heavy heart lightened. He'd remembered that night. "I am that girl, but I don't know how much of a writer I am. I'm still trying to finish the novel. Any novel actually."

He picked up a half of the sandwich and devoured it in just a few bites, chewing thoughtfully while he considered her statement. After a swallow of milk, he said, "You're not going to give up, are you?"

She remembered his words to her that night: *Be brave.* But there was so much going on in her life now. "I'm not going to give up, only things are complicated…"

As angry and upset as she was with Martin, mentioning her problems with him to Rake seemed disloyal.

He was quick to take note of her upset. "You're troubled."

She shot out of her chair and gestured to the last bite of sandwich on his plate. "You're almost done, and I have to get back to work."

"Actually, I'm still hungry and would love another sandwich. It was quite good, and since I am the boss, I'll make sure you don't get into trouble for being a little late from your break."

She met his gaze directly. His eyes were brown, flecked with gold and green, and so dark it was like she was staring into the forest at night. Mysterious, fathomless, and possibly dangerous, but also filled with all kinds of exciting life. His lips had grown harsh as he sensed her earlier upset, but slowly they broke into an enticing smile.

"Please, Josephine. You wouldn't let a man starve, would you?"

With a playful huff, she grabbed his plate and returned to the stove to make him another sandwich. As she worked, she heard him rummaging around in the kitchen, opening and closing drawers. Pots and cutlery clanged and clinked.

She glanced over her shoulder and found that he had returned to the counter, but now a bottle of champagne sat beside him along with two crystal flutes.

When she walked over with his sandwich and placed it before him, he poured himself a glass of champagne and was about to pour her a glass as well when she held up her hand to stop him.

He arched a brow in challenge. "Now, Josephine. You wouldn't let a man drink alone would you?"

"I've never had a drink before," she admitted, and his brow arched even higher.

"Not ever?" he pressed.

"Not ever," she confirmed, and he chuckled.

"Well, maybe it's time for your first," he said, but she shook her head, emphasizing that she was unconvinced.

With a chuckle, he said, "Stubborn, aren't we?" Then his eyes narrowed. "But brave, right? I don't see you as someone to turn down a challenge, whether it's writing a book or having your first sip of champagne."

For a man who didn't really know her, he seemed to know her quite well. But before she could reply, he rose from the table, walked to one of the kitchen drawers, and took out some items. He returned and laid them on the counter next to his plate: a pair of dice and playing cards that the head chef used to fleece his workers from their pay during break time.

"I don't understand," she said, peering at the items.

He picked up the dice and juggled them in his hand. "Highest roll wins. If I win, you stay and have a sip. If you win, you go back to work. What do you say, Josephine?"

Well, well, well. Now this is getting interesting.

Chapter Four

Josephine's gaze skipped from Rake's dimpled smile to the rattling dice then back to his face. "Just a sip?"

"Just a sip…if that's all you want," he said, and she had the strangest feeling he wasn't simply talking about champagne.

But Josephine Galena Valencia never backed away from a challenge. She sat down and held her hand out for the dice. He slipped them into hers and as he did so, the barest touch of his skin against hers roused flares of fire against her flesh. She jerked her hand away, brought the dice to her mouth, and blew on them as she'd seen the chef do during the kitchen gambling sessions. She supposed he did it for luck, and he won more often than not.

She could use some luck right now.

The dice clattered on the counter before coming to a stop. Two ones. The black pips on the dice seemed to laugh at her lack of skill like evil snake eyes.

"It would be hard not to beat that," Rake said as he scooped up the dice, blew on them, and then rolled.

A one and a two, yanking laughter from both of them.

"You barely beat it," she said.

Grinning, he poured her a full glass of champagne. "But I did."

He picked up his glass and raised it for a toast. She tentatively lifted her glass and he said, "To friends."

She was sure that men like Rake weren't interested in having a woman as a friend, but she obligingly tapped her glass against his and echoed him. "To friends."

My first sip of champagne, she thought with heady anticipation as she brought the glass to her lips and drank. The aroma of it teased her nostrils a moment before the taste of it exploded in her mouth and bubbles played on her tongue.

"Delicious," she said and set the glass down.

"See what you've been missing?" He nearly drained his own glass. "Drink up," he said with a wave of one hand while he picked up the grilled cheese sandwich with the other.

She nodded but used restraint as she took little sips while he ate and peppered her with questions about her studies at the convent. She answered him, explaining that she was almost done with the classes and hoped to be able to get a job shortly.

"We will miss you," he said, his tone sincere and filled with emotion.

Heat worked up from her core with his words. She grabbed the champagne and took a bigger sip of the chilled wine to fight the traitorous warmth. As she put the glass down, she realized it was empty and didn't get a chance to protest as Rake immediately refilled it.

"And then you'll work on your novel," he said, more statement than question.

Buoyed by his optimism, she nodded. "I will."

He raised his glass for another toast and she joined him as he said, "To your novel."

"To my novel," she repeated, elation filling her with the thought.

"Tell me about your book," he said.

The words spilled from her as she relayed bits and pieces about the new story she wanted to write about her *abuela* and *abuelo*'s courtship in Venezuela. As she did so, she sipped at the champagne little by little until her glass was once again empty. Rake quickly refilled it as time flew by with them chatting and laughing. They drank until the bottle was empty, and Rake went for a second.

Since her head was already swimming from a combination of the wine and his charm, she waved him off, but he merely gave her that rakish arch of his brow.

"My dear Josephine, is it time for another bet?" He reached for the deck of cards and although she was vehemently shaking her head no, he shuffled the deck and held it out to her to choose one.

My, my, this is getting even more intense, isn't it? And that champagne, so tasty and so liberating, right? Maybe too liberating, my friends?

Angel and devil wrestled with each other on her shoulders, fighting for her attention.

"Think of Martin," the angel said, and the devil added, "who betrayed you this morning."

The angel broke free of the devil, stamped her foot, and said, "Don't touch those cards!"

"You can't lose every bet!" the devil teased.

Josephine drew a card, earning a joyous shout from the devil before they both disappeared.

The Queen of Hearts, a sure winner, she thought before the queen's face morphed. Suddenly it was her *abuela* staring at her, shaking her head in a chiding manner and saying, "*Niña*, no good can come of this."

She placed the card on the counter so Rake could see her choice and smiled.

"Feeling lucky, aren't you?" he said and shuffled the cards.

"I am," she confirmed with a wobbly, possibly inebriated nod. Since she had never had a drink, she wasn't quite sure if the lightheaded, slightly fuzzy way she was feeling had to do with the champagne or with the handsome man who had been so incredibly captivating and attentive for the last few hours.

Rake drew a card and laid it down over hers. The King of Hearts.

"Fate?" he asked and stared at her intently, his dark gaze glittering with amusement and something else. Something decidedly dangerous.

A blast of heat raced through her body and up to her face. She covered her cheeks with her hands, trying to hide her response.

He grinned that enticing smile and reached out, gently taking hold of her wrists and applying pressure to lower them.

"Maybe it's time for some fresh air?"

It was definitely time for lots of fresh air, she thought. Maybe a walk in the cool of the night and out in public would be just the thing to prevent this all from getting out of hand.

"Yes, that sounds good," she said and whirled to escape the intimacy of the kitchen and the nearness of Rake.

Out in the lobby, the hotel manager came running over, his anger apparent at her tardiness, but he must have caught sight of Rake trailing behind her because he stopped short and returned to the front desk.

The heat in her cheeks intensified and she raced from the lobby and across the veranda that was virtually empty at the late hour. The sound of the river and a cool breeze beckoned her, and she hurried over until she was at the railing by the start of the marina. Rake joined her just seconds later.

"Beautiful, isn't it?" he said, but as she looked up at him, she realized he wasn't looking at the river.

"Mr. Solvino—"

"We're well past that stage, Josephine. Rake. My name is Rake."

"Rake," she said, finding that his name slipped way too easily from her lips. "I-I need to walk." She hoped that if she kept on moving it would keep things on an even keel.

"Of course, Josephine," he said and as she rushed from the railing, he matched his pace to hers and placed his hand at the small of her back.

No, that spot wasn't tingling, she told herself, but imagined fireworks bursting from that point of contact directly into the night air.

Gritting her teeth, she fought the sensation, but it was like swimming upstream as the waves of sensation swamped her.

"Rake," she said, pulling away from him and off to one side of the path along the marina.

"I like hearing you say my name. Say it again," he said, the tone of his voice low and seductive as he came closer.

She backed up to avoid him, but he kept on walking toward her until her back was against the rough bark of one of the large poinciana trees lining the path.

"Rake," she said, but it was part protest and part plea.

"Josephine, you can't imagine what you do to me," he nearly groaned as he cupped her face and laid his forehead against hers.

"Rake," she repeated again, unable to find the words to tell him what she wanted. Mostly because she wasn't sure of what she wanted.

Rake eliminated that uncertainty for her. He pressed her against the trunk of the tree and a magical shower of white petals suddenly rained down, the petals soft against her bare skin. The subtle fragrance mingled with Rake's very masculine sandalwood scent and was intoxicating.

Before she could protest, he covered her mouth with his, the kiss tentative at first, but quickly growing more demanding.

Her head swam with the kiss and the feel of his hard, lean body against hers. It was the champagne, she told herself. But as he engaged her lips over and over, it occurred to her that maybe it was more about the man than the wine. And once more, she knew that this was absolutely something that she should not be doing, yet found herself powerless to resist.

Resist, Josephine, resist. Think of Martin. Kind, caring, gentle, patient…unfaithful Martin. No, no, remember Martin, Josephine. And the snow falling. Josephine? Josephine, are you listening?

Unaware of anything but the feel of her hand in his, Josephine walked with Rake along the marina path, the stars shimmering above.

Josephine gazed at them, thinking that they had never shone so bright, lighting the way back to the entrance to the hotel. But as they neared, Rake flagged down one of the horse-drawn carriages that sat waiting for guests.

At her questioning gaze, he said, "I won the bet, and we still haven't had that second bottle of champagne."

The carriage approached and he helped her up and said to the driver, "I'll be right back."

He hurried inside the hotel and minutes later returned with the bottle. Hopping into the carriage beside her, he called to the footman, "To my railcar."

The driver took off and sent Rake falling onto the seat beside her. He wrapped one arm around her, drawing her close for the short ride to the railroad depot.

What are you doing, Josephine? she asked herself. Visions of Martin with his arms wrapped around another woman provided an answer, but not one she liked. This wasn't about retribution. And it wasn't about the champagne giddiness.

It was about a man who intrigued her. A man who dared her to chase her dream: to become a writer. A man who didn't want to keep her trapped under glass like the figurines in her beloved Viennese snow globe.

As the carriage neared the depot, the driver pulled up to the fenced-off porte cochere that led to a covered breezeway and the tall building that held the waiting room and opened onto the tracks.

Rake stepped from the carriage and held his hand out to her.

It should be explained here that one day, when Josephine Galena Valencia was still a very young girl, her abuela had handed her a pristine white gardenia and instructed her to crumple it up. Despite her utter confusion, Josephine was a good girl and did as her abuela instructed. As she unfurled her fingers around the crushed blossom, Alberta told her to try to make it look new again, but alas, Josephine could not. And her abuela warned her that was exactly what would happen when she lost her virginity. She could never go back.

This important life lesson was one that Josephine would never forget.

However, at this very moment, Josephine was not thinking about that lesson at all.

She slipped her hand into his and walked out into the night. She followed him as he led her into the depot and kept on walking through the breezeway and waiting room to the tracks where, at one far end, a number of railcars were stationed.

This is crazy, Josephine told herself, but she had never ridden on a railway car before. And she wanted to so very desperately all of the sudden.

A security guard stood by the car, but stepped aside as he recognized Rake.

"Mr. Solvino. Miss," he said in greeting and offered his hand to help her step up onto the stairs for the car.

She held his hand, her step slightly unsteady, but pushed forward onto the stairs and into the railcar. Inside the car, the electric sconces snapped to life, their light casting a golden, intimate glow over the fine leather furniture and mahogany walls and tables.

"Beautiful," she said and ran her hand across the gleaming wood beneath the windows where the curtains had been drawn against the daytime Miami sun and for privacy at night. Surprisingly, the railcar was neither stuffy nor warm thanks to a cooler night breeze that swept from one open door to the other.

The pop of the champagne bottle reminded her of why they were there at the same time the angel on her shoulder warned that they were there for much, much more.

There's still time, Josephine. There's still time. Remember your flower…

She accepted the glass from Rake but vowed to take only a few more sips. It was difficult to do as they sat on the cushioned seat together, Rake at a respectful distance at first as they chatted again, mostly about her and her desires. A rather unique experience since most men tended to want to talk about themselves.

Except Martin, the angel reminded her.

But as the minutes passed and the bottle of champagne grew ever emptier, they inched closer and closer together until Rake's thigh was tight against hers and his arm rested heavy across her shoulders. The weight and heat of it was comforting, but as he took hold of her empty glass and bent his head to meet her gaze, the moment morphed into something different.

The warning flashed at her in vivid images of her *abuela* and the crumpled white flower in her hand. She had vowed that day to stay a virgin until marriage. Marriage to Martin, her *abuela's* voice warned.

But as soon as those memories appeared, they were replaced with the vision of the fragrant white petals drifting down near the marina a second before Rake's lips met hers. And just as *abuela* had warned, there was no turning back.

She kissed Rake over and over, straining toward him until, with a powerful swipe of his muscled arm, he pulled her into his lap.

"Rake," she murmured against his lips.

"Touch me, Josephine," he said, and at her hesitation, took hold of her hand and placed it on his own hard body. When he groaned, it roused an incredible sense of power inside her.

She traced the shape of him, and she couldn't hold back her own little moan as he ran his hand over the curves still hidden beneath her prim white shirt. As she sucked in a breath, he slipped his tongue past the seam of her mouth.

The taste of Rake and champagne was intoxicating and had her straining closer, needing something she had never needed before.

In a flurry, Rake was easing off her shirt and his, leaving her upper body clothed only in a thin chemise and her corset. He skimmed his hands along the slope of her bare shoulders and up to her bun where, with the release of a few pins, he freed her hair to cascade down.

"You are so very beautiful," he said, brushing her hair back. He leaned close to drop a kiss along her neck and whisper, "So very, very beautiful and brave."

She might have been able to resist a more determined seduction, but his gentle touch, so slow and reverent, made her lose her head.

With quick fingers he undid the strings on the corset and tossed it away. Her petticoats and skirt soon followed, as he laid her down onto the wide leather seat.

The heat of his chest teased the bare skin above the line of her chemise a second before his hard muscles pressed against her. He kissed the sensitive skin along the swell of her breasts and she arched up into him, wanting more. He complied, drawing the fabric down to taste her. Skimming his hand down her body to her center, he touched her until she was writhing beneath him.

Oh my. I hope Abuela is not reading this.

Time passed in a blur as waves of pleasure like she had never known coursed through Josephine's body. When he moved his hand away she protested, but then she felt him working the fastenings on his pants and reached down to help him.

She experienced a moment of hesitation as he poised there, close to the flower her *abuela* had warned her not to lose, but then he was there, filling all her senses and crowding out every other sensible thought as he pushed past the final barrier, taking the one thing that she could never give to another man again.

The pain was sharp, but it passed quickly as he moved and murmured tender words to her.

"I'll make it good for you, Josephine. You have nothing to worry about," he said as he rained light kisses on her cheeks and moved inside her. His pace was slow at first but grew faster and faster as passion rose until that moment when something wonderful crashed over her.

She was suddenly floating high in a field of white flower petals that drifted slowly down, until the feel of the leather against her back and a strong man pressed to her body registered. In that moment, clarity returned swiftly and sharply, and Josephine Galena Valencia asked herself: *What have I done?*

Well, Josephine, I think we all know what you've done, but the question now is, what will you do next? You've just hit the bump in the road full on, and when you land, will you take the Rake detour or try to get back on the path to Martin?

Chapter Five

Josephine tiptoed carefully across the veranda, avoiding the squeaky floorboard. The front door groaned as she opened it, and she bit her lip, praying that neither her *abuela* nor her mother had heard the low sound. But as she entered, Zara was sitting at the kitchen table, sipping a cup of *café con leche*. She looked up as Josephine entered, eyed her directly, and said, "I never thought I'd live to see this day."

"*Mami*, please. You sound just like *Abuela*," she said and glanced around nervously for her grandmother.

"You're lucky that she had to go to work early today," her mother said and gazed at her over the rim of her coffee cup. "Want to tell me why you look like you slept in your uniform and are sneaking in at this hour?"

She slogged to the table, her conscience heavy and dragging her down. "I don't know how it happened, but…" She sucked in a breath, and then the words exploded from her mouth. "I spent the night with Rake Solvino in his railcar."

"I beg your pardon?" Zara said and shook her head to clear her ears and make sure she'd heard right.

"I don't know how it happened. One second I was making him sandwiches and drinking champagne—"

"Drinking champagne is probably a good explanation for how it happened," her mother said dryly, but with an obvious note of amusement in her voice.

Shamefaced, Josephine looked away and shook her head. "Maybe it was that, but maybe it was also that I saw Martin with another woman. I was so confused and hurt, and Rake was so charming and attentive."

Zara moved around the table and wrapped an arm around her daughter.

"I don't know what to do. I always wanted to wait to be intimate with a man until I got married. A man I loved and wanted to spend the rest of my life with," Josephine said and thought of the petals that had rained down last night, only this morning it was an avalanche of crushed and mangled gardenia flowers.

"Sometimes things happen that we don't expect. It was that way with me and your father."

The mention of her father drew Josephine's attention from her own problems and to the ones her mother must have faced so many years earlier.

"What was he like?" She'd wondered about that for a very long time, but Josephine understood it was something her mother normally didn't want to discuss.

As sadness crept into Zara's expressive brown eyes, much as it did at any mention of her father, Josephine said, "I'm sorry, *Mami*. I know it hurts you to talk about him."

Zara nodded and swiped at an errant tear. "It does, but maybe it's time we talked. Your father was so handsome and charming. Talented."

Josephine shot her a puzzled look. "A talented soldier?"

Zara stumbled as she replied, "He was very good at marching and shooting."

It seemed odd, but Josephine decided to press about something much more important. "Did you love him?"

With a heartfelt sigh, Zara said, "I did love him. Do you love Martin?"

If anyone had asked her before yesterday morning, the answer would have been an unequivocal yes. As she searched her heart, she wanted to believe there was a reasonable explanation for what she'd seen in the park. That she could get past the unexplainable attraction to Rake and still have a life with Martin.

"I think I do, but I'm so confused, *Mami*. I made such a big mistake."

Zara cupped her chin and gently urged her face upward. "When you're hurting, you sometimes make bad decisions, but they don't have to define your life."

As she met her mother's gaze, shimmering with unshed tears, it was obvious her mother wasn't just referring to last night. Zara had made her share of mistakes, but she'd picked herself up after every one to follow her dreams and take care of her family.

At her confused hesitation, Zara said, "Say nothing about what happened, Josephine. Not to Martin or to your grandmother. Not a thing, and try to get on with your life."

Josephine didn't know what was worse. Martin possibly being unfaithful. Her *definitely* being unfaithful. Or keeping both of those things from her *abuela*.

"Josephine?" her mother prompted.

"I have to go and get cleaned up for work," she said and shot to her feet. "I have to think about this. About what to do. About what's the *right* thing to do."

She hurried away as fast as she could with the weight of her conscience dragging on her leg like a ball and chain.

The server placed the high tea service on the table in Rake's suite and after the man had left, Rake smiled at the beautiful woman sitting across from him. "It's good to see you again," he said.

Now, who saw this coming?

"I'm so glad I came down before Sondra and Father. I wanted to have you all to myself, if only for another day or two," said his sister, Lucia.

Okay, friends. It's not as bad as we thought.

Lucia reached across the narrow width of the table and grasped his hand. "I've missed you so. Palm Beach is not the same without you."

"I've missed you as well, and I'm so proud of you. My sister, the nurse. Mother would be so happy to see what you've accomplished."

Lucia smiled with pleasure, but then grew serious. "I just had to do it. When I saw how those nurses took care of you while you were sick, I realized I wanted to be able to help others like that as well."

The mention of his illness stole some of the joy of spending time with his one and only sister. Especially since once his father arrived, things had a tendency to get…difficult.

"And where were you last night? I came by to see you as soon as I got in, but you weren't in."

Much like things were going to get difficult if he told Lucia where he'd been, but he had never been one to keep anything from his older sister. "I was with a young woman. One of the concierges in the hotel."

Lucia's teacup rattled against the saucer as she set it down. "Rake! Haven't you learned anything from watching our father?"

He shook his head, picked up one of the delicate ham and watercress finger sandwiches, and jammed it in his mouth. "I'm not like Ernesto," he said around chews, unable to stay silent. "I have better sense than to chase after every woman in sight and then end up with someone like Sondra."

"She's really not all that bad," Lucia replied and dabbed some clotted cream onto the scone on her plate.

With a shrug, he said, "I'm sorry. I forgot that she was your friend in boarding school."

It might be time to mention that it was an all-girls boarding school and that when the young ladies got bored, they'd practice kissing with each other like they would do with the boys. Except Sondra and Lucia discovered that they liked kissing each other way more than they liked kissing the boys. Uh-huh.

"She is…my friend," his sister said, an odd tone in her voice that had him examining her more carefully as if he were seeing her for the first time.

Lucia blushed under his scrutiny and reached for another sandwich, avoiding his eyes.

"Lucia, is there something you want to tell me?"

"I think our father is having an affair. He's been secretive and distant. He's been traveling a lot lately, and I worry about what's happening with him and Sondra."

"Because she's your friend," he said.

She dropped her knife and shot back angrily, "Of course because she's my friend. And I don't want her to be hurt, just like I don't want you to be hurt."

Rake had no clue what she meant by that. "Hurt? Me?"

"Father isn't just coming down for a visit, Rake. He wants to see how you're running the hotel, because he doesn't believe that you can do it."

"I *can* do it. I have invested too much time and money in this hotel to have it fail." He needed to prove to his father that he was capable of taking over the family business so he could wash his hands of those other, illicit operations.

Lucia met his gaze directly. "I know you can do it. Do you remember that time father left us for two weeks with that horrible nanny? The one who would lock us in our rooms alone at night even though she knew I was afraid of the dark?"

He remembered all too well. For the first day or so he could hear his sister crying miserably in her room. Luckily his father had gotten him a book on magic that contained instructions on how to pick a lock. He'd stolen a hatpin the next day and picked the lock on Lucia's door so he could sneak in at night and keep her company before returning to his room in the early morning.

"I'm glad father got rid of her as soon as he came back from Europe."

"I'm glad, too, and I never forgot what you did for me. If there's anything I can do for you, just let me know."

"I appreciate that, Lucia. It means the world that you believe in me."

His hunger restored, he dug into the high tea with renewed vigor, but found himself thinking of gooey melted cheese sandwiches and the luminous Josephine from last night.

Maybe he was more like his father than he wanted to admit.

The single red rose sat on the concierge spot along with a playing card: the King of Hearts.

Heat rose in Josephine's cheeks and she looked around, hoping no one would notice as she grabbed the rose and stuffed it into the wastebasket.

She wanted to try to forget the other night and all that had happened with Rake until she could get a handle on what she was feeling and how she was going to deal with the situation. Something that might be hard to do since she worked in Rake's hotel.

At the desk, she opened her secret drawer and pulled out the snow globe. Josephine shook it and peered at the snowflakes dancing around the smiling couple at the center of the globe, walking hand in hand along a path. Frozen in that perfectly romantic moment, they had no cares or doubts, much like she'd always felt with Martin. But as she'd recently discovered, their relationship was not quite as picture perfect.

Jamming the globe back into the drawer, she saw a folded square of paper. Martin had left another note! She opened it eagerly but it was short, bordering on terse, and said only that he was sorry he'd missed her again last night, but that he'd had a lead in the case and had not been able to come by. He would try to visit today.

But she didn't want to see either him or Rake anytime soon.

Straightening out the papers on the desk, she caught sight of Rake at one side of the lobby chatting with a woman that Liana had mentioned was his sister, a troubled look on his face. At one point, he glanced in her direction and offered up a weak smile, but then returned his attention to his sibling. When he finished chatting with her, he started walking toward Josephine, but before he could make it across the lobby, an older gentleman came up to the desk, asking her for directions to the solarium.

Josephine snared that opportunity to personally walk the man to the spot, neatly avoiding Rake.

By the time she returned to the desk, Rake was gone, and he didn't return for the rest of the morning. Near lunch hour, her friend Liana came by, obviously bursting with more news to share. As she stood next to Josephine, she said, "You're not going to believe what I heard."

"What did you hear?" she asked, praying it had nothing to do with her and Rake or her and Martin.

"They found a body last night upriver. They think it's Mr. Slayton."

"Oh no, that's horrible! The poor man," she said and wondered if that was the lead Martin had mentioned in his note.

Liana laid a hand on her arm and was nearly jumping with excitement as she said, "But there's more. Someone saw Rake with a woman by the marina the other night, and then he got into a carriage with her and they sped off into the night."

We hadn't really sped, Josephine thought. "Do they know who the woman is?" she asked, praying that whoever was spreading the gossip had not realized it was her.

"No. It was too dark."

Thank God, Josephine thought as Liana plowed on with her gossip. "It gets better and...well, here comes trouble," she said and jerked her head in the direction of the front desk where Lucia was greeting a beautiful young woman who had arrived with a mountain of luggage.

"It looks like she plans on being here a long time. Who is she?" Josephine asked.

"Oh, that's Rake's wife."

The air left Josephine's lungs and for a moment the world spun around dizzily. She sucked in a deep breath, but it brought on a coughing fit.

Liana clapped her on the back, trying to help her breathe. "Are you okay?"

"Yes, yes, of course," she said in a strangled voice. But as she watched the woman kiss Rake on the cheek, nothing could be further from the truth.

Now, who could have seen this coming? Well, possibly me, but no wonder Lucia thought it was a big problem that her little brother had spent the night with our dear Josephine.

Rake had found himself with the unenviable task of trying to avoid one woman all day long while trying to see another woman who was obviously trying to avoid him.

Since tea with Lucia, he had been preparing himself for the arrival of his father and Sondra, but luckily that had apparently been delayed for several weeks due to something that had come up with his father's business dealings. He was grateful for the reprieve since, despite Lucia's friendship with the woman who was his stepmother, Rake couldn't seem to forgive his father for dallying with a string of women even before his mother died, then marrying one that was his daughter's age so quickly afterward. Plus, he had always thought there was something slightly off about Sondra.

To add insult to injury, his wife Penelope had decided to surprise him and come for an extended stay at the Regal Sol. It was the last thing he expected or wanted since, as far as he was concerned, his marriage to Penelope was as good as over. If not for the demands and time spent the last few months getting the hotel back on course, he would have long ago started the paperwork to divorce his wife. Even though he had once loved Penelope and she had been at his side during his illness, he had discovered that his wife had been unfaithful with multiple men over a number of months.

And then there was Josephine. Smart, spunky, and surprisingly sexy Josephine.

Something inside him that had been long dead had come alive last night as they'd talked and much later, as they'd made love. It had been more special than he could have imagined.

Only now Josephine had been avoiding him all day long.

Determined to discover what was troubling her, he hurried to the door of his suite and threw it open, only to find the young woman already standing on his doorstep, about to knock.

"I've been trying to see you all day," he said, stepping aside and inviting her to enter.

She hesitated for a moment, but then with a resigned sigh, she walked in, but didn't take a seat.

"I think we have to talk about what happened the other night," she said and wrapped her arms around herself, her stance defensive.

He hurried over to stand before her and said, "I agree. I think we have *a lot* to say to each other. That night was very special to me."

She raised an eyebrow and straightened her spine as her gaze became steely. "Really? So special that you didn't think to mention that you had a wife?"

Rake looked away from that penetrating gaze, hating that he'd been less than truthful with her. Shaking his head, he said, "It's a complicated situation."

"So you're saying you're *not* married, because there was a woman at the front desk today who says you are."

He gritted his teeth and forced out, "Penelope *is* my wife, but our marriage has been over for some time. We haven't been together for quite a while."

"Considering the pile of luggage she came with today, she plans on staying for quite a while," Josephine countered. She quickly added, "And by *been together*—"

"Yes, that kind of together," he said on a rough breath. "I was sick with a tropical fever and discovered afterward that Penelope had been unfaithful to me. I couldn't stay with her once I found out. That's why the other night was…so very, very good, Josephine. And not just what happened in the railcar. Everything. Talking. Eating. Just spending time together. It's been a long time since it's felt so right with anyone."

"But it's not right if it's based on a lie, Rake."

"I'm going to end it," he said and held his hands out in pleading. "I'm going to make it right by you."

She shook her head vigorously. "Not on my account, Rake. I feel guilty enough about what happened, and I already have a—" She cut off abruptly, then simply said, "You barely know me. And I don't know you. We just made a terrible, foolish mistake."

He didn't get a chance to reply as she bolted past him and raced out the door, leaving him to wonder how he'd made such a mess of things.

Possibly by not telling Josephine that you were married before crushing her flower. And what's this about his illness again? Could it be we're in for yet another surprise on that front?

The alligators had done quite a good job making it difficult to identify Richard Slayton. If not for the fact that what was left of the body was wearing a Regal Sol uniform and that Martin had found the water-logged remnants of a note on hotel stationery addressed to Slayton in the man's jacket pocket, it would have been hard for Martin to recognize the man.

The state of decay along with the other facts that Martin had been able to put together all pointed to when Slayton might have been killed. He had failed to show up for his shift for the first time a week ago, and no one had seen him after that.

That information combined with a series of occurrences a few years ago all seemed to be directing Martin and his partner to identify one possible suspect as the mysterious Sin Sombra: Rake Solvino. There had been several murders in Palm Beach when Rake had returned there to work with his father. After Solvino's arrival in Miami to direct the building of the Regal Sol, there had been a break in the activity in Palm Beach, but a few murders had taken place in Miami. Then there was another gap of several months that coincided with Solvino's supposed illness until his return to health and the recurrence of issues in both Palm Beach and Miami.

Not to mention, Solvino hadn't been seen around the hotel the night before Slayton failed to report to work. The night he was likely killed.

His gut tightened with the thought that Josephine's colleague was dead and that she might be working for a murderer. And if Martin hadn't been pulled away to work for the mayor, he might be too, since Rake had hired the Pinkertons to protect the hotel.

Thanks to the investigation, he had been unable to see Josephine the last couple of days, and he hated how they had parted the last time. She had clearly been upset about something, and even though he'd tried to make things right with the notes he'd left, he knew it wasn't as good as explaining to her face-to-face. Which he planned to do that night. While he couldn't tell her everything, he was willing to risk telling her enough so that he could keep her out of harm's way. She was too important to him, and he'd risk losing his job if it meant Josephine would be safe.

He was just finishing up his report on Slayton and the time lines that he and Nita had worked out when someone knocked on his office door. He looked up to find Josephine standing in his open doorway.

"Josephine," he said and popped to his feet.

"I hope I'm not interrupting. I know how busy you've been," she said, and his gut tightened at the upset tone in her voice and the sadness in her gaze.

"I am…was. I had planned on going to see you tonight." He gestured to the chair in front of his desk and with a nod, she walked over and sat down. Her hands were clenched tightly on the handle of her small reticule and tension radiated from every part of her body.

He closed the door to his office and sat in the chair opposite her. Leaning forward, he reached out to lay a hand on her knee, but she shied away.

"Josephine, what's wrong? Something has been bothering you, and I can't figure out what it is."

Her head snapped up, and she said, "I saw you the other morning."

Martin narrowed his gaze, trying to figure out what was causing her anger, but was unable to. Shaking his head, he said, "When? Where?"

"By the Royal Palm. You were there. With a woman," she said and plucked at her purse nervously.

He flashed back to that moment. Nita had just gotten some bad news from home and had been upset. He had given her a friendly hug as a friend and colleague, but Nita had surprised him by deepening the embrace and attempting a kiss. He could see how Josephine had gotten the wrong impression.

"That was my new partner, Nita Alvarez. She had just gotten word that her mother was ill and well, she's a strong woman. Like you. I knew it had to be serious when she got that upset, so I was just being supportive," he said and raked a hand through his hair in frustration. He should never have let the situation with Nita get so out of hand that morning.

"I can see how you might have gotten the wrong idea, but I thought you knew me better. Trusted me."

Josephine's color paled to the point he thought she might faint, but instead she straightened and shook her head. "Your partner? A woman?"

He nodded. "She's actually not the first female detective Pinkerton's hired. Would you like to meet her? She's right next door." He paused and tilted his head. "Although I'd like to think that you might have more faith in your fiancé. After all, I've never given you any reason to doubt me, have I?"

Josephine shot to her feet and backed away from him, a shaky hand pressed to her stomach. "I'm sorry, Martin. So, so sorry," she said and his heart clenched at the pain visible on her features.

He stood and walked to her. Took hold of her hands that were icy and trembling. "Please, Josephine. Whatever is wrong, you can tell me."

"It's just that… I saw you together, and I was upset. So upset and feeling so alone. And then there he was, so charming and understanding. And we had champagne, and I've never had champagne before." She looked so distraught, and her words were coming faster and faster.

A sick feeling was coming over Martin, but he tried to keep calm and understanding. Cradling her cheek, he brushed his thumb across her wan skin and urged her on. "You can tell me anything, my darling. Please, tell me."

"I didn't mean for it to happen." She almost wailed the words, and in that moment, his blood ran cold.

"What…happened?" he ground out, nearly growling. "Who gave you the champagne?"

She couldn't quite meet his eyes. "Rake Solvino."

His stomach flipped nauseously even as he told himself that he was thinking it was much worse than it actually had been. "You… kissed him?"

She bit her lip, and tears welled in her eyes as she finally met his gaze and shook her head ruefully. "I… I was…inappropriate with him."

The air rushed out of Martin's lungs suddenly, and he swayed a bit, gripping the desk to steady himself. It was far worse than he'd imagined.

He looked at her as if seeing her for the first time. His beautiful, smart, innocent, had to-wait-for-the-wedding Josephine. *Only she hadn't waited.*

"You told me about your grandmother…and the flower…and how we had to do things in the right order… We had plans," he said, floundering for the right words as the anger built inside him.

She laid a hand on his arm and pleaded, tears sliding down her cheeks. "Martin, I am so sorry. Please forgive me! I know that I did something just awful, but it was because I was hurting and not thinking clearly. Please."

"Are you saying that he…he took advantage of you when you were drunk?" he pressed, his voice rising as the rage burned hotter.

But as a condemning flush worked across her cheeks, it was clear Josephine had not been that indisposed. Terrible images of her passionately entangled with that robber baron were seared into his brain.

"I can't believe this. How could you? I-I have to go." He rushed out of his office, so furious that he was afraid of what he might say. What he might do.

For at that moment, our patient, kind, caring, and gentle Detective Martin was sorely tempted to find that heel Rake Solvino and beat the other man to a bloody pulp. But despite his hurt and anger, Martin knew one thing for sure: no matter what had happened, no matter how badly she'd broken his heart, he could never allow Josephine to be involved with a criminal.

Josephine rolled over in bed and stared at the moonlight streaming in through the window and onto the wooden floor of her room. Another sleepless night to add to the others she'd experienced over the last two weeks. Finding rest had proved difficult with her guilty conscience about both Martin and Rake. She hadn't seen either of them in all that time since Martin was ignoring her and she was avoiding Rake.

Little by little the room brightened until the distant chime of church bells warned she should be rising. Even that light sound made her head pound. She sat up and the room spun around crazily, bringing a round of nausea. With a deep breath, she brought the dizziness under control and forced herself to rise, wash, and dress for work.

Her mother and grandmother were both downstairs in the kitchen and greeted her sunnily at first, but her sickness was impossible to hide from both their eagle-eyed gazes.

"*Mi'ja*, you look a little pale," her *abuela* said as she placed a steaming cup of *café con leche* before her on the table.

"You don't have a fever, do you?" her mother asked and laid the back of her hand on Josephine's forehead.

"I just haven't been sleeping well. I'm a little tired."

Alberta laid a dish of toast on the table and jammed her hands on her hips. "I'd ask if Martin was keeping you out too late, but we haven't seen him around lately. Is something wrong?"

Zara and Josephine shared a guilty glance and Zara hastily replied, "Martin has been busy at work."

"And I have too," she said, and wanting to escape before her *abuela* truly got wind of something being wrong, she jumped to her feet. Unfortunately, another round of dizziness had her head reeling and she fell back onto the chair, a clammy sweat erupting all across her body. Sucking in a few rough breaths, she restored control.

"You came in late last night. Did you have a chance to have supper?" her *abuela* asked.

"I didn't get a chance to eat after I left work." Her gaze connected with Zara's, who clearly understood that her attempt two weeks ago to track down Martin and speak with him hadn't gone well.

Bustling around, her *abuela* laid a hand on her forehead and said, "No fever, so that must be why you're not feeling well. Let me make you something to eat."

But as her grandmother walked away to begin making breakfast, her mother peered at her intently and then started counting something on her fingers. The count hadn't gone far when Zara wrapped an arm around Josephine's shoulders and called out "Make her some eggs, *Mami*."

"Of course, some eggs are just the thing to settle her stomach," her grandmother said, but there was a look on her mother's face that said otherwise.

Josephine wondered what eggs had to do with anything, but when her *abuela* put them before her, her stomach revolted violently and she dashed to the bathroom to avoid embarrassing herself.

When she emerged, both women were standing near the doorway, staring at Josephine in horror.

"It's probably just a little stomach upset. I'm sure it'll pass in a few hours. I'll have to send Mr. Adams a message somehow—"

But she broke off as Zara took her arm gently, a look of despair on her face, as she steered Josephine to the sagging well-worn sofa in the living room. "No, honey. Sit down."

"I can't. I have to be at the hotel—"

"*Sit down*, Josephine," her grandmother said sharply.

Josephine sat. "Please don't worry, *Abuela*. I'll be just fine in—"

"Nine months," Zara cut in urgently, squeezing her arm.

Confused, Josephine stared at her mother as recognition slowly dawned in her still-fuzzy head. A chill swept through her. Was her mother saying… Could she actually be…?

"No, Zara, you're mistaken. Josephine knows how important it is to not ruin her flower." Her *abuela* looked in her direction and said, "Right, Josephine? Tell your mother…" But her voice trailed off at the guilty look on Josephine's face. "No, Josephine. *No.* You understood about the flower. About how you can never get it back!" she said harshly.

"Maybe it's something else," Josephine said, trying to count down as her mother had done.

"Josephine, I thought you understood. That you saw how hard it's been for your mother. The way some treat her and even how they treated you," her *abuela* urged.

"*Mami*, please. This isn't what she needs to hear right now," her mother said and urged Alberta to calm down.

"No, I'm sure it isn't. But I am sorry, Josephine. I had hoped for more for you," she said and rushed from the room.

Josephine stared at her retreating back, the sight fuzzy from her tears. "*Mami*, I'm so sorry, but maybe it's just a cold."

Zara grabbed the plate of eggs and brought it closer, making Josephine's stomach twist in revolt again. "*Mija*, I have no doubt. You're pregnant."

With that proclamation, the dizziness descended on Josephine once more and for the first time in her life, Josephine Galena Valencia fainted.

Oh my goodness! Josephine is having the boss's baby? Alberta is truly not happy about this. Martin won't be either.

Chapter Six

When she stirred, Zara led her back to bed, tucking the covers in around Josephine's legs. Her *abuela* had not returned to the room and was probably on her way to work already. Or maybe she was so disappointed in Josephine she just couldn't bear to face her unmarried, pregnant granddaughter right now.

Pregnant. The word bounced around inside Josephine's skull like a bagatelle ball ricocheting off its game pegs.

Her mother grabbed the plate with the dry toast from the nightstand and handed it to Josephine. "Eat this. It will settle your stomach."

She took a bite but protested as she chewed. "How can you be sure I'm with child?"

"Your *abuela* couldn't eat eggs while she was with child. I couldn't either. That's how she knew I was pregnant with you."

"It's not possible." She and Rake had only made love once that night. Okay, maybe twice, but she knew lots of girls who were far more inappropriate and had been spared this fate.

Zara cradled her cheek. "It's more than possible, Josephine. I should know."

Josephine was surprised Zara was willing to talk about this, when she'd been so upset and uncomfortable sharing part of her story weeks earlier. But she was eager to hear more of her mother's past.

"You've never told me how you got pregnant with me."

Zara hesitated, still slightly uncomfortable, but began talking. "I thought he loved me. We had known each other as children, in school together, but then he…left. He moved around a great deal…"

Her voice trailed off as she hesitated and looked away, her pain obvious.

"*Mami*, it's okay. You don't have to say more," Josephine said and covered her mother's hand with hers, squeezing it reassuringly.

"You know he was a…soldier," Zara said and continued. "He came back and we were together, but then… Well, I thought that once I told him about you, he would stay, but before I could, he was called away."

"And he never came back?" Josephine asked, wondering what kind of man would just walk away from the woman he loved. Would Martin? Would Rake? But then she recalled Rake's wife and fear gripped her hard. Rake could be that kind of man. Maybe Martin could too; he'd walked out of his office without a backward glance at her nearly a fortnight ago. How could he ever want to be with her again if he knew she was having another man's baby? Panic filled her at the thought.

"No, he didn't come back," Zara said, "and I had no idea where he went. I always hoped that he would return one day, only…"

Her mother shook her head and suddenly pushed to her feet. "Why don't you finish up that toast and get some rest? I'll walk you to work when you're feeling better."

Josephine nodded and watched her mother rush out the door. In truth, she was already starting to feel better physically because the food had helped to settle her stomach. Mentally, however, she was at sixes and sevens. She didn't want to believe that her mother was right, but doing a quick calculation in her head, she knew she was several weeks past the time when she should have gotten her monthly menses. Josephine pondered how she could tell the two men in her life about the pregnancy. She felt sick imagining how they would respond. And her *abuela* would be even more disappointed in her when she found out how it had happened.

Plus, she was worried about what kind of mother she could possibly be and how that would affect all that she wanted in life. She had only one more course to complete in order to be able to tutor, but what respectable family would hire a young woman whose virtue had been compromised? Her job at the hotel could likewise be in jeopardy, especially if Rake responded negatively to the news. As for her lifelong dream of writing a novel, how would she find the time if she had to also add caring for a baby to work and finishing her class?

But she had never been one to just sit and take things lying down, like she was doing now. She tossed off the covers, grabbed her reticule, and marched downstairs to the kitchen where her mother was cleaning up.

"I'm going to work," she said.

"I'll walk with you." Zara tossed aside the towel she had been using to dry the dishes and met Josephine at the door. Smoothing her hand across Josephine's upswept hair, she said, "It will be okay."

"I wish I could be so sure about that. Were you sure?" Josephine asked as they started on the short walk from the cottages to the Regal Sol.

Zara shook her head. "Not at all. I had so many doubts and worries about raising you alone."

"Not entirely alone. You had *Abuela*." Josephine's heart clenched. "*Mami*, do you think she'll ever be able to forgive me?"

"In time, she'll come around, you'll see. She forgave me. Eventually."

Josephine shot a half glance at her mother from the corner of her eye, hearing the upset in her tone. "Did you ever wish you had done it differently?"

Love shone from her mother's eyes as she smiled and said, "I'm glad I had you."

"That's not what I asked," Josephine said, though truthfully she felt relieved at her mother's answer.

"I know." Zara stopped short suddenly, the anguish apparent on her face. "Do you wish I had?"

Since Zara was her best friend in addition to her mother, she had to be truthful. "I always wished I knew my father. It's why I have to tell Rake about the baby."

Her mother looked discomfited at her confession. "What do you plan on doing about Martin? Do you plan on telling him as well?" Zara said, her tone filled with concern.

"I think I owe it to Martin to be truthful and tell him what's happened." She started walking again, and Zara matched her pace to Josephine's.

As they neared one of the entrances to the hotel, a small billboard heralded an upcoming show by a well-known troupe of actors and singers. The handsome male lead, Ronaldo de la Sera, beamed a toothy smile from the billboard and Josephine could swear that there was a real twinkle in his eyes a second before he suddenly winked at her.

She blinked, clearing her vision, and stared back at the billboard, but it was just paper and ink pasted on wood.

Surprisingly, some excitement rose up at the thought of seeing the troupe and its handsome male lead. Ronaldo had been one of her *abuela*'s favorites since she had heard him sing many years earlier. Whenever her *abuela* could afford it, she would visit the phonograph room in town to listen to one of his latest recordings and take Josephine with her.

Josephine clapped her hands and said, "Look who's coming to the Regal Sol. *Abuela* will be so excited, *Mami*." *If she ever speaks to me again,* Josephine thought.

"Yes, she will," Zara replied, but there was a flatness to her response that caused Josephine to peer at her mother intently.

"Are you okay? You look like you've just seen a ghost."

Zara just shook her head and said, "We need to go. You don't want to be too late for work."

The Valencia women seem to be having a very difficult morning. Even the great Ronaldo de la Sera couldn't help! Maybe we should see how Josephine's ~~employer~~ ~~paramour~~ ~~love child's father~~*... Ahem, how Rake is doing this fine day, shall we?*

❄

Penelope ran a finger along the edge of Rake's desk and scrunched up her nose in distaste. With a regal tilt and pivot of her head, she glanced around his suite and with an indignant sniff said, "This place really needs some style. It's so…pedestrian."

Rake laid down his fountain pen and peered at his wife as she strolled around the room examining the various furnishings that he had chosen. "This is my suite, and I like it just the way it is," he said, trying to fight the anger that Penelope could rouse in him so easily.

Penelope made that face again, as if she were smelling something bad. "If you want to impress your father—"

"I don't," he shot back, although secretly he very much did want to make his father take notice of his accomplishments. Penelope knew that and never failed to find a way to use that for her own advantage.

His wife—soon to be ex-wife—arched a perfectly shaped brow and said, "Come on now, Rake. We both know that everything you do is to prove to your father you're just as good as he is, but you're not, are you?"

Rake pictured wrapping his hands around that long, elegant throat and squeezing it tight just to shut her up. Instead, he fisted his hands on his desktop and inhaled deeply, battling that urge. He wasn't a violent man by nature, but Penelope brought out the worst in him. It made him wonder what he'd ever seen in her until the inner voice inside him that sounded too much like his father said, *That blonde hair like silk. That face and body and those legs. Dear Lord, those long, delicious legs.*

"Why are you here, Penelope? Did you come to Miami just to torture me?"

Penelope beamed him her siren's smile. The one that used to move him but no longer did since he'd learned just how fake it was. How fake she was.

"Come now, Rake. Don't tell me you don't miss me? Miss what we can do together?" she said and sashayed sexily toward him. When she reached the desk, she sat on its edge and leaned toward him, giving him a clear view of the creamy skin and plump bosom above the line of her bodice. She laid her hand on his chest and trailed it down, but he snared it before she reached her desired destination.

"Miss you lying to me? Being indiscreet with the manager at my father's hotel in Palm Beach?"

She pouted, slid her hand back up to his chest, and splayed it directly over his heart. "It was a mistake, Rake."

He picked her hand off his chest as if he were removing a distasteful bug. "A mistake that went on for how long? A year? Two? And what about all the other men?"

"I took care of you while you were sick all those months," she reminded him, her cajoling voice changing to crisp and icy on a dime.

He couldn't deny that. "I appreciate what you did, but everything changed after that. We're not the same people anymore. We're not good for each other."

"We are," she insisted, but her words lacked conviction.

"As I told you months ago before I returned to Miami, our marriage is over. As soon as I can get some business things settled, I plan to file for divorce."

She flounced off the desk, her crystal-blue eyes flashing. "I won't agree to it. You owe me for all I've done for you."

He couldn't argue with the fact that he did owe her in some ways. They had loved each other at one time. They'd had plans together until he'd gotten sick, and that months-long fever had changed so many things.

"I will take care of you, Penelope. You needn't worry about that, but if you fight me…" He didn't need to finish for her to understand what he meant.

"I love you, Rake," she said, but it lacked the vehemence with which she'd once professed her love. It was almost mechanical, as if she said it because it was expected she say it.

"No you don't, Penelope. It's why it's better that we go our separate ways."

With an elegant sniff, she regally tilted her head up and said, "You won't get rid of me that easily."

Without waiting for his reply, she hurried out of his suite, leaving Rake to ponder just what it would take to be rid of his troublesome and unfaithful wife.

※

The small fishing boat rocked side to side beneath Martin's feet as he peered through the binoculars, searching for the caves that supposedly existed along the riverbank. He and Nita had been keeping an eye on some saloons of interest in North Miami when he suddenly noticed a group of Tequestas had appeared near one of the locations. After some digging around, one of his informants had mentioned that the native people had tunnels that led down to the river, which they used to bring their goods to market.

He scoured the riverbank as the boat chugged upstream; however, there was little but rock, sand, mangrove roots, and tangled underbrush. As they neared the North Fork, the vegetation thinned and the rock outcroppings grew more abundant. Suddenly, he caught sight of an opening in the rocks.

"Over there," he pointed to the riverbank and shouted to the boat captain to be heard over the noise of the engine.

"Do you see something?" Nita asked, coming to stand beside him.

He gestured to the spot and handed her the binoculars. "Over there. That opening."

Nita took the binoculars and raised them. With a nod, she said, "It looks like the entrance to a tunnel or a cave."

"I've seen the Tequestas paddle up to them in their canoes," the boat captain said.

Martin and Nita looked at the man in surprise. "Who else knows about them?" Martin asked.

The boat captain shrugged. "They're not common knowledge if that's what you're asking. Besides the Tequestas, maybe those white folk who've worked the waterways for years," he said and brought the small ship as close as he could to the edge of the bank and the rounded opening in the limestone. "The river is high now on account of last night's rain, but normally you could anchor on the riverbank and walk right into the caves. They exit a little way up in North Miami."

And from there, it's just about a dozen or so blocks to reach the heart of Miami and the Regal Sol, Martin thought.

He and Nita shared a glance that said she was thinking the same thing as he was.

"Could you please take us back to the Regal Sol marina?" she said, and the captain steered the boat around and toward Miami. With the current moving in their direction, they returned to the hotel's marina in under fifteen minutes. Someone with a powerful yacht could do the trip upstream to the caves in about the same time, Martin figured. If a crew of men was waiting, they could unload their contraband and be back at the hotel in little more than an hour.

It would be easy enough for Solvino to disappear for that length of time without calling much attention to himself.

Once they were back on land, Martin and Nita walked toward the Regal Sol and ran over the evidence they had so far.

"You say this Sin Sombra came to the attention of the Palm Beach office about four years ago?" he asked, just to confirm he had the timeline correct.

"Yes. Right around the time Solvino returned from Miami. I talked to some of the workers in his Palm Beach hotel, and they say he had some kind of tropical fever that he contracted while he was overseeing the construction of the hotel."

"And right around the time that Sin Sombra's activities in Miami went quiet," Martin said. "We also know that when Solvino and the other railroad barons started building the hotels, nearly six years ago, the first problems and murders began in this area," he added.

"We do, and while it's all circumstantial—"

"Cases have been built on less," he urged, anger kindling in his gut at the hotel owner who had seduced Josephine.

"You really don't like Solvino, huh? Are you sure there isn't more to this that you're not telling me?" Nita said and paused as they reached the steps of the veranda.

Martin was tempted to spill it all out to her, but Nita was so by-the-book that he was certain she'd report him to their superiors and get him kicked off the case. "I just want to catch Sin Sombra and put an end to his crime spree."

Her gaze narrowed, but then she dipped her head and visibly relaxed. "I'll take your word on it…for now. It's almost time for supper. Would you like to get something to eat?"

Martin was a little taken aback at her forward suggestion, but then again, Nita was an independent woman. She wasn't afraid of pursuing what she wanted, and as he examined her features, it occurred to him that since the other morning when he'd comforted her, there was something different there.

His bruised ego was tempted to grab at it eagerly. Nita was smart and attractive and having her interested in him was a salve on the wounds from Josephine's actions. But he wasn't ready just yet to move on.

"I appreciate the invitation, but I still have a few things to do around the Regal Sol."

She eyed him speculatively and smiled sexily. "Some other time maybe. I'll see you in the morning, Martin."

"Have a good night, Nita."

He waited for her to walk away and then he bounded up the steps, intending to explore every nook and cranny of the hotel. He was determined to discover whether the caves extended farther than they'd been told or if there was some other kind of secret passage from the marina into the hotel that would make it even easier for Sin Sombra to come and go without being seen.

For the next hour he scoured every entrance in and out of the hotel in the basement area as well as each and every closet and storage area.

He found nothing.

He headed up to the main floor and was making his way toward the now closed kitchen when he ran into none other than Rake Solvino.

The hotel owner stopped short, surprised at finding him there. "What are you doing back here?" Rake asked.

Martin pulled back his lapel to display his badge. "Investigating, Mr. Solvino. It's what you pay my agency to do, which you might remember if you weren't so busy seducing my fiancée."

Rake's eyes widened in surprise. "Your fiancée? I'm not sure—"

"Which of the women it was that you seduced?" he said and grabbed hold of Rake's shirtfront, anger overriding his common sense.

"Since I'm only aware of one woman with whom I've been intimate—"

"Other than your wife up in the Empress Suite?" Martin shot back and tossed Rake away like he weighed nothing.

Rake hit the wall but easily bounced back and nonchalantly dusted off his shirtfront. "What's happening between my wife and me is none of your business. For that matter, neither is what's happening between Josephine and me."

A red haze swept across Martin's gaze and he lunged at the other man and pinned him against the wall, his forearm tight against Rake's throat. He got up so close to Rake's face that his nose nearly brushed across the other man's as he said, "She's my fiancée."

"Funny that she never mentioned you at all," Rake challenged and grabbed hold of his wrist. "And you may want to consider taking your hands off me if you want to keep your job."

"Martin! Martin, what are you doing?" Josephine shouted as she raced down the hall and forced her way in between the two men.

Rake arched a brow and glanced at Josephine. "I understand this man is your fiancé."

Josephine grimaced at the condemning tone in Rake's voice, and as Martin manhandled Rake again, she pleaded with him. "Please, Martin. This isn't going to help the situation."

Martin reluctantly released the other man and stepped back. Staring hard at Josephine, he said, "Is that what this is now? A situation?"

She laid her hand over his heart. "I'm sorry I hurt you. I never meant to, but this is not going to solve anything."

Maybe it won't, but it sure had felt good for a moment, Martin thought. And what would feel even better was telling Josephine what he suspected about Rake, but he needed more proof before he did that. Still, he had to warn her.

"He's not the kind of man you think he is, Josephine. You can't believe anything he tells you," he said and cradled her cheek gently.

Josephine smiled at him tenderly. "I know you only want what's best for me, Martin."

He nodded, then glared at Rake. "You know who you are, Sin Sombra."

Rake examined Martin as if he had two heads, then laughed heartily. "Sin Sombra? The criminal? Sorry to disappoint you, Detective, but I don't know a thing about him."

Martin scoffed. "I will prove it's you, Mr. Solvino."

He returned his gaze to Josephine. "I'm here for you whenever you're ready to talk, Josephine," he said and walked away without waiting for her reply.

Whoa. What happened to our patient, kind, caring Detective Martin? I think he's reaching the limits of that famous patience. And exactly what will happen when Josephine drops her little bombshell? Oh baby!

Chapter Seven

Rake watched Josephine as Martin walked away. Her face was a kaleidoscope of emotions. Pain. Anger. Confusion. Love. That didn't bode well for his chances.

"We need to talk," he said and offered her his arm, intending to lead her up to his suite for the conversation.

"We do," she confirmed, but ignored his offer and marched into the empty kitchen.

He followed her and trying to relieve some of the tension, he said, "We have got to stop meeting like this."

The ghost of a smile flashed across her lips before they thinned into a tight line. "Charm won't help me forget the fact that you lied to me. And that you're a married man," she said.

Rake leaned against the counter and crossed his arms. "Seems to me you weren't totally truthful either. You never mentioned you had a fiancé."

Bright color erupted across her cheeks. "I am engaged, and I love Martin, but… There's something I have to tell you."

He waited, wondering what it could be for a moment until she blurted out, "I'm with child. *Your* child, Rake."

It took him a second to process what she'd said because he didn't dare believe it. He didn't dare hope that it was true. "Are you sure, Josephine?"

"That I'm pregnant?" she asked, and at his nod, continued. "Apparently the Valencias have a surefire way to know."

He couldn't picture what that might be, but he could picture how she'd react to this next question: with a solid slap of his face. But even as he pictured it and didn't want to hurt her, he had to ask.

"But is it mine?"

Her hand flinched as if to slap him, but she held back. "You know what you took from me, Rake. I have never slept with another man."

"Not what I took, Josephine. What you freely gave."

"I should have known better than to trust you. To think you could be a gentleman," she said and started to walk out.

He grasped her arm gently and said, "I'm sorry, Josephine. I know I'm handling this badly, but...I never thought I'd be able to have a child. The doctors said it would be a miracle if I could after my illness."

She shot him a puzzled look, and he explained. "While I was here overseeing the building of the hotel six years ago, I contracted a tropical fever, probably from being bitten by the mosquitos. It didn't seem like much at first, but then it got worse, and I spent months fighting it. Afterward, Penelope and I tried for months to conceive, but it didn't happen. The doctors told us the high fevers had likely made me sterile."

"I don't know what to say except that this is your baby. I guess miracles do happen," she said.

Joy suffused him from head to toe suddenly. He couldn't believe he was getting another chance at fatherhood. "I want to be involved with this baby, Josephine. With you. I want to help you take care of it."

"Only you're still married and never told me." The joy dampened like a rain cloud had passed over him. "It makes me wonder what else you haven't shared. I'm not sure that I can trust you."

He took hold of her hand. "What Penelope and I had is long over, Josephine. And you can't deny that there is a powerful attraction between the two of us."

She shook her head. "I can't deny it, but it's not the same as what I feel for Martin. I want to make things right with him, and if he'll have me and the baby, I want to marry him. I'm sorry, Rake."

"I'm not going to give up so easily. This is my baby, and I know you have feelings for me, Josephine. I'm willing to fight for you and to be a part of my baby's life."

"Don't. Don't fight for me, because it won't change how I feel. I want *my* life to be with Martin."

This time when she walked away he didn't try to stop her. But no matter her assertions, he wasn't going to give up on her. On them.

Quite a quandary, isn't it? Penelope loves Rake, but Rake loves Josephine. Josephine loves Martin, but Martin is beginning to like Nita... Oh, wait. Now where did that come from? It looks like things are going to get quite complicated around here.

Josephine hastily scribbled the ideas in her journal. She was working on a story that she had started and set aside years earlier while she had explored a new concept for another novel. But there was something about the tale set in Venezuela during the civil wars, a story loosely based on her grandparents, that was drawing her back to it. There was something grand about two people fighting for their love while the country around them was in turmoil.

But even though it was much more emotional than her other stories, it needed more. She had already added a touch of her mother's zest for life and love of song.

She leaned back in her chair and chewed on the pencil as she let her mind wander, but then the ideas began to come to her hard and fast. She rapidly jotted them down before they slid away from her.

Love lost. War and violence. A hero in jeopardy. A woman praying for his return, forced to fend for herself. Maybe giving herself to her lover before he leaves for war. Finding herself with child, alone and wondering how she will raise the child should her lover not return.

Sniffling, Josephine realized she was crying and swiped at the errant tears slipping down her cheeks.

She'd let her life bleed onto the pages, and maybe that was a good thing. Maybe she could exorcise her ghosts that way. As she committed the first scene to the page, the spirits danced around her, urging her on as the tears came again and streamed down her cheeks.

Josephine was so lost in the story that she didn't notice her *abuela*'s entrance into the room until her grandmother sat beside her and wrapped an arm around her shoulders. As she had so often, Josephine turned into that embrace and finally released all the emotions that she had pent up. She cried until her body shook and there were no tears left.

"I'm sorry, *Abuela*," she said, and it wasn't just about the crying jag. They hadn't spoken about the pregnancy—or really anything at all—since that morning. Josephine hoped this comfort was a sign that her grandmother would be able to forgive her.

"I didn't listen to you and made a mistake," she said, and a cascade of crushed and broken gardenias fell around them while she continued her story.

Her grandmother sighed. "*Mi'ja*, do you know why I told you that story?"

"Because God wants us to remain pure until we're married?" Alberta was quite religious.

"Well, yes. But also because I saw how difficult it was for your mother. The people who judged her without knowing her, and the way some looked at you, a bastard child."

Josephine shook her head, trying to remember, but couldn't. "I didn't realize it was that way."

"We both did everything we could to shield you. And I didn't want you to have the struggles she had, or that I did."

Josephine frowned. "But you were married to *Abuelo* when you had *Mami*, weren't you?"

Alberta sighed and patted Josephine's hand. "I was, but that doesn't mean it wasn't very difficult. We did not have much money. Your grandfather worked very hard and very long hours, and I...well, I had to set aside my dreams."

"You did?"

Alberta smiled wistfully. "When I was younger, I dreamed of becoming a famous dancer. But then I met Marcos, and your mother came along, and then there was the war, and the journey here..." She shrugged and sighed. "You are young. You cannot comprehend yet how fast the time goes."

They were quiet for a moment and Josephine marveled at all she hadn't known about her grandmother.

Her grandmother squeezed her shoulder and leaning close, she said, "Your mother told me the baby is not Martin's, but Rake Solvino's."

Shamefaced, Josephine could only nod.

"How could you share such intimacy with a stranger, Josephine? And our employer at that!"

"He wasn't a stranger, though, *abuela*. Not exactly." She told her grandmother about that first kiss with Rake when she was just sixteen, and she thought she saw a small light of understanding dawn in her grandmother's eyes. "Plus," she added quickly, "I was upset because I'd seen Martin with another woman. And Rake was so understanding." *And charming,* she thought, but wouldn't say.

Josephine told her *abuela* about their meal, the gambling, and the champagne. The walk in the moonlight and carriage ride to his railway car. More of the champagne, although she knew that was neither an excuse nor a reason for what had happened. She had to acknowledge that there had been attraction there and a need she had not experienced so fiercely before.

How it had all felt like something out of a dream. A magical dream.

Her *abuela* was silent for a too-long moment, then she said, "But now we have no choice but to deal with reality. What will you do, *mi'ja*?"

"Martin is a wonderful man. I know I don't deserve his under-standing, but I hope that when I tell him—"

"He doesn't know yet?" her *abuela* interjected.

Josephine shook her head and felt like she was strangling beneath the weight of the mangled flowers that were now as high as her chin. Sucking in a deep breath of air scented with the stench of rotting gar-denias, she blurted out, "I will tell him. And I pray that he'll forgive me and be willing to help me raise the baby."

Another seemingly endless and telling pause followed her state-ment. "And Rake? What role will he play in the baby's life?"

Josephine had pondered that ever since Rake had told her the day before that he intended to fight for her. That he wanted to be a part of her life and the baby's.

"He has a right to know his child, but not to interfere in what I want for my life. I have plans for what I want, and Rake is not part of those plans."

Her *abuela* dipped her head in a slow, thoughtful nod. "While we may have plans, sometimes He has other designs for us. We can fight against them and find ourselves always at odds or we can adapt and find peace."

A harsh breath escaped her with her disbelief. "Are you saying that God thinks I should be with Rake?"

"There is a reason why he came into your life at this moment. Maybe it is a test of what you feel for Martin and Martin for you. It doesn't mean you have to give up on your plans, only that you may have to adjust them for this gift you've received."

A gift? The baby? She pondered the idea until a flutter like butter-fly's wings beat inside her. She covered her still-flat belly with her hand and imagined the flutter growing stronger. Pictured her belly growing rounder and bigger, and those visions chased away the mounds of crushed flowers.

"It *is* a gift, *abuela*. Maybe it didn't come when I expected it, but I will accept it and find a way to fulfill my dreams."

A broad smile lit her grandmother's face, awakening the crinkles of deep lines forged by a lifetime of joyfulness. "That's my Josephine."

Yes, that's our Josephine. Smart and spunky and determined. It's good to have her back, isn't it? And good to have Alberta back in her corner.

Martin's search the night before had been interrupted by the altercation with Rake. He still regretted losing his temper and, worse, letting Josephine see that dark side. It was totally unlike him, and he didn't recognize that side of himself.

The side that was still driving him to prove that Solvino was the notorious Sin Sombra crime boss. He told himself it was all about solving the crime, but as Nita had so wisely hinted the day before, maybe there was more pushing him on this mission. Especially since they'd gotten word that morning that a murder had occurred the night before in Palm Beach. One that might be connected to the crime boss.

He returned to the hotel's kitchen. It was closed once again and quiet. He entered and searched the room, but found nothing. Exiting the area, he went in and out of the various back rooms and caught sight of someone entering the manager's office. Odd at this time of night. He walked down to the office and leaned his ear on the wooden door. He heard a loud scrape and thud before silence fell.

He knocked on the door, but no one answered. Entering the room, he saw that it was empty. Impossible. He'd definitely seen someone enter.

Walking around the dark office, he peered at the walls and floors, searching for a hint as to where the intruder had gone. As he neared one wall, something crunched beneath his foot.

He bent down and peered at the floor. Sand like that along the riverbank and in the Tequesta limestone caves and tunnels. Near the wall, a bright-colored bit of foliage. He picked it up and examined it. A poinciana flower. Although there were poinciana trees all through the grounds between the Regal Sol and Royal Palm, they also lined the walk along the marina.

As he leaned closer to the wall, it became apparent there was a gap in the plaster, barely noticeable, but definitely there. He pushed on the wall and it gave a little. Standing, he pushed harder and with a click, the wall suddenly popped open to reveal the tunnel behind it. The echo of footsteps as it opened told him that the intruder he had seen earlier was not that far ahead.

He charged into the tunnel, intending to catch up to the person, but as he did so, the footsteps ahead of him changed pace. They became a run, and a second later, the shout of voices warned him that they must have heard his footsteps and realized someone else was on their trail.

Hastening his steps, he reached the end of the tunnel at a full run. But all he caught was a glimpse of a faraway man dashing into the poinciana trees while a small boat sped downstream toward Biscayne Bay.

Frustrated, he jammed his hands on his hips and paused to catch his breath. Something illegal was clearly going on at the hotel. Whether or not it was Solvino behind the deeds, he needed to warn Josephine to be careful.

With a quick glance at his watch, he confirmed that it was not too late to visit. He headed back toward the hotel and circled around to the street that led to the cottages where so many of the hotel employees lived. The small folk homes were dressed up with the elaborate gingerbread trim that graced the hotels, giving them a fancier air even though they were little more than basic shelter. For the most part the cottages were well kempt, although the Miami heat and humidity made it a challenge.

It reminded him of his first meeting with Josephine, bringing a smile to his face as he recollected the crumbling plaster ceiling landing on them, like snow falling. He'd vowed that once he and

Josephine were married he'd take her somewhere that she could see real snow falling.

Armed with that happy memory, he was ready to face her after yesterday's uncomfortable incident. He knocked on the door and a second later Josephine answered, eyes red-rimmed. The stain of tears on her cheeks still visible.

"Are you okay?" he asked, concern for her automatically overriding every other emotion.

She nodded and gestured for him to enter. "I'm glad you're here. There's something we have to talk about."

He stepped through the doorway and slipped off his boater, holding it nervously as he waited, but when she hesitated, he took the lead. "I'm not happy about what happened with Rake."

Tears shimmered in Josephine's eyes again and with a sniffle, she said, "You have every right to be angry and to tell me you don't want to marry me anymore."

"I love you, but…it's not easy to think about you and that man. He's not a good person, Josephine. I don't trust him."

"I understand how you feel, and I'm not sure I trust him either. He's a married man and didn't tell me before we—" Color flamed across her cheeks and she covered them with her hands. "All I can say again is that I'm sorry for what happened."

He believed her, and he wanted to try to move on from that mistake. He cared for her far too much to just walk away. She was everything to him. Martin laid his boater on a nearby chair, reached up, and took hold of her hands. Twining his fingers with hers, he smiled at her for the first time in what felt like ages and said, "Together we can find a way past this, Josephine."

The tears in her eyes grew brighter and then spilled over, running down her cheeks copiously, confusing him because from the sadness in her gaze, they weren't tears of joy. "Josephine?"

"There's more, Martin. I'm—" She inhaled a hard breath. "I'm with child. Rake's child."

Martin shook his head to clear his hearing, unable to believe what she'd just said. He dropped her hands, turned away, and dragged a hand through his hair. When he faced her again, he said, "You're pregnant? With his baby? Do you know who he is, Josephine? What he's done?"

"I know you want to believe he's this Sin Sombra—"

"I am going to prove he is, and then I'm going to make sure he's locked up for a very long time," he said, the tone of his voice hopefully making it clear that he would do just that.

"Martin, are you sure you're not letting jealousy cloud your judgment?" Josephine challenged.

That red haze from the night before returned, coloring everything he saw. His fiancée, pregnant with another man's child. A criminal's child. Her defending that criminal.

Him raising that child if he could not only forgive her, but learn to trust her again.

"You think you know him? Know that he's better than that?" Martin challenged.

Josephine reached out and laid a hand on his chest in a gesture so familiar, it made his heart ache at the thought of never feeling it again.

"There's a side to him you don't want to see. He's not the rogue you want him to be."

Her words shredded that heart into little pieces. "Because I'm jealous and unreasonable? I guess I know who you think is the better man then."

Josephine shook her head vehemently and more tears came to her eyes. "That's not what I meant, Martin. Please try to understand."

He had been trying to understand since she'd first confessed her indiscretion. But all that he'd heard tonight had him wondering if there truly could be a future for them still. In that instant, it was obvious what he had to do.

"I have a lead about Sin Sombra that I have to follow. It's not in town, so I'll be going away. Maybe for a few weeks." He paused. "Maybe more."

Maybe when I come back, I'll know what to do about all this. About whether you still love me, he thought.

"It's what's best," Martin said, and without waiting for a reply, he turned and left the cottage, wondering if this would be the last time he saw his Josephine.

Sniff. Sniff. Sniff. Does anyone have a handkerchief? True love cannot be dead. I cannot believe that our Martin and Josephine will not have their miracle!

Chapter Eight

Rake juggled the bouquet of flowers in his hands, nervous about seeing Josephine. Slightly unsettled since he'd just had another fight with Penelope about the baby and whether or not it was really his. Penelope's words still clung to him like an oil slick on the water.

"Do you really think it's your child? The little gold digger just sees a way to move up in the world."

Nothing Josephine had done before their night of passion would lead him to believe that she'd been trying to use him to improve her lot in life nor had her actions since then. If anything, she seemed determined to do it on her own. Or rather, with Martin. Even if a different Pinkerton had been working at the hotel of late. He wondered where the good detective had gone and what that meant for his relationship with Josephine. Maybe she'd broken their engagement. The thought lightened his spirit and quickened his steps.

When he passed by the concierge desk though, only Mr. Adams was present. The man told him Josephine was on a short break, so he hurried down to the small spare room where the employees sometimes gathered for rest.

The door to the room was open and when he peered inside, he realized Josephine was there, sitting at a table and sipping tea along with two other women. They jumped to their feet when they spied him.

She looks tired, he thought as he approached, the bouquet tucked behind him since he didn't want to be too obvious in front of her friends and his other employees. It wouldn't be good to be seen favoring one of his workers, especially not with the recent layoffs.

"Mr. Solvino," she said, with a respectful dip of her head.

With a look at her friends, he said, "Miss Valencia. And who might these other young ladies be?"

Josephine gestured to each of them as she introduced them. "Miss Duarte and Miss Garcia."

"Ladies, it's a pleasure to meet you. Would you mind giving us a moment?"

The two young women murmured their consent and hurried away, tittering to themselves and closing the door behind them.

Handing Josephine the flowers, he said, "I've missed our night-time talks in the kitchen."

She glanced at the bouquet, but didn't take it. "They've found another employee to fill Mr. Slayton's position, so there's no need for me to work a double shift anymore."

"That doesn't mean we can't see each other," he urged.

She held up her hand and pointed to the pitiful little diamond ring on her finger. "This means we can't. I'm engaged to Martin."

"Funny, but I haven't seen your detective around lately," he chided, earning a glare and uplift of her chin.

"What do you want, Rake?"

Ah, there was the spunk he liked so much. Though it wasn't quite as appealing when directed so dismissively at him. "I told you, Josephine. I want to be with you."

Wagging her head back and forth, she said, "That's not going to happen."

As determined as she seemed to be, he could be just as determined. And if he couldn't push straight through the obstacle, he certainly intended to find a way around it no matter how long it took.

"That may be, but I deserve a chance to get to know my child. Surely you don't intend to deny me that, especially since the odds are that I can never have another."

It was obvious his point had struck home. Pressing that point further, he cupped her cheek. Her skin was so smooth beneath his fingertips and palm. So familiar even in so short a time that if he closed his eyes, he would know her just with a simple touch.

She sensed that connection and swayed toward him, the moment shimmering between them with possibilities.

"Rake," she said, her tone filled with want and doubt. "We can't. This could never work between us."

Because he was a patient man, he said, "We'll see, Josephine. All I want is a chance to be in my child's life."

The door shot open behind them, and they jerked apart as a trio of hotel workers burst into the room. His employees stopped short as they saw him, but he smiled at them and said, "Carry on. I was just thanking Miss Valencia for filling in when we needed her."

With another smile in her direction, he thrust the flowers into her hands and hurried from the room, not wanting to spark gossip by lingering too long.

After all, there would be talk enough when Josephine began to show.

Francesca and Liana were waiting for her when she ended her shift, their faces alight with questions. Her friends would have made wonderful interrogators during the Spanish Inquisition. They often walked home together, as Francesca and Liana lived with their parents in the cottages as well. Josephine acted as if nothing unusual had happened earlier.

"That was nice of Mr. Solvino to bring you flowers," Liana said as she walked beside her friend.

"Who says he gave me flowers?" she said.

"Lily, Monica, and Abigail. They said they walked in on you and he handed you the flowers he had with him when we met him," Francesca piped in.

Flowers that she'd tossed into the wastebasket the moment she returned to the desk. "They were a thank you for filling in for Mr. Slayton."

"God rest his soul," her two friends said in unison.

She stopped short. "He's dead?"

"They found a body in the river. They think it's him," Liana said.

"Didn't Martin tell you?" Francesca asked.

"No," she murmured shakily and started walking again.

Her friends were silent, the night quiet. The sounds of their skirts rustling and soft footfalls joined the call of night creatures. The hushed noises created a rhythm that was smooth, almost soothing, until Francesca said, "Where is Martin? I haven't seen him around lately."

"Shhh," Liana chided.

Josephine paused once again and inhaled deeply. "He's on assignment in Palm Beach. He may be there for a few weeks."

Liana and Francesca shared a concerned look that turned conspiratorial.

"I think it's time for us to do something different tonight. I hear the Women's Club is doing readings from Miss Austen's works at the public library," Liana said.

Francesca clapped her hands with glee. "And Mr. Seybold is keeping his lunch counter open late so that the ladies might visit after. This is so perfect."

"Well, Josephine? Will you join us?" Liana prodded.

Inside Josephine, her heart warmed with the love bathing her. "A night of Jane Austen, sweets, and my two best friends. What more could I ask for?"

Almost nothing else, she discovered later as she finished the slice of chocolate cake and listened to her friends chatter about Mister Darcy and the readings they'd heard at the Women's Club earlier that night. In truth, she'd rather preferred the snippet from *Sense and Sensibility* and the roguish John Willoughby. Josephine always enjoyed reading about the scoundrels a bit more than she should.

"It's so romantic," Francesca gushed. "Isn't it romantic, Josephine?"

"It is. That's why she's my favorite."

Liana leaned forward to see her down the length of the counter. "She's wonderful. I'm so glad we did this. It's been too long."

It has *been too long what with dating Martin, working, and trying to write,* she thought. It had been fun to get all dolled up with her friends, who had also put on their Sunday best. They'd done their hair in chignons secured with their finest barrettes. Swan-bill corsets completed their outfits, giving them the pleasing curves that were all the rage.

"Let's do this again," she said, rising and standing behind her friends so she could hug them. Hard. "Soon. We need to do this again soon."

Really soon, because she hadn't felt so normal in a long time. It gave her hope that maybe things could get back on track quickly.

Chapter Nine

The feeling of returned normality that Josephine had experienced with her friends that evening made her heart blossom with hope as they walked back to the cottages. She hurried home, picked up her pen and paper, and decided to write a letter to Martin.

> Dearest Martin,
>   You've only been gone a few days and I miss you already. I hope things are going well with your investigation and that you will be home soon...

She continued, asking for his forgiveness. She posted the letter the next morning and waited, but days went by without a response. She buried herself in her correspondence classes, work, and most of all, writing. Her novel and letters to Martin. Letter after letter to Martin.

> My dearest Martin,
>   Life here has been ~~difficult~~ different without you. I'm almost done with the correspondence class, and Sister Elizabeth is hopeful that she'll be able to find a family that ~~can overlook my situation~~ will hire me. Things have been good at work ~~even though my skirts are a little tighter and I worry my belly will soon show~~. I hope we can see each other soon.

Josephine hesitated as she inserted the letter into the slot of the cast-iron mailbox in the hotel lobby. The postman would be by later in the day to pick up the mail and drop off correspondence at the hotel and the nearby cottages.

But nothing came for her at the hotel or at home. Again.

Another two weeks went by without a response and as she sat at the kitchen table late one night finishing a short story, it occurred to her that perhaps she'd made a horrible mistake by writing to Martin. Maybe he hadn't been ready to hear from her. Maybe she'd sounded too needy. Maybe he didn't want to hear about her baby. Maybe…

Maybe it was time she turned her attention to other things. Like getting ready for the baby. Maybe it was time that she stopped keeping Rake at arm's length because, if truth be told, he'd been a great source of support over the last several weeks.

He hadn't pressed for anything other than friendship and sharing an occasional grilled cheese sandwich with her. He asked often how she was feeling and made it clear he would take care of whatever she needed.

Yet he couldn't give her what she needed most: to hear from Martin. To know that he was okay. To know whether she should move on with her life.

It was with those thoughts that she went to sleep that night, determined that in the morning, somehow, some way, her life would change.

But Josephine had no idea what was heading her way and just how her life was about to change. Batten down the hatches, because Hurricanes Ronaldo and Sondra are on the way!

"Are you sure you're up to this?" Rake asked the next morning, as she perused the papers he'd handed her at the front desk.

"You want me to coordinate the shows with Ronaldo de la Sera and his troupe?" she said just to make sure.

"You're our best concierge, and I understand that Ronaldo can be…difficult."

"I'm honored that you trust me to do this," she said and was truly flattered. And of course, her *abuela* would be ecstatic that there might be a possibility of a personal meeting with her favorite singer.

Rake leaned back in his chair and smiled. "I trust that you can do whatever you say you will do. Like the novel. How is that going?"

With a shrug, she said, "Still working on it, but I finished a short story last night."

"I understand the *The Miami Metropolis* is looking for stories. Have you considered sending your story there?"

She eyed him thoughtfully, wondering at what game he was playing with the new project and his helpfulness. But there was nothing to suggest he was being anything other than the supportive self he had been for the last several weeks.

"I hadn't, but I will think about it. And if you're serious about this," she said and waved the contract for the group, "I'll do that as well. I'm always up for a challenge."

Little did she know just how much of a challenge it was going to be to deal with the dashing dynamo Ronaldo de la Sera.

Josephine dashed through the hotel lobby, heading to the rotunda where the troupe would be performing for the next few months. It had turned out to be a lot of work over the last week, and with the troupe set to arrive in just a few days, she was still coordinating with the carpenters on the stage setup that had been requested by Ronaldo. It seemed a little…elaborate, but based on the notes that had been arriving on an almost daily basis from the troupe, that was par for the course.

Ronaldo also wanted a room facing west because he didn't want the morning sun to wake him after a late-night show.

Fresh mangoes were to be brought to him as a post-show snack as well as steak and eggs for breakfast so he could maintain his lean and muscular build.

Josephine was busy skimming through the notes when she almost ran into Penelope as she walked out of the rotunda.

"I'm so sorry," she said. "I didn't see you."

Penelope regally lifted her head and looked down her nose. "Maybe you should pay more attention to what you're doing. Like that mess in there. That will never be ready in time for the troupe."

Josephine shook her head and bit back the response she wanted to make. Like that maybe Penelope should have paid more attention to her husband to keep him from turning to another woman. "Thank you, Mrs. Solvino. I'll keep that in mind."

With a sniff, Penelope walked away. But as she did so, something washed over Josephine. Sympathy for the other woman because she knew what it was like to love someone and not have him love you back.

Or maybe it was more accurate to say not write you back, *because if Josephine could see Martin up in the Pinkerton Palm Beach office, she'd know that he'd picked up a pen time and time again to write her. That he'd read her letters so many times the ink had smudged, and the paper was wearing thin from being handled. She couldn't see that, of course, but that didn't stop her from trying to be nice to Penelope.*

Because that's just the kind of person Josephine was.

She laid a hand on Penelope's forearm, earning another down-the-nose stare.

"Excuse me, Penelope, but I need your help." She intended to ask her advice on the stage setup for the performers.

But the other woman's head jerked in shock. With a sneer, she said, "Why would I help a floozy like you? You're carrying my husband's child."

She understood Penelope's anger. She'd suffered the bite of the green-eyed monster of jealousy when she'd caught sight of Martin with his partner and misunderstood the situation. Because of that, she tried to put things to right with Penelope.

"But I don't want to be with Rake. I want to be with Martin," she said and yet, Rake had been there for her these last several weeks, while Martin…

"It doesn't matter anymore," Penelope shot back. "I thought we could fix the things that haven't been right for years. No one could be happy with a man like Rake who seduces woman after woman."

Josephine didn't want to believe that Rake could be, well, a rake, and as Penelope sensed that, she lashed out again. "So you thought you were special? The first woman he's cheated on me with? Think again, Josephine. There have been many, many others."

With a flounce of her skirts, Penelope whirled and stalked away, leaving Josephine staring at her retreating back. Also leaving her to wonder if the man she thought she'd come to know was really a scoundrel like Penelope had said.

Well, he did seduce you, Josephine, even if he had a wife. And there is the child you carry, and he might never be able to have one with anyone else. Not to mention that those late-night talks with him always seem to end with him going out into the night, but to do what? If Martin were around—but of course he isn't…yet—he might warn you that Rake is not the man you seem to want to believe he is.

Martin stared at the stack of letters from Josephine. Guilt slammed into him at the way things had ended with her. *No, not ended,* he thought. As angry and upset as he was with everything that had happened with her and Solvino, he couldn't imagine not having Josephine in his life.

She had been his world for the last two years. Two wonderful, loving, fun, and fulfilling years, and he didn't want to throw away those two years or his future with her.

Surprisingly, he could even forgive her for what had happened, because he'd become so focused and obsessed with finding the elusive Sin Sombra that he'd not only lost sight of what was important, he'd stopped treating Josephine like the smart, independent woman that she was.

She had no need of him protecting her, wanting to keep her under glass like the delicate figures in the snow globe he'd gifted her. Josephine was sensitive and a little naive, always wanting to think the best of people, but she wasn't delicate or fragile, and as she'd told him, she could take care of herself.

But that didn't mean she had to go it alone with this child, he thought.

While the many weeks away on the investigation had yielded little information to discover the identity of Sin Sombra or conclusively prove that it was that cad Solvino, the separation had shown him that his life was far better with Josephine in it. Because of that, he had to start to make things right with her.

He picked up his fountain pen, a piece of stationery, and began to write.

My dearest darling Josephine,

Unlike you, I have never been good with words, but I pray that I can convey my deepest regret at all that has happened in the last several weeks, and all that I hope for our future.

Yes, our future, my darling, because I cannot imagine a world without you.

My friends, he's back! There he is, the caring and patient Martin we all know and love. I knew that he would not be one to stay angry for long and desert our dear girl just when she needed him

*most. Now let's hope Josephine can see past Rake's numerous charms
to what really is important in a man.*
    And I don't mean a love of grilled cheese sandwiches.

He paused, hesitant about how to continue. Afraid that he would
either say too much or too little, but then he plunged forward.

> I must confess that I was sorely hurt by what occurred because for
> years I dreamed of our being together and how special it would be.
>   I still dream of the day that we will be one, if you can forgive
> me for the hurt I've caused you by not being there for you, my love.
> Understand that not a day has gone by that I haven't thought about
> you. Not a day has gone by that I wonder if you are well and how
> the baby is doing.

He stopped and took a deep breath, thinking about how far along
Josephine was and pondering if she was showing yet. If he were there,
could he lay his hands on that small mound and feel the baby move
beneath them? Would her breasts be heavier as they prepared to sus-
tain that new life in the months ahead? What else would be different
after so many weeks away? He wondered and knew then that it was
time to go home.

> As I write this, it is my most fervent wish to be with you again, if
> you'll have me. I expect to be returning to Miami shortly and I pray
> that when I arrive, you will give me a chance to make things right.
>   All my love,
>   Your Martin

He sat there for a moment, reading and rereading the letter and
hoping it would be enough to convince Josephine to talk to him. To
possibly forgive him for leaving her when she likely needed him the
most. That tore at his gut and he hoped with all his heart that they

both could find forgiveness and a path to the future they had envisioned at one time. A future together.

He laid his pen down and as he did so, Nita walked into the office. "Still burning the midnight oil?"

Martin glanced at his partner as she strolled to the chalkboard with their notes on the case. "I might say the same of you."

She studied the board, then sighed in frustration. "We seem to have reached a dead end. Do you have any new ideas?" she asked and glanced toward the papers on his desk.

"None, and actually, this is a letter to Josephine," he said in the hope that his astute partner would get the message. In the last several weeks, Nita had made it clear she would be open to more with him, despite his putting her off on a number of occasions.

"Oh," she said and wrinkled her nose. "I had assumed you were done with her since…" She gestured to the pile of letters on his desk.

"I'm not. I just needed to find the right things to say. Josephine will always be the woman who has my heart, Nita."

His partner considered him, took a deep breath, and nodded. "I understand, Martin. If you should ever change your mind—"

"I won't," he said in a tone that brooked no disagreement.

"I'll see you in the morning," she said.

He was about to fold up the letter, but then after a brief moment, he picked up his pen once more. He scrawled a postscript at the bottom of the page, one he knew in his heart to be true.

P.S. I'm not going to give up on us. We belong together, and I'll never stop believing that.

And for as long as Martin lived, until he drew his very last breath, he never did.

Chapter Ten

Ernesto Solvino was a man used to getting what he wanted, and what he seemed to want most of all was a son who could be as ruthless, cunning, and successful as he was. However, Rake was certain that his father thought he was none of those things.

"You say the hotel is doing well?" Ernesto asked and strolled around the room, hands tucked behind him as he appraised the furnishings, his son, and his wife, who lounged on a settee in the sitting area of the suite.

With a dip of his head and a hesitant shrug, Rake said, "It's holding its own, with a little assistance. The Royal Palm provides some very stiff competition."

"I know. I've stayed there," his father said, shocking Rake with the admission.

"You've been to Miami and stayed at Flagler's hotel instead of mine?" he asked, his gaze narrowing as he considered his father.

"One always needs to know what the competition is doing." Ernesto returned to stand before Rake. "I can see that the Regal Sol has potential, but are you the man to take it to the next level?"

Warmth flooded Rake's cheeks at the less-than-subtle condemnation. He had spent his whole life dealing with his father's doubt and dismissal, but since discovering Josephine was pregnant, some things had started to change. While he still wanted his father's approval, he also had realized that first and foremost, he himself had to be happy with all that he had accomplished.

"I am more than capable of doing that, Father."

Ernesto arched a condemning brow. "Even without your other… businesses? The Regal Sol can only lose money for so long before it pulls you down and you lose everything."

"I am my father's son. I will do what needs to be done, but just like you, I understand the risks and what to do to protect myself." His tone must have made it clear to his father that he was deadly serious.

With a slow decisive nod, Ernesto said, "I guess we'll see." His father glanced at his wife. "I'm going for a walk."

Which in his father's world meant, "Come with me now."

Sondra shot him an indulgent smile. "I think I'll stay and catch up with Rake. It's been too long since we've chatted."

To Rake's surprise, Ernesto merely grunted his acquiescence and walked out of the room.

The calm demeanor that Sondra had exhibited when Ernesto was in the room disappeared the moment the door closed behind his back. Rising from the settee, she rushed over to Rake and said, "I really do need to speak with you about your father. There's something wrong with him."

During the last few hours since their arrival and the tour he'd given them of the hotel, Rake hadn't noticed anything amiss.

"He seemed quite fine to me, Sondra."

"But he's not fine. At first I thought it was because he was having an affair, because you know how your father can be," she said.

He did, but it was rich to hear that coming from Sondra of all people. She had been "the other woman" to his father's third wife. Or was it fourth?

He arched a brow and said, "But you think it's more than that now?"

"I overheard him talking to his right-hand man. He said that he had to get them the money 'or else there would be problems.' Why do you think he came to Miami and stayed at the Royal Palm?"

"I thought he was rather clear as to the why of it, Sondra," he said and strolled to the dry bar at one side of his suite. He raised the decanter of whiskey, offering it to his father's wife.

"Yes, thank you," she said and walked over to take the glass that Rake poured. She downed the liquor in one gulp and gestured for him to refill the glass.

At his questioning look, she said, "You believed that? He was so agitated when he came back to Palm Beach that I was worried he'd get ill. That's why we had to delay our trip to Miami. To let Ernesto take some time off, not that he did. I'm really worried, Rake."

As Rake sipped his own whiskey, he considered what Sondra had said and a bit of worry sprung up inside him. His father's visit to Miami would have been right around the time that Slayton and Rake's liquor had both disappeared. Not to mention that Ernesto's return to Palm Beach seemed to coincide with Detective Cadden and his partner being sent there because of a lead on the Sin Sombra case. That was just too much coincidence to ignore.

"I think you're overreacting, Sondra," he said, strolled to the chair next to the settee, and sat, trying to maintain a veneer of calm when his gut was roiling with apprehension. He gestured for her to sit once more, but instead she paced back and forth nervously and emptied her second glass of whiskey before pouring herself a third. Only then did she sit, but continued to manically shift her glass from hand to hand.

"Truly, I'm not. What if he's involved in something criminal again? I had hoped he'd put that all behind him years ago," she said, her voice barely above a whisper.

He had thought the same as well, but his father had also not been one to pass up an opportunity to make money. "I'm sure there's an explanation for what he's been doing. I could ask him if you'd like."

"Would you?" she said, overdramatically. Come to think of it, most everything about what she'd said and how she'd acted had been a trifle theatrical. As he met her gaze, he detected the shadow of a sly look before she controlled her features and said, "Ask him about Cuba.

I overheard him speaking with someone about that right around the same time he was loading a suitcase with a lot of money."

She laid a hand on Rake's thigh to emphasize her plea and said, "Please, Rake. I'm really worried."

Something about that touch made his skin crawl, and he shot to his feet and paced as he thought about Sondra's worry. His father had asked to borrow the yacht for a quick trip to Cuba in a few days. Although it was going to slow down some deliveries to the North Miami saloons, he had planned to have his crew take advantage of the visit to load up on some fine Cuban rum to sell upon his father's return.

Facing her, he said, "I already know about the trip, Sondra. My father told me that he's meeting with some investors about a new hotel on Varadero Beach. If he was trying to hide something—"

"What better than to hide in plain sight, Rake? You have to believe me. I'm worried for his safety," she urged and took another big gulp of the whiskey.

Since it was clear that Sondra would not be appeased by just his assurances, Rake said, "I will keep an eye on my father to make sure there's nothing untoward happening."

She set the almost empty glass on the table before her and, after a beat, slowly pushed to her feet. "Thank you, Rake. I know Ernesto has his doubts about you, but I trust you to take care of this situation."

It occurred to Rake as he watched Sondra leave that she always managed to find a way to stick a knife in him while couching it with support. It just added to his dislike of the woman and made him wonder what his sister Lucia saw in her.

And thinking of Lucia, he recalled his sister's words from a few weeks earlier that their father had been secretive and traveling quite a bit. Lucia had worried that it meant he was having an affair, but now with Sondra's concerns, he was fearful that it might be more. With the seeds of doubt planted in him, he set off to find his father and try to discover just what his father had planned during his upcoming trip to Cuba.

Ah, Cuba. A country celebrating the end of war and the birth of a republic. Cigars, rum, and women with dangerous curves. Although, a man with no shadow might not fare so well under the bright Cuban sun...

Josephine's shift was just about over when Zara arrived unexpectedly at the concierge desk. Her mother wasn't due to perform for a few hours, but upon seeing the very serious expression on her face, worry twisted Josephine's stomach into a knot. "*Mami*, is something wrong? Did something happen to *Abuela*?"

"No, *mija*," Zara replied and raised shaky hands to hold out an envelope to Josephine.

She recognized Martin's neat handwriting and the return address of the Palm Beach Pinkerton office. She stared at the envelope as if it were a cobra about to strike. Afraid to take it and suffer its bite, she just looked at it until Zara gave it a little shake and said, "You must read it, Josephine."

But not now. Not when the bite from that snake would either paralyze her or stop her heart. A heart that was already racing unsteadily as she considered what Martin might have to say. His lack of response over the last several weeks had her worrying that Martin could not forgive her and now this. Did he intend to end things with just a letter?

Uneasily she took the envelope from her mother and tucked it into the wide, deep pocket of her skirt.

"Josephine," her mother admonished, but she held up a hand to stop her.

"I will read it as soon as my shift is over."

Zara opened her mouth to speak, and for a few seconds, it flapped open and closed like a fish out of water, but then she shut it tightly. With a grim smile on her face, she said, "I am here for you if you need me, Josephine."

She nodded. "I know."

Her mother walked away in the direction of the rotunda where the show would be held later that night on the newly finished stage designed for Ronaldo de la Sera's troupe. The troublesome entertainer would be arriving the next day, and Josephine was already dreading it. If the man could be so demanding via the incessant notes that a messenger delivered every few days, how much worse would it be once he arrived?

Although she had only another half an hour until the end of her shift, time seemed to stand still. What made it worse was that with it so close to the dinner hour, there were few guests needing assistance to provide some distraction from the letter burning a hole in her pocket. When Mr. Adams finally arrived for the late shift, she hurried off to do one last walk through the dining room and then dashed out to the back path.

Josephine pulled the letter out of her pocket as she walked and ran her hands over the surface of it, as if by doing so she could touch him. She drove away a vision of the hurt and anger on Martin's face as he'd stormed out and recalled an image of him smiling instead, hoping that the fact that he'd written her at all would bode well for their future.

Gingerly she opened the envelope as she ambled along the path, weaving past patrons strolling on the way to the rotunda and pool area, but she paused as she extracted the letter. When she saw it was addressed to "My dearest darling Josephine," optimism blossomed in her heart like a lush gardenia offering its petals to the sun.

Excited, she skimmed the first few lines anxiously, and certain phrases jumped out at her, kindling the hope burning in her heart: "my deepest regret," "hope for our future," "my darling"…and then, there it was:

I cannot imagine a world without you.

Joy spread through her like a wildfire, and she hurried along the path, reading Martin's missive, unmindful of where she was going. Hope and pleasure filled her as she read of his plans for a life with her and the baby and, even more importantly, that he would soon be returning to Miami.

But how soon? she wondered and turned the letter over to see when it had been mailed. As she peered at the postmark, she saw it was dated five days earlier. Martin would be back within a few days!

Overwhelmed with excitement, she couldn't resist a little hop of pleasure, only to find herself suddenly flying through the air as she landed on the edge of the Regal Sol's swimming pool, lost her balance, and went crashing into the chilly water.

The tangle of her sodden skirt and petticoats made it difficult for her to find her footing. She struggled to right herself and bring her head above water, as the weight of her skirt and undergarments kept on pulling her down. Water filled her mouth as her breath escaped her, and she flailed her arms, fighting to reach the surface.

Oh no! Truly it cannot end like this, just when it seems as if our dear Josephine will finally get her heart's desire!

Chapter Eleven

As the water dragged her down, Josephine snatched at her skirts with one hand, trying to free her legs of the tangle of wet fabric, while clutching Martin's quickly disintegrating letter with the other. A second later, strong arms surrounded her and hauled her to the surface. Josephine inhaled, sputtering as she coughed up pool water.

"Next time you might inquire about obtaining bathing attire from the hotel gymnasium," Rake teased with a devilish smile. Drops of water, tinged gold from the setting sun, glistened in his dark hair and thick lashes.

The hand holding Martin's letter was trapped against his chest, and she looked at it and said, "I didn't see where I was going. I was reading a letter from Martin."

His smile evaporated, and Rake shot a glance at the now sodden piece of paper but said nothing. With powerful strides, he carried her out of the pool and up onto the surrounding deck. When he released her, she began to shiver, as the early evening air had cooled a bit. She wrapped her arms around herself and, teeth chattering, said, "T-t-t-hank y-y-ou."

Rake grimaced, ripped off his suit jacket, and wrapped it around her shoulders. "Let's get you out of those wet clothes—"

"And into something dry," she warned, too aware of what had happened the last time she'd been immodest with him.

"Yes, of course. Something dry and warm before you catch a cold," he said, although she sensed he might have been wishing for another outcome.

He led her back into the hotel and to the elevator so they could go up to his suite. Once they were inside, he guided her in the direction of the bathroom. "Get out of those wet things, and I'll order up some tea."

"I'd prefer some warm milk," she said.

"Bossy, aren't you? Warm milk it is. Now please, go get dry," he said, then gently urged her into the bathroom and shut the door.

The powder room was one of opulent luxury and nearly as large as the cottage Josephine shared with her family. Marble gleamed everywhere along with gilded fixtures that she realized might be actual solid gold. Against one wall sat an immense claw-foot tub big enough for two. She wondered if Rake had ever shared it with anyone, and her angel appeared on her shoulder to chastise her about such thoughts.

Not to be outdone, her little devil urged, "Why not at least warm up with a nice bath?"

"Alone," her angel reminded sternly.

A warm bath would be nice, she thought, but first, she carefully peeled apart what remained of Martin's letter and tenderly blotted the pages with a towel as thick as her mattress. Then she set them to dry on the immense marble vanity and walked to the tub. She turned on the water, letting it run over her hand until the temperature was just right, and slipped inside. Josephine let herself soak blissfully, the warm liquid chasing away the lingering chill from the pool water. Nearly half an hour of bliss passed before a knock came on the door.

"Do I have to rescue you again?" Rake asked through the thick wood.

"Just taking a bath," she called out.

"Do you need some help?"

"No!" she said adamantly and gazed at Martin's letter, reminding herself that what she had with him was far, far more important than any physical attraction to Rake. She hurried out and dried herself, marveling when the incredibly soft towels didn't scratch her skin like the ones at home.

Glancing at her still-wet clothes, she grabbed the large robe that hung on a towel rack instead. It was warm inside and she wrapped the lush fabric around herself tightly. She'd have to find something else to wear for the walk home and hang her clothes to dry once she got there.

Reentering the suite, she realized Rake had ordered more than just the hot milk. Even though the kitchen was normally closed at this hour, he'd somehow managed to procure thick roast beef sandwiches and fried potatoes. At her questioning glance, he said, "I sent someone to Mr. Seybold's lunch counter, and they managed to catch him before he closed for the evening."

He gestured to a women's hotel uniform draped across a nearby chair. "Fresh clothes for you, but first: dinner."

"Rake, this really isn't necessary," she said, but her stomach betrayed her by loudly growling.

"Dinner," he insisted, "and then you can go, if that's what you want to do." Rake offered up a little-boy pout that was far more endearing and dangerous than his sexy dimpled grin.

"*Just* dinner, and then I have to go." She was heading toward the small bistro table on one side of his suite when he gently grasped her hand and led her to the settee.

"It's too formal," he explained, urging her to sit, and then wheeled over the serving cart with the food. In no time he had laid out dinner on the Louis Philippe marble-topped coffee table and they ate, mostly in silence as hunger took over. He devoured the food, finishing his meal well before she did.

When she was done, she leaned back on the settee next to Rake. "Thank you. That was very tasty."

Smiling, he said, "But not nearly as tasty as your signature grilled cheese sandwich."

Josephine grinned and wrinkled her nose. "The three cheeses are the secret. One-third white Cheddar, one-third yellow Cheddar, and one-third grated American. It's my mother's recipe."

He reached out and twined a long strand of her hair around one finger. "The two of you are close."

She nodded emphatically. "My *abuela* also. The Valencia women stick together. What about your mother?"

His smile dimmed, and sadness slipped into his gaze. "She left when I was four."

Josephine couldn't imagine not having Zara in her life. She shifted on the couch to face him, trying to understand how he might have felt. "Why did she leave?"

He shook his head and looked away. "I don't know. I woke up the morning after my birthday, and she was gone."

So sad! But don't let that open a crack in your heart, Josephine. Think Martin. Think Martin.

"That's all?" She cupped his jaw and applied gentle pressure to urge him to face her once again. "What did your father say?"

With a shrug, he admitted, "He said she was gone, she was selfish, and that we had to move on."

Just like that. *Move on* to a four-year-old who had just lost his mother. The pain of it was clearly reflected in Rake's dark-chocolate eyes, lending him a solemnity and depth she hadn't previously seen in the glib charmer. It made her wonder what else she didn't know about the man who was the father of her baby.

Wanting to move the conversation away from such sadness, she said, "Let's play a game. What's your least favorite food?"

"Caviar. I can't stand it," he replied without hesitation and with some obvious relief. "What's your favorite food—besides grilled cheese?"

"Gumdrops, but not the spicy ones," she answered, which launched a question and answer game that went on late into the night until things started getting a little more serious.

"What do you want to name the baby?" he asked.

In truth, she hadn't given that a thought with everything else going on in her life. "I don't know."

"Let's pick some boys' names."

She quickly shot back, "No, no need. We are having a girl. The Valencia family only has girls. My grandmother, she had six sisters. All of them had daughters."

He paled, maybe because he was thinking of what it would take to keep so many young ladies away from men like him. "Six girls?" he echoed, swallowing hard.

"Six, so no need to pick a boy's name."

"Duly noted," he said and revived their earlier game, asking her question after question until she grew drowsy and yawned.

"I should go…" she said, but her eyes were drifting closed already, as were Rake's. Her little angel popped up once more on her shoulder, her tone urgent. "Wake up, Josephine! You cannot stay the night with this man again!"

Just then, Rake wrapped an arm around her and urged her close, pillowing her head on his shoulder.

As her angel did a panicked dance, the devil emerged and with a satisfied smile said, "But his shoulder is so strong and warm and just too comfortable to resist, isn't it, Josephine?"

It is just too comfortable to resist, she thought, and her angel grabbed the pitchfork from the devil and jabbed her, but it was too late.

Josephine had drifted off to sleep, Rake beside her.

Oh dear. So, if you're keeping score at home, that's two nights with Rake, and none with Martin. Something tells me that he's not going to be too happy about this when he gets back to Miami.

It was late the next morning before Josephine awoke. She was tucked against Rake's chest on the settee, their legs intertwined. Awareness dawning slowly, she shifted uncomfortably, trying to extricate herself gently, but Rake tightened his arm around her waist and drew her even closer. It was impossible to miss that he was all too ready for them to share another inappropriate moment.

Slightly panicked, Josephine jumped off the settee and when Rake stirred, offered a babbling excuse for not having breakfast with him and hurried off, carefully trying to make her way home without attracting too much notice. While she was grateful for all that he'd done the night before, Josephine worried there might be even more talk around the hotel should she be spotted leaving his room in yesterday's clothing.

Still, she had to resign herself to the idea that wagging tongues were inevitable; she would soon be showing. Besides, the extra sleep had been sorely needed. With the dance troupe arriving later that afternoon, it was going to be a busy day.

Josephine spent most of her shift reserving seats for hotel guests for the premiere show. Her *abuela* popped in before going home, and with a slightly disapproving glance, she said, "We missed you for dinner, *mi'ja.*"

Leaning close, she whispered, "Nothing happened, *Abuela.* I've learned my lesson."

Her grandmother narrowed her gaze, and Josephine must have passed her test. "Are you working late tonight now that Ronaldo is arriving?"

Excitement had crept into her grandmother's usual no-nonsense tones. Josephine wanted to tell her *abuela* just how difficult and self-centered Ronaldo was, but she didn't want to shatter her illusions. "I will have to get them settled and…" She reached into her desk and pulled out two tickets. "For you and *Mami.*"

Elation beamed from her grandmother's features. "Oh, how exciting! Thank you, Josephine."

"I have to be backstage in case anyone needs anything, but I'll look for you and *Mami* after the show. Maybe we can arrange for you to meet Ronaldo."

A totally girlish giggle and titter escaped her *abuela* before the older woman rushed off, clutching the tickets to her chest like a schoolgirl with a note from a beau.

Like the cherished letter tucked into her own skirt pocket. It was crinkled now that it had dried and a bit mangled around the edges.

There were some ink smudges here and there, but to her, it was the most perfect thing she could possess. Besides the snow globe, of course.

If she could, she'd pull out the letter and read it and reread it, but the rush of people wanting tickets began again. Then, with only a couple of hours left before the troupe's arrival, a stack of notes from Ronaldo were delivered by a messenger.

> I will need fresh spring water in my room, please. Not too cold and not too hot.

> Please do not forget the mangoes for after the show and the steak and eggs for breakfast.

> I would like to take a nap before the show so, for that, I will need a different, east-facing room to avoid the afternoon sun. I would like your biggest, most grandest room, please.

Josephine gritted her teeth but made arrangements for all the entertainer's demands. Rake had put her in charge of making sure everything went well for the troupe's stay and gave her some time away from the concierge desk. That would be welcome since she worried about what some hotel patrons might think when she started to show, as well her fellow employees. No matter what, she intended to fulfill all her duties, especially since so far Sister Elizabeth had not been able to find anyone willing to hire her as a tutor. Josephine had been deemed too inexperienced with children. Ironically, in a few months she'd be showing, and once that happened, there was no way the sisters would help her find a job or that families would want a compromised young woman in their home.

But maybe once Martin was home and they could be married, that would change. A proper married woman was employable as a tutor, but maybe her short story would be published by then. If that happened, she might be able to sell more stories and not have to take on another job.

She had just returned from the rotunda and was doing a last check of the stage and the temporary backstage area when the entry doors banged open and loud voices spilled into the hotel's lobby. The troupe had arrived.

Ronaldo was in the lead, head held high. Dressed in an elegant charcoal frock coat, double-breasted black vest, and black pants with a faint gray pinstripe, he cut quite a figure. If *Abuela* had been there, they might have needed to get her some smelling salts. A silver-headed cane rested over his arm, and as she approached him, he swept his silk top hat off his head and bowed gracefully.

"Miss Valencia, I presume."

"Mr. de la Sera," she said and held out her hand.

He surprised her by grasping it and dropping a kiss on the back of her hand. "You are the angel who has been so kind to deal with my many needs. Is all in order?"

Despite her annoyance at his demanding requests, Josephine found herself softening at his sweet words. As he smiled and met her gaze, there was genuine warmth there, creating an immediate connection with the entertainer. She extracted her hand, returned the smile, and nodded. "It is, sir. Let me show you to your rooms."

As they walked, he kept up a steady stream of chatter about the trip to the Regal Sol, and Josephine found there was something charming about his exuberance and enthusiasm, even with his enlarged ego and dramatic affectations. She managed to get Ronaldo and the rest of the troupe members settled and take a slight break before she had to return for the big opening night.

Which gave her time to read Martin's letter again and revive herself with the promise that they would soon be together once more.

Later that night, as she stood just off stage, it was easy to see why Ronaldo was so popular. He had a strong voice, and while the act itself could only be described in one word—flamboyant—it was appealing and had the audience laughing and clapping at the various skits. Judging from the sold-out performance and those standing along the back walls, the show was a huge success for the Regal Sol.

The fact that it went on without any problems was a success for her.

As the final skit came to an end, her mother rushed up to her as Josephine stood in the wings. She looked around for her *abuela*, thinking that her mother might have thought to sneak her backstage to meet Ronaldo, but her grandmother was nowhere to be seen. In fact, rather than excited, her mother seemed quite flustered and almost nervous.

"*Mami*, is something wrong?" she asked, growing worried.

Her mother shook her head and glanced over Josephine's shoulder at the players on the stage. "No, I just thought we'd get out of here before the rush at the end of the show."

Puzzled, she said, "But I thought *Abuela* wanted to meet Ronaldo."

Zara waved her off. "No, not at all. She's fine and we thought you might be tired after such a long day at work."

She was, but then again, the success of the show and the promise of Martin's return had given her the energy she needed to last through the day.

"I'm fine," she said, but to her surprise, her mother took hold of her shirtsleeve and tugged her in the direction of the exit.

"We should go so you can get some rest," she explained.

"Zara? Zara, is that you?" Ronaldo called out exuberantly as he flounced off the stage and rushed over to them. "It *is* you! I cannot believe it after all this time," he said and wrapped Zara up in a tight and enthusiastic hug. He dropped a number of kisses on her cheeks.

Josephine watched in amazement. Although her mother looked stricken and rather much like she wanted to die, Ronaldo kept up his high-spirited greeting. "I never thought to see you again, and now here you are! How wonderful!"

The beaming smile on Ronaldo's face was a stark contrast to her mother's anxious features.

"*What?* Do you two know each other?" Josephine asked, incredulous. All the times *Abuela* had waxed poetic about Ronaldo, her mother had never given a hint that she actually knew the man.

Zara shot Ronaldo a nervous glance and slid from beneath the arm he had tossed over her shoulders. "It was a long time ago. We should really go—"

"Go? But we have just found each other again, my dear Zara!" Ronaldo grasped her mother's hand again and drew her close. "You cannot leave. Please, you must stay and tell me what has happened to you since we shared that impossibly perfect night together under the stars!"

Josephine's eyebrows rose dramatically. *An impossibly perfect night under the stars?*

Zara was trying to unsuccessfully extricate her hand when Josephine turned to Ronaldo and asked, "So, Mr. de la Sera, the two of you were...close?"

"Very close, Miss Josephine. When I was a younger man, only slightly younger of course, I was very much in love with Zara."

Her mother screwed her eyes shut, just as Josephine's own popped ever wider in surprise. Before she could ask another question, *Abuela* hurried over, a beaming smile on her face, and took hold of Josephine's arm. "*Mija*, wasn't that just the most wonderful show? Ronaldo is even more handsome in person than I expected."

Ronaldo preened with the compliment. "Thank you, kind lady! You have very good taste, I must say."

Her *abuela* turned in surprise, and her jaw dropped as she realized Ronaldo was standing there. Her face went pale, then flushed with color. She covered the blush with her hands and stammered, "Mr. de la Sera. You were very—I-I really enjoyed the—Is it—Is it warm in here?" She waved a hand to fan the heat of her blush from her face.

Josephine bit her lip in amusement. She had never seen her grandmother so tongue-tied in all her life.

"*Abuela*, Mr. de la Sera was just telling me how he knows *Mami*." Her *abuela* whirled to face Zara in shock. "They do? You do?"

Josephine's mother covered her face with her hands, but as Alberta started to ask another question, she was cut off by Ronaldo's bewildered voice.

"*Mami?* Excuse me, Miss Josephine, but did you just say that Zara is your...moooo-ther?" He stretched the word out as if it were foreign and unfamiliar on his tongue.

"Yes, I did. Zara is my mother, and I'd love for you to finish the story of how you know each other."

Silence stretched for a few long seconds as a funny look came over Ronaldo's face, but he didn't answer her. Instead he tenderly urged Zara's hands from her face. He held them in his own, his thumbs rubbing gently across her mother's knuckles. "Zara?" he asked, his usually booming voice now a hesitant whisper.

Her mother raised her gaze to Ronaldo's and nodded, tentatively. Then, she heaved a shuddering sigh and, without turning back to Josephine, said the next words very calmly, very quietly, as they continued to stare into each other's eyes.

"He's your father."

Oh my, Ronaldo is Zara's long-lost traveling "soldier"? And Josephine's long-lost father? Who could have foreseen this? Well, yes, of course, I could have, but I think everyone else is pretty surprised about now. Just wait until Ronaldo finds out he's about to be a grandfather!

Chapter Twelve

Martin could barely contain his excitement as the miles of pines, mangroves, and coastline passed before his eyes as the train chugged toward Miami. The railcar was moving at a reasonable clip, but to him, it was as if it was standing still.

In less than an hour they'd arrive at the Florida East Coast Railway depot, and from there, he was going to head straight to the Regal Sol to see if Josephine was at work. If she wasn't, he'd go to the cottages next in the hope that they would have time to talk and sort out the issues between them.

Then he'd have to head over to the local Pinkerton office so that he and Nita could brief their superior on the information they'd been able to gather in Palm Beach. Unfortunately, despite some promising leads, the trail of Sin Sombra had disappeared into the shadows much like the man himself. He was hoping that they could find the trail again once they returned to Miami since rumor had it that a huge shipment of illegal liquor would soon be arriving from Cuba.

"Do you think there's some truth to that rumor about the contraband coming in?" Nita asked as she flipped through the small leather journal where she kept her notes on the case.

Martin shrugged. "Unfortunately, it's the only semi-credible lead we've got. Plus, it fits the pattern of what we've seen Sin Sombra do in the past."

Nita arched a manicured brow. "So we hit the ground running once we get to Miami?"

He hesitated. That hadn't been his game plan. In the last several weeks, he and Nita had spent a lot of time together on the case, and he knew she wanted more of his time and attention of a personal nature despite his telling her he had no interest.

Looking away, almost shamefaced, he said, "I need a little personal time before heading to the office."

Nita pursed her lips, obviously discomfited. "Josephine?"

"I just need a few hours, that's all," he said.

Nita nodded. "Whatever you need, Martin. I mean that. Whatever you need."

As he met her gaze, the meaning beneath the words was abundantly clear, only Martin had no interest in anyone but Josephine. Even though some might think him a fool for wanting her back, she made him feel things that no one else did. In Josephine, he had a true friend as well as someone who challenged him intellectually. As for physically...well, for two years he'd imagined what it would be like to be with her. The pleasure to be had from the feel of her creamy skin and lush curves against him. From the taste of her lips and the way her dark brown eyes melted like chocolate in the Miami sun with desire.

As upset as he was that another man had experienced that pleasure first, and that a child had been the result, he was man enough to forgive that. Man enough to raise another man's child as his and hopefully create more of his own.

The woo-woo of the train horn sounding their arrival pulled him from his thoughts and made his heart beat more rapidly with anticipation. As the train stopped, he rose, grabbed his valise and Nita's, and helped her down the steps and onto the train platform. They walked through the waiting room and breezeway out to where a number of carriages were waiting for patrons.

Luckily they had little time to wait before a carriage freed up and they were on their way to the Regal Sol...and Josephine.

True love is alive once again! But Josephine has just had quite a shock. Can she handle Martin's arrival at such a delicate moment?

✱

Josephine stared at her mother as if seeing her for the first time.

Ronaldo stared at Josephine, seeing his daughter for the first time.

Zara stared at Ronaldo, thinking he didn't look all that different from the first time she'd seen him.

"Y-y-ou t-t-old me he was a soldier," Josephine said after a long, uncomfortable moment.

Ronaldo seemed startled at first, but then he threw back his shoulders and puffed up his chest. "Not just a soldier. I was playing a general, if I recall."

Shock at his prideful statement rendered Josephine silent, giving Ronaldo time to continue. Hands held out before him in pleading, he faced Zara and said, "Why didn't you tell me that you were with child? That I had such a lovely daughter?"

Tears shimmered in Zara's eyes, but she managed to hold them back. "I didn't realize I was pregnant until you'd left, and then I didn't know how to find you."

Ronaldo held his hands wide in disbelief. "I am everywhere, *mi amor.*"

"Which is why I could not track you down, Ronaldo," Zara insisted. "You would be one place one day and another the next."

But her mother had known for weeks he would be coming to the Regal Sol, Josephine thought, surprise at the revelation being replaced by anger. But before she could lash out, Ronaldo reached out and cupped her mother's cheek tenderly.

"I am here now, Zara. And I never stopped wondering where you were. Never stopped thinking about you and how it was between us."

"I'm so sorry, Ronaldo," Zara said as the tears finally slipped down her cheeks. Her mother faced her and said, "I'm so, so sorry, Josephine. I never meant to lie to you."

But she had. Josephine couldn't stand there another minute.

"I can't…I-I have to go," she said and raced off, leaving the two lovers to finish their reunion.

✳

Martin hopped out of the carriage in front of the Regal Sol and sent Nita on to the Miami Pinkerton office.

He hurried to the concierge desk, but her supervisor told him Josephine had been given responsibility for making sure the hotel's entertainment was in order that night. Thanking the man, Martin charged along the path to the rotunda, but the show had already concluded. He snuck into the wings off the stage and caught a glimpse of Zara and Alberta with one of the stage performers, but no sign of Josephine.

Hoping that she'd headed home, he raced back onto the path and nearly sprinted to the Valencia cottage. There was a light on inside, and his heart stopped for a beat as he imagined Josephine there, just beyond the wood of the door and glass of the windows.

His hand was almost trembling as he raised it and knocked on the door. A second later, it jerked open and the sharpness of the movement sent flakes of white paint drifting down again.

A good sign, he thought, and then a second later, she was flying through the door and into his arms.

More snow! It's another miracle! True love will always win out, my friends.

Josephine held on to Martin tightly, almost unable to believe that he was finally there. The tears of sadness and frustration she had shed on the way home from the Regal Sol were now replaced with tears of joy.

"I am so glad you are home," she said and kissed the side of his face.

"I am glad to be home, my darling." He cradled her cheeks and wiped away the trail of tears. "You've been crying."

"Happy tears now that you're here," she said, taking hold of his hand and urging him into the cottage.

"Did something happen? Did that cad hurt you?" he said, his growing anger visible on the tight lines of his handsome face.

"No, Rake didn't do anything. It was my mother who upset me. And my father," she explained and guided him to a chair at the kitchen table. Needing something to do, she set about preparing tea while she told him what had happened just a short time earlier.

Martin had been silent, but as she placed a cup of tea before him, he said, "Maybe she just wanted to protect you."

Josephine slammed her cup on the table a little more forcefully, causing it to rattle and the tea to spill. "Maybe I don't need protecting."

Martin laid a gentle hand over hers. "I know you don't. If I've been overprotective, it wasn't to smother you, Josephine. It's because you're so important to me."

"You're important to me too, Martin, but we need to allow people to grow, and if they make a mistake—" She stopped short, aware she was heading onto dangerous ground.

Martin squeezed her hand reassuringly. "We *all* make mistakes. I erred in trying to keep you from what was happening with the investigation. There were things I could have shared with you without compromising my obligations."

Josephine smiled and twined her fingers with his. "I made a *big* mistake, Martin. I let misguided anger drive me into doing something…irresponsible, and I hurt you. I hope you can forgive me for that."

A full-lipped smile erupted on Martin's face. He brought her hand to his mouth and dropped a kiss on it. "I can, Josephine. And I hope you can find it in your heart to forgive your mother. She loves you so, and I'm sure she never meant to hurt you."

She thought of her mother and Ronaldo staring at each other. Seeing each other after more than twenty years apart. What could they have been feeling, and how hard might it have been?

As hard as it was right now to have Martin here after so long. Caring, patient—yes, always patient—and kind Martin, willing to forgive her, to give her another chance.

She wanted that so badly, but she also needed to be honest with her fiancé. She took his hand into both of hers and held it tightly. "I know my mother didn't mean to hurt me, and I didn't mean to hurt you. I hope you can believe that."

With a quirk of his lips and dip of his head, he said, "I want to believe it, Josephine. I truly do. It hasn't been easy to forget what happened, and I know we have to rebuild the trust that we once had."

She did know, which was why she had to tell him everything that was in her heart. "In the weeks you've been gone, I've felt so alone. You were always there for me."

"And I'm here for you now, Josephine. If there's anything you want to tell me…"

"I need you to know that since that night, I haven't been unfaithful to you, Martin. But Rake and I have come to know each other well. He's become a close friend, and we have spent some time together. I had to tell you that. I want you to trust me again."

He frowned at the mention of Rake, but then simply said, "I want that also, Josephine. So tell me how you are. How are your classes?"

She smiled that he had remembered, but was also sad at the same time. "Getting a job as a tutor may be hard right now. But I've been writing."

"In your journal?" He smiled. "You must have dozens of them filled by now."

"Well, yes, but"—she took a deep breath before continuing—"stories too. Romantic ones like—"

He grinned and said excitedly, "I suppose just like Miss Austen. I know she is a favorite of yours."

"Yes, just like Miss Austen's," she replied and waited expectantly, unsure of what Martin would think about her spending her time so frivolously. He was such a hard worker, and his job was so important and serious.

"It's not an easy thing to write a novel, I imagine," he said, and there was no doubting that his interest was real.

"No, it's not easy. It's taken me a lot of hard work," she admitted.

He smiled and nodded. "Well then, it is truly wonderful that you've accomplished that, Josephine."

"Really?" her heart soared, confidence imbuing her at his encouraging words. "Because I—I think I'd like to be a writer."

"Well, I'd say you already are."

She breathed a sigh of relief at his support and said, "I just finished a novel and sent it off to some publishers up North."

"I am so happy for you, my darling, but why didn't you tell me before? I hope you know you can confide in me about anything, don't you?"

"I guess I was worried that you would say I was setting my hopes too high. That I wasn't being practical; I was just dreaming."

He shook his head and reached out to caress her face. "That's one of the things I love the most about you." Martin leaned in and touched his lips to hers, and the minutes fell away as they kissed.

When they finally broke apart, Martin asked, "How are you feeling? How has it been at work for you?" And for the next hour or so, they chatted about all that had happened in the many weeks since Martin had left for Palm Beach. As the time wore on, the lantern that Josephine had set on the kitchen table grew slowly lower, warning them that it was time for Martin to go.

"I'll be by tomorrow, my darling," he said as they stood together at the door.

"I'll be waiting for you," she said, rising on tiptoes to kiss him.

And as she did so, the light in the lantern sputtered and blew out for a moment before jumping to life again, brighter and stronger than before. Highlighting the flakes of peeling paint drifting down around them in the warm glow of the light.

They broke apart, and Josephine noted the big white flakes on Martin's shoulders. She brushed them away, smiling, as Martin reached up and plucked a fat flake from her hair.

Martin peered up toward the source of the paint flecks. "We really need to fix that ceiling."

Josephine chuckled. "Not ever."

Aw, the lovebirds have found their way back to one another at long last! Sniff, sniff. This was truly the most romantic night ever, and maybe, just maybe, the path of true love was finally a smooth one.

Chapter Thirteen

With his father's trip to Cuba set to happen the next day, Rake decided that it was time for a family dinner. He'd wish his father a safe trip and also try to pry more information from him on why he was going. Since his stepmother had shared her concerns about his father, he had in turn been worrying that Ernesto might somehow be the Sin Sombra that the Pinkertons were chasing. He wondered if the real reason Ernesto was heading to Cuba was to avoid the Pinkertons breathing down his neck. It had become impossible to rid himself of the fear that stuck with him about his father.

No matter how difficult their relationship could be at times, he still loved him and cared about his well-being.

He, Lucia, Sondra, and Ernesto were all gathered around the table in his suite while one of the hotel servants served the first dish of the elegant ten-course meal he'd planned with the hotel chef.

The servant placed the hors d'oeuvres plate with caviar on brown bread before them. While he disliked caviar, it was one of his father's favorites.

"Won't Penelope be joining us?" Sondra asked, earning a glare from Rake.

"Penelope is no longer a part of this family," he said curtly, but he had no sooner said that when the door to the suite burst open and Penelope sauntered in.

"I heard we were having a family dinner," she said with a charming smile and walked over to greet everyone except Rake. She shot him a challenging look, as if daring him to toss her out.

While he had no desire to spend the evening with Penelope, he was too much of a gentleman to make a scene. Especially in front of his father, Sondra, and Lucia.

"Please, join us," he said through gritted teeth and gestured to the empty chair beside Lucia, seating her as far away from him as possible.

Dinner resumed, and Lucia started the conversation again. "This is delicious, Rake. Thank you so much for thinking of having this dinner to wish Father a safe trip."

"Yes, thank you, Son," his father added, although it sounded too reluctant to Rake.

"My pleasure, Father. So tell us what you plan for your trip," he said, hoping to draw information out of Ernesto.

As the servant removed the plates and placed the second course of a beef consommé on the table, Ernesto explained his plan. "Cuba is stabilizing, and Havana and the nearby coastline are only ninety miles away. It's a perfect time to see if Varadero Beach has the potential for a new Solvino hotel. It's been too long since we built one."

"The Regal Sol is only a few years old," Rake said, earning a tut-tut from his father.

"This is *your* hotel, Rake. And quite frankly, I'm still not convinced that it will prove to be profitable in the long run," Ernesto said.

Maybe this dinner was a big mistake, Rake thought but bit his tongue.

As the *vol-au-vents* came out, Penelope said, "Actually from what I can see, the Regal Sol has quite a lot of potential. It wouldn't surprise me if it was profitable soon."

The support from his soon-to-be ex-wife was unexpected. He wasn't sure what game she was playing, but it was nice to have someone else deflect his father's condemnation.

It actually restored his hunger and let him enjoy the warm savory pastries, which had two different fillings, a hearty beef and mushroom mix in one and a creamy crab mix in the other.

"The Regal Sol is quite lovely. I'm sure that in time it will hold its own," Sondra said, likewise surprising him. Until of course, she added, "It's just the kind of place to appeal to tourists."

Lucia coughed uneasily, drawing his attention. She shared a supportive look with him and said, "Didn't the Astors stay here a few weeks ago? Mr. Deering, also?"

"You're quite right, Lucia. High society seems to think the Regal Sol is just their cup of tea," Penelope said, shocking him yet again.

A disbelieving grunt erupted from his father, and the meal went downhill from there despite a lovely offering of courses from the kitchen and a constant stream of support from Penelope and Lucia.

Cold poached salmon with a rich velouté spiked with herbs.

Roast beef with farm-fresh green beans.

A beautifully seared duck breast accompanied by a wine demiglace.

Wonderfully ripe French cheeses on a fine china serving tray and a hearty port in his best lead crystal came out next.

And finally, thankfully since he couldn't wait for the dinner to end, delicate lemon ices that were nowhere as chilly as the silent freeze that had settled over the room.

When the dessert dishes were cleared away, they almost simultaneously jumped to their feet, obviously intending to forgo the traditional coffee and liqueurs that had been prepared for them in the front parlor of Rake's suite.

At the door, Rake hugged his sister warmly and whispered in her ear, "Thank you, Lucia."

Ernesto was next, and he held out his hand stiffly. "Father. Safe travels." He hadn't learned much tonight about what his father was truly doing, but he intended to find out. His father had hired his own captain for the trip on Rake's yacht, but Rake intended to have some of his own men on the crew to watch what was happening.

Rumor had it that Sin Sombra was bringing in a huge load of contraband shortly, and if that load was coming in with his father on Rake's yacht, he intended to know.

When Sondra came to the door, she shared a knowing look with him, seeming to say that Rake had better keep a close eye on his father.

Last to leave was Penelope. She strolled to the door slowly, obviously waiting to have her moment alone with him.

"I should thank you," he said because she had been in his corner during the meal.

With a soft laugh and a smile, she said, "Yes, you should. When I heard you were having your family for dinner, I thought I should come. I remembered how difficult it could be with your father and that woman."

"Thank you for tonight. Dinner with my family is never easy," Rake said.

"Then why put yourself through it?" she asked.

With a shrug, he opened up to her the way he once had when they were together, explaining to her his concerns about his father. She listened patiently, but then shook her head. "It's not your father you have to worry about. If I were you, I'd keep an eye on Sondra."

"Really?" His stepmother had been notably more pleasant since sharing her concerns about Ernesto with Rake.

"Trust me, Rake. I know her type, and she's nothing but trouble. Have you seen the way she's been kissing up to your sister the last few weeks?"

Her intuitiveness and concern surprised him. "Well, Lucia and Sondra were schoolmates and have always been close." *Perhaps unusually close,* he thought but kept that to himself.

"I'm telling you. She's definitely up to something."

He smiled at her vehemence, remembering how much he'd liked her staunch confidence in her own opinions once upon a time. "I'll keep that in mind."

An awkward silence followed until Penelope said, "Well, it's late. I should go."

"Good night, Penelope. Thank you again for everything." With a chaste kiss on her cheek, he ushered her out the door, shut it, and leaned back against it, the weight of all that was happening dragging on him. His father. Sin Sombra. Penelope. Josephine.

Josephine, Josephine, Josephine, he repeated, using it as a mantra that lightened his soul from the darkness that was his family.

Just this week, she had started to show and he wished he could lay his hands on her belly and feel the child. His child. A miracle. Since the doctors had told him years earlier that he was likely sterile, he had given up hope of having children and put all his energies into the Regal Sol and proving to his father that he had what it took to run the Solvino business empire.

Tonight had been enlightening in many ways. He could always count on Lucia's support, but Penelope's defense had been surprising. It had also helped him to realize that his father was impossible to please, and so he was done trying to please him. With that decision, something freed up inside him and he knew it was time to focus on more important ventures.

He had something he had never thought he would have: a child. And then there was Josephine. A wonderful and amazing woman.

It was time to grow and build the life he'd already created for himself here in Miami. Time to make the hotel profitable, put an end to his less scrupulous enterprises, and stop worrying about his father's approval.

But what if his father was involved in illegal activities once again, or worse. What if Ernesto *was* the deadly and dangerous Sin Sombra?

Well, he had his family to protect. If Ernesto was the crime boss, Rake would do whatever it took to keep the Regal Sol and Josephine safe from Sin Sombra.

In the lavish suite that Ronaldo had politely demanded, Josephine sat across from the entertainer—her father—as he ate the steak and eggs breakfast he'd likewise courteously demanded.

She nibbled on some dry toast and sipped the tea that seemed to be the best protection against the morning sickness that still plagued her well into her fourth month of pregnancy.

"Please tell me about yourself, Josephine," he asked, which surprised her since for the last half an hour, he'd talked about nothing but himself and the many shows and cities he'd visited since leaving Zara twenty-some-odd years earlier.

"Well, I work here at the hotel," she said.

"Obviously," he said with a dramatic circle of his knife.

"I've finished some correspondence classes, and Sister Elizabeth was attempting to secure me a position as a tutor with a nice family only…"

She hesitated, not sure just what to tell her father about her life. A life he had not been a part of ever. But at his theatrically raised brow, she pressed forward.

"That's proved impossible since I'm with child."

Ronaldo stopped chewing and eyed her carefully. "I wasn't sure."

She rose and held her skirts tight to herself to mold the fabric to her rapidly growing belly. "You weren't sure?" she asked, dubious.

With a dramatic flare of his hand, he said, "A gentleman such as myself would never assume that or make a woman feel that she might be, well…looking particularly plump, should we say? Not that you are, by the way. You look quite ravishing, brimming with the glow of new life, like a finely sculpted Madonna one might find on a golden pedestal in the pope's grandest basilica."

Not sure he was serious, she examined him carefully, but as his clear-eyed and wide gaze settled on her, she realized he truly was serious. He might be a little self-centered, but he had a childlike honesty about him. She was learning that he said what he thought without hesitation or dissembling.

"Thank you," she said and sat back down.

"May I ask who is the father? Of course, I plan on making sure that he is doing the right thing by you," he said with assuredness.

"Like you did?" she responded with a bit of smartness and regretted it instantly as sadness slipped over his very expressive features. "I'm sorry. I shouldn't judge you since I really don't know you."

With a poised and stately nod, he said, "That is something I hope we can rectify in the next several weeks. And trust me that if I had known about you, I would not have stayed away."

Surprisingly she believed him. When he asked about the father again, she said, "It's a complicated situation."

At the subtle arch of his brow, she continued. "Rake Solvino, the Regal Sol's owner, is the father, but I'm engaged to a Pinkerton detective—Martin Cadden."

The arched brow shot ever higher, forcing her to try to explain—no, *justify*—what she had done. "I saw Martin with a woman, and I was angry. Hurt. Rake was suddenly there, and he was so charming, and there was champagne…" The words spilled from her as she retold the story of that life-changing night. Well, most of the story, since she kept the more intimate details to herself.

"And both men still want a place in your life?" he asked after his shocked silence faded.

"Yes, they do. But Martin thinks Rake is this mysterious crime boss, and well, Rake isn't too fond of Martin and his insinuations. And Rake dared me to be brave, and I find myself attracted to him, but Martin is the man who has always had my heart."

Eyes opened wide again, he said, "A triangle that's quite more sensational than any drama I've been lucky to play. But as the Bard himself wrote: *All's well that ends well.*"

Josephine wished she could be that optimistic, but it still all felt way too complicated and uncertain.

Ronaldo must have sensed her upset. He reached out, took both of her hands in his, and in a booming voice, said, "Do not worry, Josephine. I am here now, and I will make sure that *both* of these men do right by you. Never fear."

So this was what it was like to have a father, she thought suddenly. Josephine realized that Ronaldo really did want to try to make things right and not just with Rake and Martin. She truly believed he had not known about her and was determined to remedy that situation.

And she wanted to get to know him. Despite his demands and drama, there was something endearing and charming about the man.

As they sat there and finished breakfast, she realized she was looking forward to the next few months that the troupe would be performing at the Regal Sol. She had wished for a father so many times as a child. One who was kind and gentle and would read stories to her like her *abuela* had. One who she could tuck herself against for a good cry like she did with Zara.

Alberta and Zara had always been there to fill the void of not having her father, but despite their best efforts, she had always felt his absence. But Ronaldo, dramatic, extroverted, and flamboyant Ronaldo, was nothing like what she had imagined as a father.

Sitting there, listening to his stories, sharing her own, and thinking about his behavior over the last few weeks, it occurred to her that he was a man with a big ego, but with a bigger heart. He was kind and caring. Determined to make up for his absence and to be a part of her future. She imagined that he would be patient and playful with her daughter and take great pleasure in being a grandfather.

He was in another word—imperfect—but in a delightfully entertaining way. She was looking forward to having her father in her life and was hopeful that he and Zara would maybe find their way back to each other.

Josephine might be pleased, but would Zara be so enthusiastic at having her former lover in their lives once again? And what about Alberta? Could she reconcile the fact that her favorite entertainer had been the one to crush her precious daughter's flower? This is just like a telenovela!

Another load of illegal liquor had made it into the North Miami saloons. Worse, word on the street was that a load of cocaine had likewise made an appearance. While not technically illegal, there were many pushing for it to be outlawed because of its dangers.

Conveniently, the appearance of the contraband happened just around the time that Rake Solvino's father returned from a trip to Cuba, Martin thought. Convenient because it seemed to turn the direction of the Sin Sombra investigation away from Rake being the criminal mastermind and toward his father. But that didn't mean that Rake wasn't assisting his father in his nefarious activities. His hope was that if they cut off the head of the snake, the rest of the syndicate would die off.

"I know you don't want it to match up, but it does, Martin," Nita said as she stepped back to look at the chalkboard where they had laid out the timelines of the various murders and events against the presence of the two men in both Palm Beach and Miami.

Martin hated that Nita might be right. He had no doubt that Rake was up to something illegal, and it worried him that a man like that might be in Josephine's life—and his—on a more permanent basis. In his heart of hearts, he truly believed that Rake was Sin Sombra and he had been determined to prove it, but he was also a man who dealt in facts. The facts written in chalk on the board before him said that Rake might not be the crime boss, except for one thing.

He rose and gestured to one gap in the timeline where Rake was present in Miami and his father had still been in Palm Beach. A gap that also coincided with Richard Slayton's murder. "If Ernesto Solvino is Sin Sombra, how do we account for this?"

"You're grasping at straws, Martin," Nita said with an exasperated sigh.

"But the gap is there, Nita. You can't deny it," he urged and stepped back to look at the chalkboard and review all the details again. "The timeline fits him better, and he has more reason to do it. He's had to lay off people at the hotel because he's in a financial bind. What better way to get the money than by selling illegal liquor and drugs?"

Nita came to stand beside him and narrowed her gaze. "The drugs are a new element. That bothers me, Martin."

It bothered him also. It was a big diversion from the crime boss's original dealings unless… "What if it isn't new?"

Nita shot him a puzzled look, and he explained. "Rake charmed Mrs. Tuttle into giving him a license to sell alcohol. So he brings in more than he can use at the Regal Sol and sells the rest to willing buyers, but how much can he make that way? Is it enough to keep the hotel afloat?"

"Or enough to kill for?" Nita added, catching on to what he was suggesting. "How could we have missed something like that?"

He hated to say it, but maybe because he'd been so fixated on one thing—proving Rake was Sin Sombra—he might have lost sight of the bigger picture.

"When the mayor came to us, he was worried about the liquor and prostitutes and all the violence. We've managed to curb some of that activity, but not all. Maybe the reason is that we've all been focused on the alcohol when there's something more dangerous going on."

"And you think Rake Solvino is behind it?" Nita asked.

Martin just pointed to the gap in the timeline and the latest murder. A victim connected to the Regal Sol at a time when Ernesto Solvino was in Palm Beach. No words were necessary to convey to his partner who he thought was behind the murder.

Chapter Fourteen

Josephine sat beside Martin on the cottage's front porch, tucked into his side with his arm wrapped around her shoulders. He'd had more time to spend with her lately, as his big investigation had gone quiet. It was always so peaceful being with him, even with the chaos of everything else going on in her life.

Throughout the past six weeks she had been spending time learning more about her long-lost father, who was considering putting down roots in Miami. He'd said he didn't want to miss a moment more of his daughter's life and not a second of his granddaughter's.

Rake was a constant in her life, dropping by often to see how she was doing and leaving little gifts. At times his presence stirred up emotions that made her feel like she was being unfaithful to Martin all over again. Especially when he turned that dark gaze on her and heat flared to life inside her.

The baby kicked her, dragging an oomph from her at the force of the blow, as if the baby was upset by Josephine's thoughts.

She laid her hand over her belly and rubbed gently until the movements ceased. "Easy girl," she said.

"Are you okay?" Martin said and went to lay his hand over hers, but hesitated.

"It's okay to touch her," she said, and he relented and covered her hand, but she reversed their positions so he could feel the movement of the baby beneath his palm.

An astonished look passed over his face, but then it became tinged with a hint of sadness. "I used to picture this in my mind. How you would look when you were carrying my baby. After we…you know…"

She cradled his cheek and urged him to look at her. "I did too. I'm sorry it happened this way."

"I still want that, my darling. I want it so much," he said.

Her heart skipped a beat, and as her gaze met his, the need there mirrored her own. She took hold of his hand and drew it upward, over her breast. "I've been dreaming of this. Of you touching me."

He sucked in a breath and his body tensed beside her, but he caressed her and leaned closer to whisper, "You don't know how hard it is not to do more with you."

"You want to do more? Even now?" she said with surprise. How could any man want someone who looked like her, all round and swollen?

"I do, Josephine. So much, but we had always talked about waiting until we were married. That it would be the right thing to do. I want to honor that promise, no matter how much I want to be with you."

She sighed at his words, wishing for once that Martin wasn't *always* so honorable and patient. Images from her night with Rake flickered quickly through her mind, fueling her growing need as Martin tenderly caressed her and kissed her temple. She forced the thoughts of another man away, turned her face and covered her mouth with his, wanting to show Martin just how much she wanted him.

The baby kicked again, dampening her passion. "She's so active," she said.

Martin laughed and placed his hand over the baby, this time without hesitation. "Be gentle, little one. You'll be here soon enough."

She would, which made Josephine think about something else. "I thought we might be married right after the baby is born. I don't want to wait too long." Josephine was tired of her life being so dramatic. The sooner she could get back on track with her plans, the better.

"I don't either, my darling. If we could, I'd say let's do it now, but I know how much you wanted to wear your grandmother's wedding gown."

"I always dreamed of walking down the aisle in her dress; it's so beautiful. And I want the wedding to be all about us starting our lives together and the baby…" Her voice trailed off, but she knew he understood. The baby was Rake's, and her belly was not something she wanted front and center at her wedding to Martin.

"You are going to look lovely, and I'm counting the minutes until then, my darling."

She smiled and kissed him, her caring, gentle, and patient Martin. He was truly the kind of man worthy of being her husband and a father to the daughter who would be here shortly. And Rake could only be a friend and nothing more.

She had to believe that and stick to it because anything else…

Anything else? Anything else, what? You can't leave us hanging, Josephine! Josephine?

With a final yank of the wrapping paper, Rake unveiled the brand-new crib that he'd ordered. The wrought-iron crib had been handmade in Paris with decorative scrollwork that was painted in an emerald green and gilded with gold. Casters made it easy to move the crib around. *Not that there is much room,* he thought as he looked around Josephine's tiny bedroom.

He had ordered two of the cribs, as well as the horsehair-stuffed mattresses and down pillows, so that he could also have the same crib in the Regal Sol. He wanted his daughter to be comfortable no matter where she stayed.

"It's so…extravagant. You really didn't have to do this," Josephine said, obviously uneasy.

"It is not a bother. I want my daughter to be at home wherever she is, although, I confess," he said, gathering his courage to speak plainly, "I wish she didn't need two sets of everything. Or two homes."

"Rake, we discussed this—" she began, and he hated the conciliatory tone in her voice, so he cut her off.

"It's just hard not to think about it, Josephine. About us being together. After all, you're having my baby."

He cleared his throat and went on, feeling apprehensive. This wasn't going the way he'd expected, but he intended to show Josephine he was serious about a future with her and their child. Rake reached into his suit pocket and pulled out the papers he'd had his attorney prepare days earlier. He laid them on the table and scooted them in her direction.

At her puzzled look, he said, "For you. Read it."

She hesitated, but he shifted the paper ever closer. "Please, Josephine. For the baby."

She picked up the papers and unfolded them. As she read, her eyes opened wide and the color slowly drained from her face. "You've made me and the baby part owners of the hotel?" she finally said in a shaky voice.

He nodded, and puzzled by her reaction, he said, "I had hoped this might prove to you that I'm serious about our future together."

"Rake," she said hesitantly, clearly searching for the right words. "This is incredibly generous...*too* generous. It's—It's too much. Far too much."

He frowned, disappointed and confused by her reaction. Maybe he was just too used to people who thought money was the most important thing in their lives. "I just wanted you to know that I can provide for you and the baby."

She looked at him strangely, shaking her head. "*I* can provide for the baby, Rake."

"But I want to give you and our daughter the best that money can buy," he urged, and as bright color erupted on her cheeks, he realized he was making a mess of this.

"So you think you can *buy* me and our baby?" she gestured to the crib, anger clearly evident in her voice now. She shoved the paperwork over to him. "Do you think we're just like another piece of property that will go to the highest bidder?"

"What? No." Alarm flooded through Rake. He'd never expected this kind of reaction or just how upset she would be. "Not at all, Josephine. I just wanted you to see that we can make a beautiful future for our family. Our daughter can have all the things you never had growing up."

Her eyes narrowed, and her lips thinned into a sharp slash. Her next words cut him to the core. "Having a lot of money doesn't make you a family. You of all people should know that, Rake."

He did, and he was beginning to realize how badly he'd mishandled the situation. "I do know that, Josephine, and I want better for my child. *Our* child," he hastily corrected.

She tilted her chin up defiantly. "And I do too. I want our child to work hard and learn right from wrong. And I don't want her growing up thinking that being wealthy will solve all her problems in life!"

"She won't!" He crossed the room to take hold of her shoulders gently. "We will teach her that. We'll teach her all those things. Together," he said, pleading with her to understand.

She shook her head, moving away from him and wrapping her arms around her belly. "How, when I don't think you really understand that yourself, Rake? Just look at this." She gestured to the room full of expensive baby gifts. "From everything I can see, you think that money *can* solve any problem."

"That's not true," he said, but hated that there was some truth to her accusation. From his relationship with his father to the problems with the hotel, and yes, even to Josephine and the baby, he had sometimes thought that with enough money, all those problems would vanish.

She must have sensed that he finally understood, since her stance softened a little. "I know you only want what's best for me and the baby, Rake. I truly do, but the kind of man I need in my life is one who puts his family first. One who is honorable and will be there for us when we need him. Can you be that kind of man, Rake?"

A sick feeling came over him since there was no doubting the sincerity of her conviction.

"I can try," he said, but sadly, he knew he wasn't that kind of man. Not yet anyway.

With all joy gone, he gave Josephine the remaining gifts he'd purchased. She accepted each one with a forced smile and a dutiful thank you.

At the door to the cottage he hesitated, not knowing how to end their day together. She likewise stood there awkwardly until, without another word, he left the Valencia cottage, crushed and heartbroken. For the first time in his entire life, Rake Solvino felt incredibly, utterly helpless.

Well, it's a horse race, my friends! Rake and Martin have left the post, and it looks like Martin is ahead by a length going into the far turn. Rake will have to use some muscle to take the lead. Bets, anyone? Does baby make the odds two to one in Rake's favor? We shall see.

Martin stared at the whiskey as if it would have the answers to all the questions rattling around in his head. More than a month had passed since he'd returned from Palm Beach, and so much had happened with Josephine during that time. Little by little, they'd started to rekindle the friendship and trust that they'd shared during the two years that he'd courted her. Little by little, they'd shared what passion they could before breaking apart because they'd decided to wait. But as soon as the baby came, they could be married and then he'd finally get to be with the woman who had filled his dreams for so long.

Although it seemed like forever until the birth of the baby, every day that he saw Josephine and her growing belly reminded him that he only had to wait another few months for his dreams to be fulfilled.

He'd soon be her husband, but also a father, though not in the way that he'd once imagined. It was impossible not to remember that when every day some token of Rake's impending fatherhood stared him in the face, like the fancy new crib that was now sitting in Josephine's bedroom.

His hand shook as he picked up the glass and took a sip, thinking about the real father and how Rake intended to be a part of their lives after the birth. Even though he'd told Josephine that he could handle that, he worried about how he would. This situation wasn't like the family he'd grown up in. A loving and faithful mother and father.

He always enjoyed when they would come down for their yearly visit closer to the Christmas holidays. The workload on their Ohio farm was usually lighter then, and a farmhand could be trusted to manage it. He knew his parents had wanted him to stay on the farm, but the Pinkertons had drawn him away because they hadn't been able to place him in the area.

The allure of the big city had called away his older brother, not that they had much in common. Where he normally toed the line, his brother delighted in dashing past it, frustrating his parents with his errant ways. Come to think of it, his brother was a lot like Rake.

Rake, he thought with a grimace as the liquor's bite and heat slid down his throat.

He had hoped that they would have made a break in the case by now. A break that would have proved that Rake Solvino was Sin Sombra, but so far no luck. The only luck they had was that Ernesto Solvino, who was suspect number two, was still in Miami. If either of them made a mistake, Martin intended to be there to make him pay for that error.

A strong clap on his back drew him from his dark thoughts.

"Detective Cadden. So good to see you," said Ronaldo de la Sera as he sat on the empty stool beside him.

"Mr. de la Sera," Martin said respectfully.

With a flourish of his hand like a magician's reveal, and a broad welcoming smile, the older man said, "Ronaldo, please. You are family."

"Not yet, but hopefully soon, Ronaldo," he said and motioned for the bartender to come over.

"What can I get you?" the young man asked.

"Another whiskey for me. Ronaldo, what would you like?" Martin asked.

"Champagne. Chilled, of course. But not too cold. It damages the bubbles," the older man said, earning an annoyed look from the server.

"You heard the man," Martin instructed, and the bartender hurried off to fill the order.

Martin tossed back the last of his whiskey and grimaced once again at the sting of the alcohol.

"You drink like a man with demons," Ronaldo said and arched an inquiring brow.

Martin shrugged, and as the bartender placed the round of drinks before them, he picked up his glass and held it up for a toast. "To our lovely Josephine."

"To my wonderful daughter, Josephine," Ronaldo said and clicked his glass against Martin's.

"She is wonderful, isn't she?" he said, almost as if he was reassuring himself, and took a smaller sip of the whiskey. He wasn't normally a drinker and didn't want to overdo.

"You of all people should know. You're going to marry her, are you not? I must say I was both surprised and pleased by that," Ronaldo said.

He hadn't known Ronaldo long, but in the last month or so, he'd spent some time with Josephine's father. In that short time, he'd come to like the man. He'd also sensed that beneath that colorful and seemingly self-centered persona was a very caring man. For that reason, he felt free enough to share his concerns.

"I never thought she would...you know," he confessed.

"It takes a strong man to forgive something like that and to raise another man's child," Ronaldo said and glanced his way. "I think that you, Detective Martin, are a very strong man."

Martin laughed harshly and sipped his whiskey again. "I hope I am strong enough, Ronaldo. I never pictured myself in such an unusual family. Mine was rather…normal. It may take some explaining to them when they come down for the wedding."

Ronaldo shrugged and tsk-tsked his denial. "I've always thought normal was boring. You'll never be bored with my Josephine."

Martin laughed again, but this time with humor. "Yes, I won't be bored, and while I thought I knew her, she surprised me."

"Women are often filled with surprises," Ronaldo said and smiled after a sip of his champagne. "Bubbly, just like my Zara and your Josephine."

He smiled at that description of his fiancée, because she was spunky and filled with spirit. Those were just two of the many things he loved about Josephine and yet…

"How did you deal with your surprise?"

The older man smiled indulgently, sipped his drink again, and then laid a hand on Martin's shoulder. "I was shocked at first, but we were out in public, and I have an image to maintain."

"You couldn't make a scene," he said, understanding.

"Of course not, but when I went to see Zara later, it was quite a scene. I was angry. I'd missed so much of my daughter's life and Zara's. She had always stayed in my mind over the years. These Valencia women are potent."

"Yes, they are," Martin said with a smile.

"But it was not easy to suddenly find out I was a father. Just as I imagine it was not easy for you to find out you're going to be one."

"It wasn't easy," Martin agreed. It was a lot to handle, and he hadn't handled it well at first. Of course, most men who were going to be fathers had lain with their wives, so by all accounts, he had reason to be out of sorts. And then there was Rake and Josephine's "friendship" with the man and his concerns that Rake would not be content to leave it at that.

Ronaldo squeezed his shoulder reassuringly. "You have doubts, but that doesn't make you a bad man, Martin."

Martin laughed harshly. "I wonder about that sometimes," he said, recalling his earlier wishes about removing Rake from the father equation. What kind of man would want a child's father to be a criminal so that he could get him out of the way?

"I don't, Martin. I may seem a little focused on myself at times— I'm often misunderstood that way, you know—but I can see you care a great deal about my daughter. You want her to be happy—"

"I do, only…sometimes I wonder if she'd be happier with someone else."

Ronaldo released Martin with a dramatic push and a loud scoffing laugh. "Do not play with me, Martin. It is obvious who has Josephine's heart and who would make her the happiest."

As long as Ronaldo was being so understanding, Martin let himself wallow for a little bit longer. "It is not obvious to me."

With a wave of his hand, Ronaldo challenged him again. "Because you are too focused on the future instead of the present. You need to be more like me and not worry about the future."

Martin could not have been more confused, since he always worried about planning for the future. He shook his head and picked up his glass. He stared at it, wondering if maybe he'd had too much to drink, because that last statement hadn't made sense, but Ronaldo urged his hand down.

"I am not crazy, despite what some may say, Martin. Josephine needs a strong man beside her *now* to show her what's truly in her heart. If you stand by her, show her how much you love her, the present will take care of the future you are worrying about so much. For example, I wished I had told Zara that I cared about her. Maybe if I had, she would have asked me to stay and I would have known I had a daughter. Been a part of their lives."

Surprisingly, his words made sense in a crazy kind of way. "So what about you and Zara now?"

A little of Ronaldo's bluster dimmed at the mention of Josephine's mother. "I was so worried about becoming a star that I didn't see the precious gift that I had been given. I didn't appreciate Zara and her beauty. Her spirit. I do not intend to make that mistake again."

Martin considered all that Ronaldo had said and how it applied to him and Josephine. Like Ronaldo, he didn't intend to make that mistake again either. "I appreciate you talking with me, Ronaldo."

"Well, of course, Martin. We are family now, so I hope you don't mind if I ask you a very important question," the man said.

"No, sir—"

"Ronaldo, please," he reminded and swigged down some more champagne.

"Ronaldo, I truly love your daughter more than anything. You do not have to worry about that," he said, assuming what Ronaldo was about to ask.

The man laughed and clapped a strong hand onto Martin's shoulder. "Of course, you do, Martin. Only a man who truly loves a woman would forgive her the way you have my Josephine."

Confused, Martin peered at the other man. "Then what important question were you going to ask me?"

"You are ready for your first wedding dance, are you not? Latin families love to dance, and it's very important that you're ready for that big moment," Ronaldo said.

Martin was about to laugh again, but as he met Ronaldo's gaze, it was clear he was totally serious. That suddenly made him very nervous, because he had the proverbial two left feet. "I'm really not ready for that," he confessed.

"Then we must teach you!" Ronaldo slipped off the stool and held his hand out, but when Martin hesitated, Ronaldo looked around. "Ah, I understand. A Pinkerton has an image to uphold much like I do."

He flagged down the bartender. "Please send bottles of your best whiskey and champagne to my room."

The bartender eyed him dubiously.

With a twinkle of amusement in his own eyes, Martin stood and laid a hand on the server's shoulder. "Please don't tell me that you don't know who this is! It's the one and only Ronaldo de la Sera. Be sure to remember that."

The bartender rolled his eyes. "Whatever you say, Detective Cadden. I'll have the bottles sent up."

"Thank you so much," Ronaldo said, and the two of them walked out of the Regal Sol saloon and over to the elevators. Once inside, the operator expertly worked the gate and engaged the lever to move them to their floor. The ride was smooth, the operator skilled as he perfectly aligned the elevator with the doorway.

In no time they were in Ronaldo's room, and he hurried over to a small piecrust table and the Victor phonograph that sat on it. The phonograph had a large brass horn and a record was already sitting on the turntable. Ronaldo turned the crank slowly and gently until the mechanism stopped. He glanced over his shoulder at Martin and said, "Are you ready?"

He wasn't, but he also didn't want to embarrass himself, Ronaldo, or the Valencia family at the wedding. After his nod, Ronaldo placed the needle on the phonograph and immediately the sounds of Ronaldo singing to what Martin had come to learn was a very Latin beat filtered out of the large brass horn.

Josephine's father walked to stand before him and held up one hand. "Come now, Martin. It is just a simple one-two-three."

He wiped suddenly sweaty palms on his pants and grasped Ronaldo's hand as the other man counted out the beat and instructed Martin on the steps to follow. More than once, he stepped on Ronaldo's toes, but the other man didn't complain. He kept up his patient count of the beat until Martin was easily following him.

Martin smiled. "I can do this," he said eagerly.

"Yes, you can, my friend. Just one more thing to learn," Ronaldo said, and suddenly Martin felt himself falling backward before Ronaldo held him suspended just inches from the floor.

"The dip, Martin. It is very important to learn the dip," Ronaldo said with a grin.

With a quick jerk of his hand, he pulled Martin back up, and after a few tries, Martin was able to execute the all-important dip. Smiling, he said, "Am I ready now, Ronaldo?"

The other man grinned and tossed his arm over Martin's shoulders. "You most certainly are, my friend."

Friends, it looks like we now have even odds in this horse race with the start of this wonderful friendship! Look for Ronaldo to be rooting for Martin in the homestretch.

Chapter Fifteen

Repeating her C-A-L-M mantra to herself, Josephine stood behind the hotel's front desk several weeks later, smarting after another direct run-in with Penelope, although this one had not been as bad as her earlier interactions. She told herself to try to understand. Reminded herself of the pain and anger she'd experienced when she had misunderstood the embrace between Nita and Martin.

And while she didn't want anyone protecting her, as she had told Martin, it was time to speak to Rake about the situation. She hoped that he could give her some additional insights into Penelope and yes, maybe even step in and tell his wife to adopt a more civil manner toward her. Even if only in public.

She asked to be relieved from her shift slightly early, and the hotel manager kindly let her go. Her intent was to head to Rake's suite to chat with him, but she noticed him suddenly rushing toward the kitchen and back office areas. She chased after him, but her slower waddling gait made it difficult to keep up. Women who were nearly seven months pregnant were not built for speed.

She pushed through the doors to the Employees Only area just in time to see Rake rush past the kitchen area and toward the office and storage areas. Nearly skipping to keep up, she was about to call out to him when he entered the manager's office.

That's odd, she thought. She had just talked to the manager upstairs; surely the man wasn't in his office already.

She slowed her pace due to the ache in the small of her back and since she assumed Rake would immediately realize his mistake and head upstairs. To her surprise, long minutes passed, and by the time she neared the door, Rake had still not exited.

She knocked and called out his name. No answer.

Even more unusual, she thought. After another knock and a suitable delay for a response, she opened the door a crack and peered inside.

The office was empty.

Impossible. She'd clearly seen Rake enter the office.

She walked in, her hand splayed over her belly protectively, and looked around. The office was completely vacant.

Shaking her head, she examined the space carefully and was about to leave when an odd shadow along one wall caught her attention. She approached with caution, tension in every line of her body, and quickly realized it was no shadow, but rather a floor-to-ceiling ridge on one wall.

She ran her fingers along the ridge and realized that it gave a little when she pushed on it. Laying her palm along the edge, she started to shove when her angel appeared on her shoulder to shout out, "Danger, Josephine. Danger."

Surprisingly, the devil that rarely urged caution joined in with, "You may not like what you find."

She ignored both of them, and the gap opened wider. Easing her fingers into the gap, she yanked the hidden door open and found herself staring into a tunnel of some kind. She told herself it wasn't possible. Rake had said that he would try to be an honorable man and one who would be there for her and their child. The taste of betrayal was strong and bitter.

"Warning, Josephine. Warning," the angel cautioned, but she ignored her and stepped through the opening. She had to know whether or not Rake was up to his old tricks.

The ground beneath her was soft sand like that on the nearby riverbank. There were some dry leaves, like those from the poinciana trees lining the marina walk, that rustled underfoot as her skirts skimmed over them.

There was a bit more light up ahead, as if the tunnel opened to the outside. It occurred to her that the ground on this side of the hotel had been built up to create a sort of levee to keep back the river and create the marina. The tunnel likely led in that direction, but who would create such a secret entrance and for what reason?

Only a criminal, she thought. The baby kicked furiously beneath her hand.

It has to be a mistake. She tried to convince herself that Rake hadn't lied to her, but off in the distance, she suddenly heard his voice issuing instructions. His rich timbre bounced off the walls, and the slight echo made it hard to understand what he was saying.

Whatever it was, she didn't want to know. She couldn't imagine that the man who was so devoted to his yet-unborn daughter that he had put his hotel in her name was a criminal, much as Martin had said.

She whirled to rush back to the office and her family who was waiting for her at home. The sight of something bright and colorful on the ground caught her eye. She stopped her headlong flight and bent awkwardly, picking up a long piece of red ribbon. Velvet, she realized as she ran her fingers across the soft, smooth surface. Then she heard Rake's voice once more, and Josephine tucked the ribbon into her skirt pocket and continued her waddling dash out of the tunnel, the whole time telling herself that it wasn't what she thought.

Rake was not Sin Sombra. A man who could be this kind and supportive and gentle and caring could not be a murderous crime boss.

He just couldn't be.

Aye, Josephine. Did he choose that crib with the iron bars because it reminded him of where he belongs? Don't let your daughter get too used to places like that; otherwise she might take after her robber baron father!

＊

When the Valencia women set their minds on things, it was hard to get them to change their opinions. As it turned out, Ronaldo was just as hardheaded.

Josephine sat at the kitchen table, the ribbon like a giant stone in her pocket, weighing down what should be happy emotions at having her family—or most of it—sitting around her at the table. She had imagined a moment just like this dozens, if not hundreds, of times while she was growing up. Zara, Alberta, and the father she'd wished she'd had as a child.

Only now they were all sitting around the table deciding her life for her, which she did not need. *I am entirely capable of managing my own life,* she thought and tried to ignore the comments being volleyed around the table like bullets from a Gatling gun.

"Martin is a good man, but Rake. Oh my, Rake is so handsome, and Josephine and the baby would be taken care of quite well," Zara said, clearly smitten by the rich robber baron.

"No, no, no," Ronaldo railed melodramatically. "Martin is the man for her. He's kind, caring, and so responsible. That's the kind of man Josephine needs in her life."

"Enough. Tell them that's enough, *Abuela*," she nearly shouted.

Accustomed to her grandmother generally being supportive, she was surprised when she said, "If you ask me, I'm not sure who is the right man for our Josephine."

Every head at the table swiveled to stare at Alberta.

"Excuse me?" Josephine said.

"*Mami,* you can't be serious," Zara almost wailed.

"Surely you are joking," Ronaldo challenged with an indignant sniff.

"I have my reasons," Alberta replied with a defiant lift of her chin that Josephine recognized all too well. She'd done it herself many a time.

"Would you mind sharing them?" she said since she generally took her *abuela*'s suggestions to heart.

Alberta directed her wise gaze at Josephine. "You seem to be having so many doubts, *mi'ja*, even though you say you are sure. As much as I might not like it, I think it is better for you to wait until you have the baby. After that, you will hopefully be able to decide who is the right man for you."

"I *am* sure, *Abuela*. And I don't need all of you deciding my life for me. I know I've made mistakes—"

"We *all* make mistakes, Josephine," her *abuela* said, sounding surprisingly like Martin. "It is how we deal with them that makes all the difference in our lives. Do not rush your decision. Time will prove to whom to give your heart."

Wise words from Alberta, as always. Now will our independent-thinking Josephine agree?

Rake paced nervously in his suite, awaiting Josephine's imminent arrival.

"If you keep this up, you're going to wear a hole in that Aubusson rug, which would be a real shame," Lucia teased and laid a hand on her brother's shoulder. "Come sit, Rake. It does no good to be so impatient."

Reluctantly he did as she asked, but reminded her, "You know how important this is to me, Lucia. I'll never have this chance again."

"Or the doctors might have been wrong, Rake. Regardless, the birth of any child is a miracle," Lucia said as she sat in a chair beside him and smoothed her skirts.

At the knock on the door, he shot to his feet and almost ran to the door. Jerking it open, he was relieved to find Josephine there. "You came," he said, surprise in his tone.

"I promised I would, Rake," she said and offered him a reluctant smile.

She walked over to Lucia and held out her hand. "I've seen you around the hotel. You must be Lucia."

Lucia took both of Josephine's hands in hers. "I am, and I want you to know you're in good hands."

"Rake tells me you're a nurse," Josephine said as Lucia guided her to the table where a tea service had been laid out for them.

"Lucia was at the top of her class, and she's been studying to be a midwife as well," Rake explained as he joined them and sat beside Josephine.

Lucia poured out tea for each of them and then offered Josephine her choice from the finger sandwiches, scones, clotted cream, jellies, and jams. "My favorite is the cranberry orange scone. We're so lucky to be here in Miami where oranges are so readily available."

"Thank you," Josephine said, and after a quick glance in his direction, chose one of the scones, clotted cream, and some orange marmalade. "Rake has told me he would like for you to assist during the birth."

"I hope that's all right by you. I assure you I am quite able to help. I've actually attended a number of births. Words cannot explain what a miraculous event it is," Lucia said excitedly and clapped her hands gaily.

A broad, happy smile erupted on Josephine's face at Lucia's exuberance, and Rake finally relaxed a little. This was something he could do for her and the baby, even if Josephine wouldn't consider what he really wanted: a future together.

"Thank you for relieving some of my apprehension," she said, and the talk turned to how Josephine should be preparing for the birth. Whether she was eating and sleeping well and other things she needed to do to stay healthy during the last couple of months.

When they finished the tea, Lucia excused herself, and when she left, Rake felt as if some of the positive energy that had filled the room left with her.

"Your sister is very nice," Josephine said, scooting her chair away from Rake, and looked down at the hands she had clasped in her lap. Rake noticed they were white from the pressure she was exerting.

"She is, and you can trust that she will do right by you and the baby," he urged and laid his hands over hers. "Just like you can trust that *I* will do right by you and the baby."

Her head shot up, and she locked her gaze with his. "You've said that before, but actions speak louder than words. Can I trust that you'll be there the way you say you will?"

Rake blew out a harsh breath and shook his head. "I thought you believed me when I said I would try to be honorable and be there for you, but I can see that Detective Cadden has still been planting ideas in your head."

She tilted her head up in a gesture as regal as any queen's. "I have eyes of my own, Rake." Josephine paused, then said quietly. "I found the secret tunnel in the manager's office a couple of weeks ago. I know you use it."

"But no more," he urged, his heart racing again. "I'm done with all that. I had been bringing in extra alcohol for the hotel and selling it off in North Miami to keep the Regal Sol from going under. But when I found out you were pregnant, I started cutting my ties to that business."

Josephine narrowed her gaze, scrutinizing him carefully. "You say that, but I saw you go into the tunnel. I heard you giving instructions to someone."

Rake grasped her hands and squeezed reassuringly. "I'm not in that business anymore, but I have been using the tunnel when someone needs me at the marina. It's the fastest way to get there. I swear to you on our baby's life, I am not doing anything you need to worry about. As I said before, I want to be the kind of man our daughter would be proud to call a father."

He took a breath, remembering how Josephine had bristled when he'd shown her the new deed to the Regal Sol. "Don't be upset. I changed the hotel deed back to my name, but I have set up a trust fund for Gini. I need to make sure she is protected legally just in case. I had done the same thing for Penelope when I was so ill and…well, it just makes sense."

A silent pause followed his words, but then Josephine nodded. "Gini? Is that the name you want for our daughter?"

"You don't like it?" he said and arched a brow.

"Well, if you want our daughter to be a lady of the night," she said, lightening the mood.

Rake laughed and wagged his head. "Maybe something else. Whatever you want, Josephine. I'll be here for you and our daughter for whatever you want."

She peered at him again, and it seemed to him that she was finally starting to believe it.

And it gave him hope. Perhaps his dream of sharing a life with Josephine and his daughter was still possible.

Can we really be seeing the end of Rake's illegal ways, and if so, will that mean the end of Sin Sombra? Will our bad-boy hero be able to steal the race (and Josephine's heart) from our good detective in the homestretch?

The ache in Josephine's back had become her constant companion the last week. Lucia had warned her that she might experience such pains when she was getting close to the big moment, and by her calculations, that could be any day now.

She just wasn't sure she was ready for the big moment. The time had gone by so quickly the last few months. She had spent a great deal of time with Rake and his sister as she prepared for the arrival of the baby.

She had also spent just as much time with Martin, sharing with him all that would be necessary so that he could take part in the birth. He'd been patient with her and oh so tender. Excited and gentle when he laid his hands on her belly as it grew ever bigger.

Her spirits were bolstered by his involvement, but that couldn't keep her from worrying about the continued animosity between him and Rake. She had hoped that Martin's investigation would have been concluded by now and that it would have absolved Rake, but it hadn't ended. And despite Rake's assertions that he had divested himself of his illegal businesses, contraband liquor and drugs were still making their way into North Miami and elsewhere.

Then there was Rake's other family: his father, Ernesto, Sondra, and his wife, Penelope.

All three had taken up residence at the Regal Sol and showed no signs of leaving. Well, except for Ernesto's many trips to Cuba on Rake's yacht. The rumors had it that he had bought and was renovating a hotel on Varadero Beach, but she wondered if there was more to it. She suspected Martin felt the same way, not that he would say.

She was dealing with Martin's protectiveness better these days. And she was handling his partner Nita's obvious affection for him as well as Penelope's continued antagonism. As for Sondra, it was sometimes as if the woman was a shadow since she rarely interacted with anyone other than Lucia and kept to herself. It made her wonder why someone as dynamic as Ernesto had chosen such a reserved and private woman. It also explained why Rake had such a distant relationship with the woman.

A woman who was approaching the concierge desk at that moment, a diffident look on her face. "I understand you can make travel arrangements for me," she said and peered down her long, patrician nose at Josephine.

"Of course, Mrs. Solvino. What do you need?" she said and grabbed her notepad and pen.

"My husband is returning to Cuba again, and I'm bored here," she said, snapping open a hand fan made of deep red silk that matched the velvet ribbon holding up the artful curls at the back of her head.

Wait one moment! We've seen a ribbon like that before, haven't we, my friends? But it was so many months ago, and Josephine's been so busy. Will she recall?

There was something about the ribbon that seemed familiar, but the flap of the fan called her attention back to the woman and the lips pursed in annoyance.

Hmm, I guess not.

"There are several tours I can arrange for you that you might enjoy," Josephine said and was reaching for one of the brochures when Mrs. Solvino rapped the fan against the desk. The mother-of-pearl blades of the fan clattered loudly against the wooden desk.

"I wish to return to Palm Beach as soon as possible," Mrs. Solvino advised.

"Certainly," she said and, wasting no time, checked the train schedules and made all the arrangements for the woman. With not even a thank you, she marched away imperiously, leaving her to understand why Rake didn't much care for the woman.

"Penny for your thoughts," Martin said as he came up to the desk, a smile on his face.

"You don't want to know my thoughts. That woman is so nasty," she said, and Martin tracked her gaze to catch a glimpse of the departing Mrs. Solvino. But as he did so, his gaze narrowed and he gestured to his own head. "Was that a red velvet ribbon in her hair?"

Martin remembered! Good job, Detective! I guess that's why they pay you the big bucks, eh?

"It was. Why?" she asked, but he shook his head.

"Nothing. Just wondering," he said, and the moment passed quickly, like a soap bubble bursting in the wind.

Aw. So close! Or is our dear detective just trying to protect Josephine again?

"Are you almost finished with your shift?" he asked.

"Just a few more minutes. Did you want to have lunch?" she asked.

He grinned, a carefree lopsided grin so reminiscent of Martin before what she had come to think of as "the troubles." "I have the afternoon off, and I thought we might go for a carriage ride. Are you up for that?"

It seemed like the last few months had been a whirlwind of her going to work, preparing for the baby, and trying to get some rest since she always seemed to be tired. A carriage ride would be a perfect break from the monotony of all that.

"That sounds lovely, Martin. Thank you."

He gestured with the hand holding his boater to the front door of the lobby. "I'll be waiting for you outside."

"I'll be there soon," she said, and the time couldn't pass quickly enough.

Mr. Adams, sensing her impatience, smiled at her and said, "I don't think you took all your break time today, Miss Valencia. Why don't you take that time now?"

She grinned at the man. "Really, sir? I can leave?" It amazed her how supportive some of her coworkers had been, especially now that she was in her final weeks of pregnancy. Not everyone, of course. Some former friends now looked at her with scorn and disdain, and some gave her the cold shoulder entirely. As for the Regal Sol customers, their reactions had likewise been mixed. It had helped that her role in assisting with Ronaldo's troupe had also given her time away from dealing with the public.

He nodded. "Yes, you may. Have a good afternoon," he said, and she hugged him spontaneously, then grabbed her reticule and her bicorne hat, which she jammed on her head, blowing the feathers off her face as she hurried as fast as she could to the lobby door. The ache in her back grew with her rushed steps. She took a deep breath and slowed her pace as she waddled down the stairs to where Martin waited by a small open carriage.

He approached her as she came down the veranda stairs and helped her the last few steps and then over to the carriage where he assisted her as she climbed up. She took a spot on the single bench seat beneath a simple sunshade. She was grateful for that, as she had not been handling the Miami heat and humidity all that well the last few months of her pregnancy.

Martin hopped up into the driver's seat, took the reins, and with a quick slap of the reins and click of his tongue, he urged the horses into a slow, measured trot, mindful of her pregnancy and the sometimes rutted condition of the Miami streets. Luckily the road he took was in good shape, and in no time, they were moving southward of Miami toward the countryside.

While the early afternoon sun was strong, there was a breeze coming from offshore and the movement of the carriage. "This is so nice. What made you think of doing this today?" she asked.

He moved his attention from the road for the briefest time and grinned. "You'll see soon enough, my darling."

She wondered what he could be talking about and examined the carriage, searching for a clue, and noticed the picnic basket tucked behind the bench seat. "A picnic! How nice, Martin. It's been so long since we've had a picnic."

"Too long," he said simply, and yet she sensed he was holding something back.

Barely half an hour had gone by when he pulled the carriage down a narrow dirt road and kept on driving until they were close enough to the ocean that a sea breeze swept over the flat piece of open land surrounded by citrus trees on every side. The salty smell of the sea mingled with the fresh scent of orange blossoms, producing an enticing perfume.

She inhaled deeply, pulling in that aroma. She wished she could bottle it so that she would forever remember what she knew was going to be a very delightful day with Martin. "This is so perfect. Thank you."

He turned toward her on the seat and brushed back the wisps of hair that had come loose during their drive. "Do you like this place?"

She glanced around, taking in the sight of the orchards and the wide-open grassy space between them. "Yes, I do. It's lovely."

"Lovely enough for a home? Our home," he asked, almost shyly.

She shook her head and looked all around again, enamored of the place. "Do you mean that? Our home? Here?"

He nodded. "I thought we could build the house right here in the center," he said and held his hands up to frame the view. "It could be a big house with enough rooms for Alberta and Zara to come and visit. A nursery for the baby on the sunny side of the house and a room overlooking the orchards so you can sit there and write. I know you haven't had much time to do that with everything that's going on."

She hadn't, and she'd felt a bit of emptiness at not being able to work on her stories. She cupped Martin's jaw and gently urged his head to face her. "This is all so wonderful, Martin. It's more than I could ever ask for considering—"

He laid a hand over her lips. "Shhh. The past is the past, Josephine. It's time to start our new life together."

Her heart swelled with joy, but the angel appeared again on her shoulder, reminding her that she had feelings about Rake. Perplexing feelings that refused to go away and that she needed to share with Martin, the angel warned. She waited for the devil to jump in and tell her to keep her doubts to herself, but the devil surprisingly remained silent. Dizzying emotions swirled inside her even as the ache in her back grew ever more uncomfortable. "Martin, you are my best friend, and as confused as I've been over the last few months, when I'm with you everything seems clear and I'm at peace."

His handsome face grew serious. "And when you're not with me? How do you feel when you're with him?"

She hesitated only a beat, but it was a beat too long. "Are you entirely sure about what you want, Josephine? That I'm the man to be your husband and a father to your daughter?"

She opened her mouth to answer him, not quite sure what words would spill out, when suddenly the ache in her back went from dull to a sharp pain, like someone was driving a hot poker into her back. A second later, that pain radiated forward and a sharp contraction stole her breath. Between her legs, a gush of warm water escaped her and wet her petticoats and skirts.

She gasped and laid a hand over her belly. Then she clutched Martin's hand with her other one as another powerful contraction made her hunch forward in pain.

"Josephine, what's wrong?" Martin asked and rubbed her back with his free hand.

She sat up slightly and met his worried gaze. "I think I'm having the baby."

What a time for Gini (not!) to make her appearance! Right when Josephine was about to say... Well, I don't know what, but the suspense is killing me! And poor Martin! He probably wasn't expecting his romantic gesture to end with them racing back to Miami so that Josephine can give birth to another man's baby!

Chapter Sixteen

Martin carefully scooped Josephine into his arms and lifted her from the carriage seat and down to the ground. He hurried with her into the cottage where Zara, Alberta, and Ronaldo were all sharing a late lunch.

"Take a breath, my darling. The pain will pass," he said and kissed her temple, but in all truth, the contractions had been coming closer and closer together as he'd rushed them back from the homestead.

"It's time," he said as Josephine grunted in pain again and bit her lip. All three jumped to their feet and went into action.

"Take Josephine to her bedroom and then go for Lucia and Rake. Zara and I will take care of her until Lucia arrives," Alberta said calmly.

"Do not forget that I, Ronaldo de la Sera, am also here to assist. I once played a doctor in one of my troupe's skits," he said, but as a louder moan erupted from Josephine, Ronaldo's face paled to a sickly green color.

"Or I can boil water. I understand that's something you do at a time like this," he said and hurried over toward the kitchen cabinets.

"Martin, it hurts," Josephine hissed and grabbed hold of his shirtfront.

"I know, but you're strong. You're going to do just fine," he said and hurried to her bedroom where Alberta and Zara had already turned down the covers and prepared the bed for Josephine. As he tenderly laid her on the clean sheets, something fell out of Josephine's pocket.

He wasn't going to pick it up, but the red color was like a giant warning sign.

He bent and lifted the crumpled length of red velvet ribbon. Recognizing it, he peered at Josephine, who had gone pale, but not from the pain of her contractions.

Almost afraid to ask, he knew he had no other choice if he and Josephine were ever to have a future together. "Where did you get this?"

"The tunnel. I meant to tell you, Martin. But I forgot…especially when Rake promised—oooooh!" Her voice strained, then cut off with a groan as another contraction came.

It was not a time for anger, he told himself. He had to put Josephine above everything else since she was the single most important thing in his life. As images of the velvet ribbon assaulted his brain, he pushed aside the little voice warning him that he had been wrong about Solvino.

"It's all right. Focus on the baby. I'm going to get Rake and Lucia."

He shoved the ribbon into his pants pocket, dropped a kiss on her lips, and whispered, "I love you, my darling."

Rushing from the room, he raced past Ronaldo, who was trying his best to heat some water, and leapt onto the seat of the carriage. Slapping the reins, he set the horses into the fastest trot he could along the streets until he reached the Regal Sol. He tossed the reins to the doorman, flashed his Pinkerton star, and said, "Hold the carriage for me."

He ran through the lobby to the front desk where he ordered Adams to ring up to Rake's suite and then Lucia's. Within minutes the two arrived in the lobby, Lucia with a leather physician's bag in hand. Once they were all settled on the bench seat of the carriage, he raced off again toward the cottage.

Ronaldo was waiting anxiously by the door, raking his fingers through his hair and looking disheveled. As he saw Martin pull up, he called out, "The water is boiling," and hurried over to help Lucia down from the carriage.

Rake was about to follow her, but Martin laid a hand on the other man's arm and said, "We have to talk."

Josephine sucked in a breath, gritted her teeth, and nearly crushed Zara's and Alberta's hands as another contraction washed over her body.

"*Mami! Abuela!* It hurts so much!"

"Not much longer. Try to keep breathing, slow and regular," Lucia advised. She was positioned at the end of the bed, between Josephine's legs.

"I'm trying," she said and began panting, trying to control the waves of pain that washed over her like a storm-riled ocean buffeting the shoreline. The steady, regular breaths helped a little.

As she calmed down, her mother toweled her forehead with a damp cloth and wiped away a trail of sweat along the side of her face.

"It hurts because I'm not a good person," she said, fearing that the pain was punishment for her inappropriate behavior with Rake and betraying Martin. Imagining her little angel jabbing her repeatedly in the belly with the pitchfork she had apparently stolen from her devil as she said, "I warned you, Josephine!"

"No, *mi'ja*," her *abuela* said and rubbed her hand across Josephine's belly, trying to soothe her. "This is normal. It will be over soon, and you will have a beautiful daughter."

"I don't know what to name her. Maybe Rake has a different name. I really don't like Gini. Or maybe Martin does. He's not the father, but he'll be a good one. And why am I so confused about them? Rake has changed for the better, but Martin is so wonderful. Why can't they stop fighting?" The words spilled from her lips and grew ever faster as another contraction built, and the angel went to jab her again, but then reconsidered, muttering, "I think you're beating yourself up enough." With a poof, she disappeared.

She panted and, in between breaths, said, "Why can't it be easier? I should be able to make them understand! It's so hard to choose between them!"

A loud scream came from her as a powerful wave of pain wrapped itself around her midsection and the baby moved violently in her belly.

Just then Lucia muttered, "Oh no!"

Anxiously, she strained to sit up. "What? What is it?"

"Easy, Josephine. You may feel like you have to push, but don't do it yet. The baby just shifted, and it's breech now," Lucia said.

"No, no, no!" Josephine called out and fell back against the pillows, sweat and tears mingling on her face.

Rake and Martin stood in the kitchen, eyeing each other angrily and silently. Martin finally said, "Look, I know you didn't want to hear me out about Sin Sombra. But I've found out that—"

His words got cut off when they heard Josephine's scream, and they both rushed in the direction of the bedroom door, reaching it at the same time. They stood there, jostling each other for position until Ronaldo approached and moved them back.

"Gentlemen. I do not recommend you going in there. I've heard it can be quite unpleasant," Ronaldo said and swayed a little, his face nearly ashen.

"You look like you should sit down," Martin said, wrapping an arm around the other man's shoulders and guiding him to a chair by the kitchen table.

"Thank you, my friend. It's not that I'm weak; Ronaldo is not weak. But the thought of my Josephine in such pain…" His voice trailed off, and he couldn't finish.

Martin understood. His gut was in knots as he thought about what Josephine was enduring and all because of the man standing just feet away.

He glared at Rake but fought back his growing anger, because giving into it would only hurt one person: Josephine.

"She's going to be just fine, Ronaldo. This is normal," he said, hoping he was speaking the truth. "There's nothing wrong." But another scream escaped from behind the closed bedroom door, twisting his gut.

"Yes, Ronaldo. Do not worry," Rake said, but he didn't sound very persuasive either and began to pace nervously by the door.

A second later, Alberta emerged from the room, wringing her hands and looking tired.

"How is she?" Martin exclaimed, rushing toward her.

"Is Josephine all right? The baby?" Rake said anxiously, crowding in on Alberta's other side.

The older woman looked very serious. "The baby is breech, but—"

"Oh dear! That sounds serious. We should go get a doctor," Ronaldo said and shakily got to his feet.

"Yes, I think that's a very sound idea," Rake agreed. "I trust my sister, but—"

"I'm coming too," Martin said, but he peered past Alberta's shoulder to look into the bedroom. Josephine lay on the bed, a sheet draped over her. Zara was at her side, holding her hands. She was red-faced and sweating, her eyes screwed closed as Lucia softly issued instructions and worked beneath the sheets draped over Josephine's legs.

"*Ay dios mío*," Alberta cried, holding up her hands. "There's really no need. The baby has already started to turn into the proper position. I'm sure things will be back to normal soon. Why don't the three of you go get some fresh air instead of hovering in here like mother hens, eh?"

He and Rake shared another glance. It was clear neither of them wanted to leave, but Ronaldo raised his hand and brought his thumb and forefinger together just a small distance apart. "Maybe just a short walk. For Josephine's sake, of course, not mine."

In deference to Ronaldo, Martin nodded toward the man and turned to Rake. "Maybe we should get some air. Just a quick stroll."

Rake nodded and walked toward the door. Martin went to Ronaldo's side, and as the man stood, he wrapped his arm around the older man's shoulders. "Let's go, my friend."

They left the cottage, Rake walking in front of them. The other man had been relatively silent since refusing to talk to him when they had first arrived. But for all their sakes, he had to get Rake to listen to what he had to say. But their discussion should be private, and first he had to relax the older man, who still seemed quite unnerved.

"I understand your shows have been very well received, Ronaldo," he said.

"Of course, although I cannot take all the credit. My players are wonderful, but they would be lost without me," Ronaldo gushed.

"And Mr. Solvino has provided you with a marvelous venue, has he not?" Martin said, causing Rake to abruptly look back at him.

"Yes, without a doubt." With a flourish of his hand, Ronaldo added, "The perfect setting for a jewel like my troupe, and myself, to shine."

"Josephine did a wonderful job of making sure the setting was just what you asked for," Rake said.

"Yes, my Josephine," Ronaldo said and stopped. He stared toward the cottage, his smile dimming.

"Let's go back," Martin said and clapped Ronaldo on the shoulder.

They turned around and headed toward the cottage, but as they went to enter, Martin held back and stopped Rake. At Ronaldo's questioning gaze, he said, "We need a moment."

Ronaldo looked from Rake to Martin, but then nodded and entered the cottage.

Rake shoved his hands into his pockets and rocked back and forth on his heels. "Again, Detective? I guess we need to get this done for Josephine's sake. So what is going on? What ludicrous accusations do you have to attack me with now?"

Martin wagged his head, reached into this pocket, and pulled out the wrinkled length of red velvet ribbon. "Does this look familiar?"

Rake narrowed his gaze and scrutinized the ribbon. "A mangled piece of lady's frippery? Should it mean something to me?"

He held the ribbon up higher. "Josephine told me she found this in a secret tunnel in the Regal Sol. Your tunnel, Rake."

"And? It's nothing but a hair decoration." He took the thin velvet strip and examined it for a second, then shrugged, handing it back to Martin. "Sondra wears ones like this all the time."

Almost immediately after he said the words, Rake's eyes opened wide, much like Martin's mind had when he had seen a similar bit of frippery in Rake's stepmother's hair at the hotel. It had caught his eye, as such a rich, red velvet would be quite pricey to procure and far less common than the grosgrain or satin decorations most ladies wore.

And because the first time he'd seen such a ribbon, it had been clutched in the hand of a freshly deceased Richard Slayton.

"There's more, isn't there?" Rake said and arched an eyebrow.

"As much as I hate to say this, I no longer think you're Sin Sombra." He smiled tightly. "But the crime boss *is* a Solvino: Sondra Solvino."

Oh my goodness! Sin Sombra is Sondra! The Man with No Shadow is actually a woman? I-I don't know what to say. For once, I'm as surprised as you are.

In between rough pants and words no proper young woman should use, Josephine said, "I will never do this again. Never. Do you hear me?"

"Most of the cottages hear you," Zara teased and smoothed damp wisps of hair from her daughter's forehead.

She grunted as knife-sharp pain lanced her side. "Never," she repeated and gripped her mother's and *abuela's* hands so hard she worried she would break a finger or two.

"You'll want to do this again with Martin," her wise grandmother said, her voice soothing.

Martin, she thought and nodded. "I love Martin, but I care for Rake too. I wish things were easier with them," she nearly wailed and panted again as the pain in her belly was replaced by intense pressure between her legs.

"Something's wrong," she said and surged up to peer at Lucia.

The woman's face was calm, and an almost beatific smile lit her face like that of the Madonna on the little altar atop their fireplace.

"The baby's turned. She's ready to come out. Push, Josephine. Push," Lucia said.

Josephine leaned forward and bore down, clenching her teeth as she closed her eyes and tried to do as Lucia asked. The pressure built between her legs. She moaned as agony mounted with the force she exerted.

Zara rubbed her back and laid her forehead against Josephine's while Alberta gripped her hand in both of hers and said, "You can do this, *mija*."

"Just one more push, Josephine. One big shove," Lucia urged.

Mustering every last bit of energy in her body, she forced herself to push, and almost like a dam giving way, the baby rushed out of her body in a final wave of pain.

A second later, the wail of the baby filled the room. With a tut-tut and a quick rocking motion, Lucia calmed the baby and laid the wet, wriggling infant on Josephine's belly.

"Welcome your new son, Josephine," Lucia said.

Wait one second. A son? Is Lucia sure? But then again, one doesn't have to have an A in anatomy (which Lucia had, by the way) to know boys from girls (something Lucia knew very well)!

Chapter Seventeen

Josephine cradled the baby close and peered at her son. A son! Not what any of them had expected given the Valencia women's history of having females.

"He's beautiful," she said and cooed at the baby, who opened his eyes and stared at her. They were a rich chocolate color, a perfect melding of her deep mocha and Rake's nearly black color. Soft brown fuzz covered the baby's head.

Inside, her heart glowed with happiness and that glow grew ever bigger, expanding to suffuse her body until she felt it might burst out of her chest. And then it did, bathing the baby with its warmth and spreading outward to encircle her mother and grandmother.

Alberta and Zara leaned closer and murmured their approval and astonishment.

"A boy after so long! Such a surprise," Alberta said.

Zara skimmed her hand over the swaddling blanket. "So beautiful."

"He looks like Rake when he was a baby," Lucia said and gestured toward the door. "I think it's time we let the menfolk in, don't you?"

Josephine nodded. "It's time," she said even as she girded herself for what was going to be a difficult moment.

Zara hurried over, opened the door, and invited the men to enter.

Ronaldo rushed in and to her side, gushing and gesticulating dramatically as he spied the baby. "She's beautiful!" he exclaimed.

Zara rested her hand on Ronaldo's arm and said, "She's a he."

"A boy? I have a son?" Rake said as he hurried over to Josephine's side.

Josephine smiled and tenderly transferred the swaddled baby to Rake's arms. It seemed as if his knees weakened, and he nearly dropped onto the chair beside the bed.

"A son," he repeated in wonder and glanced at her tenderly, his eyes suspiciously shimmering.

"Congratulations," Martin said, drawing her attention to him as he stood by the door, hands folded before him. His hesitation to come farther into the room troubled her until she met his gaze.

He smiled, and a halo of light surrounded him with the simple gesture that belied the sacrifice he'd made in letting Rake, the man he clearly despised, meet his son first. That glow began again as warmth and gratitude flooded her heart at his simple, but incredibly generous and selfless kindness. Martin had proven once again that he was the kind of man a woman could count on in any circumstance. The kind of man who would love her and cherish her no matter what.

She held her hand out to him, and he finally approached, glancing at the baby that Rake held. He took her hand into his and said, "You look so lovely, and the baby is beautiful."

"Thank you, Martin," she said, and within her, happiness burst forth and the radiance of it spilled over onto their joined hands.

Rake's head snapped up, and as his gaze drifted over them, he seemed to sense that there was something different happening between them. "Would you like to hold him?" he said and held out the baby to Martin, but Ronaldo jumped in and scooped the child into his arms.

"I'd love to hold little Ronaldo," he said gleefully.

"I'm sorry, *Papi*—"

He stared at Josephine in amazement; then his smile beamed even wider. "She called me *Papi*! Did you hear that, little Ronaldo?"

Zara once again settled her hand on Ronaldo's arm and said, "Marcos. His name is Marcos."

"After Josephine's *abuelo*, my dear sainted husband," Alberta said and did the sign of the cross before looking heavenward.

"Oh," Ronaldo said in both surprise and disappointment.

"Marcos Galeno Ronaldo Solvino Valencia," Josephine clarified, which made Ronaldo perk up once more.

"We can call him Marcaldo for short!"

"Thank you," Rake said from beside her and leaned down to kiss Josephine's forehead. Out of the corner of her eye, she could see Martin stiffen at the gesture, but he didn't protest, remaining remarkably patient—always patient.

Lucia stepped up at that moment and said, "Why don't we all give mama and baby some time alone?"

"I think that sounds like a very good idea," Zara said. She took the baby from Ronaldo and handed him back to Josephine. "Rest. We'll be back a little later."

The women herded the men out of the room, leaving Josephine alone with her baby. She gazed at him and tears came to her eyes. He was so perfect. Perfect little eyes, nose, and mouth. Perfect tiny hands and fingers. So beautiful, and he was hers. Well, hers and Rake's. And Martin's.

Somehow they would make it work for Marcos's sake. "We will make it work," she repeated like a mantra. As little Marcos looked up at her peacefully, her breasts tingled, signaling that it was time to think about something else.

Out in the kitchen area, Ronaldo and the women gathered around the table, smiling and chatting gaily about the new baby.

Martin laid his hands on the top rail of the kitchen chair and met Rake's gaze. "If you can excuse us, Rake and I need to go back to the Regal Sol."

"Is everything okay, Rake?" Lucia asked and laid a gentle hand on her brother's forearm.

"Yes, of course, but…Lucia, do you remember Father saying he came to Miami and stayed at the Royal Palm? Did Sondra come with him?"

Lucia paused for a moment, and then shook her head. "She didn't, but I don't think she stayed in Palm Beach, because I was there alone while I studied for one of my final tests."

"Do you know where she went?" Martin asked.

Lucia shook her head again. "No, I don't. She often travels without Father actually."

Martin met Rake's gaze and understanding passed between the two men. "If you're game, I'm ready," Rake said.

"I'm ready," Martin said.

Two sworn enemies working together? What an epic moment! Perhaps things really are changing for the better?

The joy of his son's miraculous birth was tempered by what Rake had seen on Josephine's face as she'd looked at Martin. Although she hadn't said the words, the love she had for the other man had been undeniable.

He told himself there was still hope, but in his heart he feared the worst. He drove that worry away because there was something much more important to do: find Sondra. Sin Sombra.

The image of the red ribbon he'd held earlier twined together with the image planted in his brain by Martin. One of Richard Slayton grasping the velvet trimming in his cold, dead fingers. Thinking that could have been Josephine's fate if she'd run into Sondra in the tunnel beneath the hotel chilled his body to the bone.

"How can you be sure?" Rake said and risked a glance at Martin as they raced to the Regal Sol.

"I can't, but I think that once we match her whereabouts with the timeline we have, we'll be able to confirm it. Especially once we know where Sondra went when your father came to Miami. It's at the same time when Slayton was murdered," Martin said.

When they reached the Regal Sol, they were heading to the front desk when Penelope strolled through the lobby and stopped them.

Pain glazing her features into a porcelain mask, she said, "I assume the hotel clerk had your little love child."

Rake was a little taken aback. "What makes you say that?"

"I was having a late lunch with your father and Sondra in the dining room earlier, when Lucia stopped by to let us know that Josephine had gone into labor and she was going to help."

That had been hours ago. "Do you know if they're in their suite now?"

Penelope shook her head of artfully coiffed curls. "They just got in a carriage. I think Sondra wanted to say goodbye to Lucia before she returned to Palm Beach."

"We need to go. We may be able to catch them at the cottages," Martin said and took off at almost a run.

And as much as Rake wished for Penelope to be gone from his life, he said, "Listen, you were right to warn me before. If Sondra returns, stay away from her. I can't go into why, just stay away."

He rushed off, leaving a perplexed-looking Penelope staring after him.

Josephine had been surprised and pleased initially that Rake's father and stepmother had stopped by to see the baby. But it turned out that neither of them seemed to have much interest in meeting their grandchild. Rather, Sondra and Ernesto had dropped by to bid farewell to Lucia before they left Miami.

Nevertheless, their rudeness did not seem to hamper her family's joy. Zara and Alberta invited them to come into the kitchen for tea while Ronaldo promised to regale them with stories about the time he delivered a baby in a skit. Ernesto rolled his eyes but went with them, since Sondra lingered, saying she wanted a few moments to say goodbye to Lucia privately.

Josephine was already shifting restlessly in bed, eager to join her family.

"Is it okay if I get up?" she asked Lucia.

"Of course, but don't overdo. You did just have a baby a couple of hours ago. In fact, why don't we take Marcos for you?" The woman's eyes met Sondra's, an affectionate look on her face. "We'll just go out on the back veranda for some fresh air and hopefully a little quiet. I suspect it may get a little noisy in there with all of Ronaldo's stories."

"Thank you. That sounds wonderful," she said, and although she was still a little sore, she dragged herself from bed, washed up, and went out to the kitchen area where everyone was gathered around the table.

Zara was sharing stories of Josephine as a child and for once, Ronaldo was silent, listening intently to the tales. Ernesto, on the other hand, kept blatantly checking his pocket watch. Josephine frowned and thought to herself how lucky she was to have a father as caring and affectionate as Ronaldo. She walked over to him and squeezed his shoulder. He smiled, hopped to his feet, and gallantly offered her his seat.

"Please sit, *mi'ja*," he said.

"Thank you, *Papi*," she said, and she could swear she saw a tear slip down the side of his face before he hastily swiped it away.

Her heart swelled with joy at the love surrounding her, and as she sat and listened to stories she'd heard so many times before, the only thing she wished for was to have Rake and Martin there with her.

At times it was hard to understand how she could care for two such different men in such different ways, but she did. She knew she was going to have to choose between them, however, so that they could all move on with their lives.

After getting past her physical attraction to Rake, she'd come to appreciate that he was funny, caring, and determined. And he would be in her life not only because he was the baby's father, but because he'd become her friend.

On the other hand, Martin was everything she could ever want in a man. Honorable, kind, understanding, patient—always patient. He took her breath away with just a look or a touch, and yet he brought her peace also. He knew her like no one else and had been her best friend for so long.

No matter how things turned out, she was lucky to have them both in her life. Marcos would be incredibly blessed to have such a large family who cared about him so very much.

Barely fifteen minutes had passed with Ernesto tapping his foot impatiently and looking more and more perturbed, when Martin and Rake rushed into the cottage.

"Father! Where's Sondra?" Rake asked, breathless.

Surprised, his father asked, "Why? Is there something wrong?"

Martin held his hand up to stop any further questions. "Mr. Solvino, you need to trust us and just answer the question. Where is your wife?"

Shocked, Ernesto puffed up his chest and said, "I demand to know the meaning of this! I will not be interrogated like a common—"

"We think she's Sin Sombra!" Martin shouted impatiently, cutting him off. A shocked silence followed for a few seconds, then everyone spoke at once.

"Ay dios mío!" Alberta crossed herself.

"Oh my goodness!" Zara said.

"Please. Who is this Sin Sombra character?" Ronaldo asked with obvious confusion.

"That's nonsense," Ernesto spluttered. "My wife is not—"

Josephine's strong but clearly terrified voice cut through the din. "Oh no! She's out back with Lucia and Marcos!" A gasp escaped her lips, but she straightened her spine and began walking as fast as possible to the back door.

A loud slap and sharp cry of pain burst from the back veranda. A second later Lucia lurched into the room. Her face was pale except for the bright red handprint across her cheek.

Martin rushed to her and offered support as he guided her to a chair by the kitchen table. "What happened, Lucia? Where's Sondra?"

Josephine gripped the woman's arm. "Lucia, where's the baby?"

"Sondra—" She gasped for breath, nearly hyperventilating. "Sondra took him. We overheard you say she was Sin Sombra, and she went crazy and grabbed him! She said if you ever want to see the baby again, you won't try to follow her." Lucia stared at Martin and shook her head, her gaze filled with questions. "When I tried to stop her, she slapped me and pulled out a gun. I don't understand. Why would she do that? How can she be Sin Sombra?"

"Noooo! We have to get Marcos back!" Josephine shouted, fear gripping her, but she drove it back. She had to be strong.

Quickly, Martin squeezed her hand. "I'll find him. Don't worry."

He turned to Rake, who was quietly murmuring to a very shocked Lucia, and said, "I have an idea where she would go."

"The marina?" Rake said.

Martin nodded. "The marina. Let's go."

Poor Marcos. Only hours old and already fighting for his life. Danger, Martin. Danger, Rake. Remember Slayton! Who will survive the dangerous female crime boss?

Chapter Eighteen

Even though Josephine was exhausted and her stomach was a tangled knot of dread, she couldn't sit still. With her mother and grandmother offering both physical and emotional support, she tottered back and forth across the room while Lucia, Ronaldo, and Ernesto sat there in stunned shock.

"Sin Sombra? My Sondra? I could never have expected something like this," Ernesto said, shock lingering on his features and all earlier traces of his impatience gone.

"She was my friend for so long, Father. I cannot believe I did not see her for what she is," Lucia wailed and covered the handprint on her cheek with a lacy handkerchief.

"Clearly, she's a much better actor than anyone knew. Of course, not better than me." Ronaldo tapped his chest with bravado, but his tone was flat. If he was trying to cheer them up, he was giving what was probably the first poor performance of his life.

"Everything is going to be fine," Alberta said without doubt, crossing herself again and glancing at Josephine. "You must believe that He would not let anything happen to your precious Marcos."

But what about Martin and Rake? she thought. What would she do if either of them didn't come home safely?

She couldn't imagine losing Marcos or his father. A man who had dared her to be brave and follow her dream. A man who had become a good friend.

But her heart stopped beating at the thought of losing Martin. She didn't know what she would do if Martin didn't return from this mission.

At the thought, her knees buckled. Zara and Alberta managed to get her to a chair. She raised her teary gaze to them. "This cannot be happening, *Mami. Abuela.* Why is this happening?"

Zara kneeled before her and brushed back wisps of hair from her face. "Everyone will come home safe, *mi'ja.*"

Ronaldo stood behind her, leaned down, and embraced her. "All's well that ends well, *mi'ja.* Have faith," he said and pointed an index finger heavenward.

"I pray you are right, *Papi*," Josephine said and as her *abuela* laid her head against hers, tears came to her eyes at the fact that her family circle was incomplete. But buoyed by their love, she did have faith that all the missing pieces would be home soon.

Sniff, sniff, sniff. Let us all pray the circle will not be broken by the shadow of evil.

Martin and Rake sprinted to the Regal Sol and down to the secret tunnel that ran beneath the hotel and to the river. It was the quickest route to the marina, but as they hit the path along the edge of the riverbank, Martin caught sight of Rake's yacht just beginning to pull away from the dock. He thought that he saw Sondra—Sin Sombra—at the bow of the boat holding Marcos, but his view was obstructed by the other boats moored in the marina.

He raced to the railing by the edge of the river, vying for a better view, pulled out his weapon, and called out, "Stop! By lawful authority of the Pinkertons!"

The boat continued moving away, but he didn't have a clear shot and even if he did, he wouldn't take it and risk hurting Marcos.

Rushing along the marina path, he cleared the last of the docks, dodging coils of rope and equipment lockers, with Rake right behind him. When he finally had an unobstructed view of the boat, he had no doubt it was Sin Sombra holding something in her arms. The woman's normally elegant features were twisted with evil, and as he watched, she laughed and held the bundle in her arms over the yacht's railing.

"No! Please, no! We won't follow," he said, hands outstretched in a pleading gesture. Then he dropped his weapon and raised his hands as if in surrender.

Sin Sombra tossed her head back and cackled. The cruel laugh drifted across the water a second before she opened her hands and dropped the baby into the water.

"Noooo!" Rake wailed, dropping to his knees. Fear had immobilized the man, rendering him helpless.

Martin didn't hesitate. He ripped off his jacket and boater, and raced to the railing along the edge of the river. With a last look at the bundle as it started to sink below the surface, he hopped onto the top railing and dove into the water.

The cool water was a shock to his system, but he pushed through it and the swirling currents threatening to pull him downriver. Stroking powerfully, he swam as if his life depended on it, and it did because if he lost Marcos…

When he reached the spot he'd last seen the baby, he treaded water and looked around, but didn't see Marcos anywhere. He dived down, and even with the silt of the Everglades clouding the water, the white of the swaddling cloth was visible a few feet beneath him. He kicked hard, struggling against the current until the bundle was within reach. His fingers skimmed the cloth for only a second before the current drew it away. He stroked again, stretching his fingers almost beyond imagining and grabbed a fistful of blanket. He dragged it near, scooping the bundle with Marcos into his arms. Feeling the weight of the baby's body within the cloth, he kicked toward the surface, all the time praying that he'd been fast enough.

Paddling with one arm, he made it to the riverbank and the levee by the marina where Rake waited, terror etched onto his features. He handed the baby up to the other man, who laid him down on the marina path and began to unswaddle him.

Martin climbed up and over the railing to where Rake kneeled silently, looking at the bundle of cloth and...

A big, dead fish.

No! He had to be somewhere, he thought and combed back his wet hair with his fingers in frustration. Trying not to panic, Martin's mind raced with thoughts of what Sin Sombra might have done with Marcos. He looked toward where the boat had taken off and ran in that direction, hoping his instincts weren't wrong. He hopped down onto the floating dock and hurried to the empty spot where Rake's yacht had once been moored. An equipment locker sat by the edge of the dock, its top slightly ajar.

Hands shaking, he approached the locker and knelt before it as he slowly opened the lid.

The air left his lungs at the sight of Marcos lying atop a coil of rope and assorted nets and fishing gear.

Finally breathing, relief sweeping over him, he picked up the baby and cuddled him close. The baby protested his wet clothes and let out a healthy, hearty wail of complaint, dragging a happy laugh from him.

The sound of a footstep on the wooden dock pulled his attention to Rake, who stood beside him, tears streaming down his face.

"Marcos," Rake said softly.

Martin rose and, after the pause of a heartbeat, handed the man his son. For one small moment, as Rake cradled the baby close and kissed its head, jealousy awoke in him. This man had stolen so much from him. Josephine's virtue. The baby he wanted to have with her someday.

But he could see Solvino's distress, and it touched him.

"He's all right," Martin said, his better nature rising as he stood dripping on the dock, even though it felt as if he were watching his life rush away from him like the Miami River and Sin Sombra. Josephine had said she wanted to spend her life with him. But now that Marcos was here... How could any woman resist her baby and a father who cared as much as Rake obviously did?

"Yes, he is, thanks to you," Rake said and held his hand out to the other man.

Martin shook it reluctantly and stepped back. "I have to go and report this to my superior. Brief my partner Nita. If we're lucky, we can get word to our stations in the Keys and Havana. Maybe we'll get really lucky and pick up Sin Sombra when she docks."

"Good luck," Rake said.

Martin wasn't feeling lucky. He nodded and rushed off, leaving the other man with his son. Hoping that they would be able to get to Sin Sombra before she could cause any more harm to those he loved.

Josephine held Marcos close as the baby nursed. Tears of relief filled her gaze and escaped down her cheeks and onto the baby, but that didn't disturb him as he greedily rooted at her breast. His hearty hunger gave her peace of mind that the baby truly was unharmed by the day's ordeal.

A knock came at the door followed by Martin's hushed words, "Can I come in?"

Her heart danced with joy that he was safe and finally there. When Rake had told her of Martin's selflessness and how he'd risked his life for Marcos, her heart had ached at the thought of how close she'd come to losing him.

She shifted the baby's blanket upward for modesty's sake and called out, "Yes, please. I need to see you."

The door opened a crack, and he stuck his head in, tentative. A bright flush of color worked up his neck and reddened his cheeks as he realized the baby was nursing. "Are you sure?"

She smiled because his embarrassment and thoughtfulness were so Martin. She held her hand out, beckoning him to join her. "I'm more than sure. Please come here."

As he walked toward her, she drank in the sight of him. His hair was still damp in spots, but a few sandy blond curls had dried and framed his handsome face. His normally pristine charcoal-gray suit and starched white shirt were wrinkled and likewise dampened here and there. The squeak of his shoes also had a telltale squish to them as he ambled to the bed, his dirt-stained boater in hand.

"How are you feeling?" he asked as he sat beside her, his gaze skipping nervously from her face to the towel covering the baby and back again.

"Tired. Relieved. I was so worried about you. Especially when Rake told me what happened."

"I'm fine. Just a little wet. The important thing is that the baby… Marcos, is fine."

"I don't know how I could ever thank you for what you did," she said and cupped his jaw. She lovingly ran her thumb across his lips, anxious for the feel of them, but suddenly uncertain as to where they stood.

Rake had said that Martin had been quiet and subdued after he'd rescued the baby. Rake had written it off to the fact that Sin Sombra had escaped, but Josephine worried that it was more than that. Was he having second thoughts now that Marcos was really here?

"It's my job," he said with a sheepish shrug and a bobble of his hat in his hands.

"No," she said confidently. "Some men wouldn't have done what you did. To risk your life for another man's child. A man who—"

He raised his hand to stop her. "I would do anything for you, Josephine. Anything. And for Marcos too. The instant I saw you holding him… I couldn't love him any less than if he were my own, you know."

"I know, Martin. It's what makes you so, so special," she said and gave in to the need she had been feeling since earlier that afternoon. She leaned forward and kissed him, letting him know just what she was feeling with her tender, yet demanding, caress of his lips. Feeling the glow within her expand again and bathe them both in its loving light.

He groaned and deepened the kiss, but then jerked away abruptly as the baby fussed.

"We shouldn't," he said, but glanced downward at where the blanket had slipped, revealing the baby as it nursed at Josephine's breast.

Bright color rose to his cheeks again, but she took hold of his hand and rested it on the baby's side. "Rake may be the father of this baby, but I know that you will protect him and me with every fiber of your being because you love us. Because you are the most honorable and kind man that I know."

His lips quirked up in a half smile. "And patient. Maybe too patient. You don't know how many times I've wished that I hadn't said we should wait. That we had…that you and I had made this baby," he said and gestured to the two of them.

With a relieved sigh, she said, "I've wished that also, Martin. So many times. All I can say again is that I'm sorry that I was so foolish."

His eyes met hers, and the worry in them nearly broke her heart. "You don't have to apologize anymore. And I know this may not be the right time to ask—"

"It isn't because it's *my* time to ask, Martin. My time to make things right," she said.

A puzzled look flashed across his features, before his eyes widened in understanding. "Josephine, are you proposing?"

She smiled and cradled his cheek. "I *am* proposing, Martin, but I'm afraid I'm not very good at this at all."

He shifted his head to kiss her palm and whispered, "You don't have to do this."

"But I do, Martin. Because I want you to know the reasons that I love you. I love you because you are kind and caring."

He raised a finger to stop her. "And don't forget patient."

"Always patient. And you're hardworking and responsible."

He quirked his lips playfully. "You make me sound so…boring."

She leaned close, ran her thumb across his lips, and whispered, "Oh no, not at all. In fact, I think about doing inappropriate things with you all the time."

He chuckled and closed the distance between them, kissing her until her head swam, and she had to grab hold of his shoulder to right her spinning world. As they broke apart, he said, "What else?"

With a smile, she continued, "You are my best friend. As confused as I've been over the last few months, when I'm with you, everything seems clear, and I'm at peace."

"That's quite a responsibility, Josephine," he said, growing serious.

"It is, I know, but… We can do this together, Martin. I want to marry you and have babies with you because I love you, with all my heart and soul."

He cupped her face in his hands, smiled, and nearly shouted, "Yes, yes, yes, Josephine Galena Valencia. I'd be honored to be your husband."

At the loud sounds of their joy, the baby stopped nursing and let out a querulous, mewling noise. They both laughed at that, and Martin reached out and caressed Josephine's cheek. "I've always loved you. And I was really hoping we could do a lot of inappropriate things together," he said as his half grin broadened into a welcoming smile that lit his crystal-blue eyes with joy and laughter.

She laughed and tangled her fingers in his hair. Gently cupping the back of his neck, she drew him near again and whispered against his lips, "You're my best friend and my true love. I—"

He cut her off with the determined press of his lips against hers, showing her just how much he needed her. How much he cherished her as he kissed her over and over again, until they were both breathless and broke apart, laughing and smiling.

"How soon can we get married?" Josephine said.

With another grin that made her heart skip a beat, Martin said, "Whenever it is, it will never be soon enough for me."

Aw. You see, my friends? True love wins out in the end, just like in Josephine's beloved Jane Austen novels! But what about that elusive Sin Sombra? I cannot believe we have seen the last of her!

✳

In the Valencia household things got back to normal much sooner than expected. By the next morning Alberta was off to work, Martin had dropped by to see Josephine and Marcos before going to the Pinkerton office, and Zara and Ronaldo were helping Josephine change the baby's diaper.

"I tell you, there is something wrong with Marcaldo, because it is impossible for anything to smell that bad," Ronaldo began as he waved his hand over the diaper to dispel the stink.

Josephine wrinkled her nose and grimaced. "I think *Papi* may be right. This smells too bad to be normal."

Zara rolled her eyes. With no wasted motions, she quickly dispatched the offending diaper into a special laundry pail, cleaned and rediapered Marcos, and handed him to Josephine. "He is just fine. Once he's eating regular food, it won't be as bad."

"I hope that won't be too long from now," Ronaldo said and eagerly held his hands out for the baby. At Zara's questioning glance, he said, "I want to make up for not being here for you and Josephine."

Zara shook her head, chuckled, and playfully whipped him with a clean diaper. "If you want to make up, you'll learn to change a dirty diaper."

Josephine sat at the kitchen table, loving the easy exchange between her mother and father. They were clearly content, and it was impossible not to see that there was still affection between them and maybe more. She was hopeful for that since Ronaldo intended to stay in Miami with his troupe for the next few months.

A loud knock drew their attention, and Josephine shuffled to the door, her body still tender. "Come in," she called out, not wanting to keep whomever it was waiting.

Rake stepped inside holding a bouquet of flowers and a hand-sewn stuffed monkey doll. "I just wanted to see how you and the baby were doing."

"We're doing fine, thank you." She smiled and beckoned him in farther, shutting the door. "*Mami. Papi.* Rake and I need to talk," she said and inclined her head toward the back veranda.

Ronaldo crossed his arms and said, "Well, of course you need to talk. Especially now that you and Martin—"

He let out an oomph and stopped as Zara elbowed him powerfully. "Let's step outside for some fresh air, Ronaldo," her mother said.

Ronaldo's eyes opened in understanding. "Oh, yes, of course. Of course."

After he and Zara hurried outside, Rake looked at her, puzzlement warring with concern on his handsome features. "Now that you and Martin…"

"Are getting married," she finished for him and then quickly added, "He still loves me. And I still love him."

"And you have no issue with the fact that he was dead set on proving I was a crime boss even though I wasn't?" he shot back and dragged his fingers through his thick hair. Tossing the bouquet and toy onto the kitchen table, he jammed his hands on his hips and began to pace. "And what about his job? It's dangerous work. Can you handle that?" Rake challenged.

Josephine arched a brow and, in a tone as cold as she could manage, said, "It wasn't Martin's job that put Marcos in danger. It was your stepmother, as I recall."

Rake muttered a curse beneath his breath and returned to stand before her. "What can he give you that I can't? What can he offer you?"

She sighed. "He's a good man, Rake. One who risked his life to save our son, or have you forgotten that so quickly?"

Her words were like a pin in a balloon, and he immediately deflated. "You're serious about this? Because I meant what I said, Josephine. I've never stopped loving you." He reached out to trace a fingertip along Marcos's tiny face. "This is what I want. Our family."

"I know. But I am serious," she said, no doubt in her tone. "I love Martin, and I know he will do anything to make our marriage work.

Including letting you be a part of Marcos's life. Can you say the same?"

Rake blew out a breath and shook his head. "If you were my wife, I wouldn't share you with anyone else."

Josephine took hold of one of Rake's hands and held it close. "I care for you, Rake, but my heart belongs to Martin. I need you to accept that, because I can't have animosity between you in front of Marcos. Can you do that? Can you be just my friend?"

He didn't answer for a long moment, but then he said, "I don't want to play second fiddle to Martin when it comes to my son. Can you handle that? Can he?"

"I would never hinder your relationship with Marcos," she said. Because she had utter faith in Martin and his selflessness, she said, "Neither will Martin. Can we all try to make this work?"

A long moment rife with uncertainty followed until Rake finally nodded. "I will try, Josephine. For you and for Marcos."

She smiled and squeezed his hand to reassure him. "Would you like to give your son that toy now?"

At her words, the baby gurgled, right on cue, and Rake smiled. "Yes, I would."

She watched him give their son yet another toy, his first of undoubtedly many. Rake had changed her life forever in so many ways. He'd dared her to dream and challenged her to discover what was truly in her heart. A heart full of love for Martin and the baby and yes, Rake, but not in that way. A life full with a family that was finally complete. Martin, Marcos, Zara, Alberta, Ronaldo, and yes, Rake. Life was truly wonderful.

Wonderful, yes, but let's go back a bit. Second fiddle? A man like Rake? Never. But enough about that. It's time to plan a wedding. And what about Ronaldo and Zara? They seemed rather friendly, didn't they? Could it be we'll soon be having a second Valencia wedding?

Chapter Nineteen

Three Months Later

(Which was not soon enough for either Josephine or Martin and way too soon as far as Rake was concerned)

Her grandmother smoothed the satin and lace over Josephine's hips. The fabric had aged to the color of the French vanilla ice cream the Regal Sol served in its dining room and smelled of the gardenias her *abuela* had placed in the trunk where it was stored. "It's beautiful, *Abuela*."

Alberta's eyes misted with tears as she stood behind Josephine and glanced into the cheval mirror. She rested her hands on Josephine's shoulders and smiled. "You look lovely. I am so happy that my wedding dress fits you."

Josephine ran her hands along the skirt of the gown and met her grandmother's gaze in the mirror. "I can't imagine getting married in anything else."

Zara rushed in a second later with a length of light blue satin ribbon and a silver tiara. "You have your something old and now something new and something blue," she said, madly waving both in the air.

She stood next to Alberta and artfully tucked the ribbon around the bun at the top of Josephine's head, and then twined the ribbon with some of her dark curls. After, she secured the silver tiara, a bridal gift from Ronaldo, onto the top of Josephine's head and like Alberta, stared into the mirror at the beautiful portrait of three generations of Valencia women.

"*Mi'ja*, I am so happy for you. Martin is such a lucky man," Zara said.

"A very lucky man," Alberta confirmed with a nod.

Josephine met their gazes, her eyes growing watery as she stared at her two best friends—besides Martin, of course. "I'm the one who's lucky to have you both in my life."

A knock came at the door. Zara hopped excitedly. "That must be Ronaldo. He was bringing a carriage around to get you. I'll go let him in."

Her father, God bless him, had been as demanding in helping her plan her wedding as he had been when arranging for the arrival of his troupe. Note after note had arrived via messenger with suggestions for the wedding concerning the music, venue, food, and guests for the big event. She'd understood that he was just Ronaldo being Ronaldo while also trying to make up for his absence for so much of her life.

At the sound of a footstep at her door, she turned, but it wasn't her father. It was Rake.

"I wasn't expecting you." She glanced at her grandmother and said, "Could we have a minute, *Abuela*."

With a regal tilt of her head, her *abuela* walked toward the door. When she reached it, she raised her index finger and nearly jabbing it into his face, she scolded Rake. "Do not even think of making our Josephine cry on such a special day."

Rake stayed clear of that condemning finger, but when Alberta exited, he closed the door behind her and stared at her for long seconds.

"What is it, Rake? Is something wrong with Marcos?" Lucia had offered to watch him that morning so that Josephine could prepare for the wedding. Josephine had agreed because she knew the other woman was still feeling guilt after allowing him to be kidnapped. She wanted Lucia to know that she trusted her.

"You look so, so beautiful, Josephine," he said, but then shook his head, as if to shake out cobwebs, and plunged on. "But no, there is nothing wrong. I just wanted to congratulate you."

"You did?" In the months leading up to the wedding, they had worked out a schedule so Rake could spend time with Marcos. But there was still a great deal of awkwardness between the men, so the well wishes were a surprise.

He reached for her hands and took them into his. "During these last few months, seeing you together, I realized Martin is the man who will make you happiest. It was hard to admit that to myself, but he's a good man, an honorable man. I know he's the right choice for you. And for Marcos. I know he loves our son."

Pleased, she cradled his cheek and offered him an indulgent smile. "Thank you, Rake. I appreciate how hard it must have been for you to say that."

He laughed roughly and looked down. "You can't even begin to imagine. I love you, Josephine, and I always will. But," he exhaled and shook his head, "I need to move on with my life. So I've been thinking about opening a new Regal Sol over in South Beach for those people who prefer the shore to the city. I'll have to buy some land from Mr. Collins, and it may take some time to develop the area, but I think it's going to be a great location in the future."

"Rake, that's wonderful." She rose on tiptoes and brushed a platonic kiss on his cheek. "But I thought that finances were difficult, especially with your…other businesses shutting down."

"Well, actually," he smiled sheepishly, "I hadn't realized that my shares in the railroad had grown dramatically over the last six years. The bank was willing to take them as collateral if I sold them the railcar as well. Since I have things to keep me in Miami and won't be traveling all that much, it didn't seem like such a bad idea to sell it to the bank."

She smiled, happy that Rake was turning things around.

"Josephine? Ronaldo is here," her mother said through the thin wooden planks of the door, nervous energy coloring her words.

Rake offered her his arm and walked her out and to the front of the cottage where Ronaldo stood in the center of a carriage, but not just any carriage. An elegant black landau trimmed with gold leaf sat at the curb. There were two footmen in Regal Sol uniforms sitting behind the passenger area. A team of two handsome black horses waited anxiously, pawing the ground while a postilion rode the near wheel horse to control them.

"*Mi'ja*, your carriage awaits," Ronaldo called out in a theatrical boom and tapped his silver-headed cane on the landau floor, causing the horses to prance some more until the postilion had them in check.

Her father wore a black tailcoat over a lavender vest embroidered with silver threads and black pants with a faint silver stripe. A tall pewter-colored top hat banded with a lavender ribbon sat jauntily on his head.

"He is quite a spectacle isn't he?" Rake said, but the affection in his voice was obvious.

Ronaldo stepped down from the landau and helped Josephine up into the carriage. Then the footmen hopped to the ground and assisted Alberta and finally Zara, who were wearing gowns that Ronaldo had helped them find among those in the troupe's collection of dresses. But she knew Ronaldo must have bought the gowns and snuck them in with the rest of the clothing, because they were clearly brand-new and fit the two women perfectly.

Ronaldo stared at Rake, as if questioning if he were joining them, but the other man waved him off. "This is Josephine's special day. I'll meet you back at the Regal Sol."

She leveled one last glance of warm affection at Marcos's father, and marveled when she realized that's how she would always think of Rake now. He was no longer the exciting and dashing stranger who'd encouraged her to be brave and follow her dreams, nor the playfully enticing railroad tycoon to whom she'd surrendered her precious flower. Now he was just Rake, Marcos's father. And more importantly, he was family.

Her father hopped back into the landau and took a seat beside her. With a rap of his cane on the floor of the carriage, he bellowed, "Please take us to the Regal Sol. My daughter is getting married today!"

Immediately the postilion slapped the reins against the horse's flanks and they were off.

❄

Martin grasped his hands together in front of him, nervously awaiting Josephine's arrival.

He glanced toward the back, taking in all the bouquets of orange roses, poinciana flowers, and orchids that graced the end of each row of seats. Near the door, Francesca and Liana held similar bouquets, plus a larger one for Josephine.

A murmur rose up from the crowd near the back of the rotunda that Rake had graciously offered to Josephine and her family for the wedding. Alberta had wanted them to get married in a Catholic church but since Josephine had just had a baby out of wedlock with a married man, and he wasn't Catholic, the Regal Sol seemed like an appropriate substitute. Especially since Father Juan would be there to provide the necessary holiness to the most blessed sacrament of marriage.

Martin's heartbeat sped up, eager to see her, but only Ronaldo entered. At his arrival, the members of his troupe and Ronaldo's other guests clapped. He waved at them regally and hurried toward where Martin waited.

"Are you ready, my friend?" Ronaldo asked.

Martin had asked himself that a thousand times in the last few days as the wedding preparations wound down. Was he ready to become an official father to little Marcos? As he glanced at Lucia holding the baby in the front row, he knew the answer to that question was a resounding yes.

Was he ready to spend the rest of his life with his dear Josephine?

"Martin? Are you having—what do they call them—cold toes?" Ronaldo asked, drawing him away from his thoughts.

No, he didn't have cold feet. *Not at all,* he thought, and said, "I am more than ready to marry your daughter, Ronaldo."

"I am glad, because I like you, Martin. I really like you and you will make a very good husband for my little girl." Ronaldo theatrically gulped back a sob and sniffed. "Weddings make me very emotional."

At that moment, Alberta and Zara came to the door of the rotunda and a heartfelt sigh escaped the man beside him. He snuck a quick peek at Ronaldo and noted the intensity of his gaze as it settled on Josephine's mother.

"And what about you, my friend? Will there soon be nuptials in your future?"

Ronaldo smiled. "Remember what I told you that night in the saloon? The present will take care of the future, so for now, Zara and I will enjoy our time together and see where it leads."

A louder murmur arose from the crowd as Francesca and Liana stepped outside.

Ronaldo wrapped an arm around him and said, "I think it's time for me to get my daughter, Martin."

Martin smiled and said, "Please do me a favor, Ronaldo."

At that, Josephine's father glanced at him, puzzled.

"Please don't take too long."

Martin couldn't wait to get started on the rest of his life with his new wife and child.

Chapter Twenty

Josephine hugged Francesca and Liana as her two friends swarmed her when the footman helped her down from the landau parked at the door of the rotunda.

"You look beautiful," they both said in unison and oohed and aahed over her grandmother's gown, the satiny ribbons, and gleaming silver tiara.

"You both look lovely as well." Her friends were wearing matching outfits in pale shades of lavender and although the color wasn't traditional and should have clashed with the bright-colored tropical flowers in the bouquets, there were enough hints of purple and pink in the orchids to harmonize the hues.

Francesca handed her a larger floral arrangement with the same combination of flowers, and a second later, her father slipped back through the entry to the rotunda, his smile as bright as one of Mr. Edison's lightbulbs. He stepped to her and took hold of both her hands. "*Mi'ja*, I am so happy for you."

She smiled. "I am happy, too, *Papi*. I am so glad you could be here the last few months and for this very special event. It would not have been the same without you."

With an accepting nod, he said, "No, it would not. But I plan on being here for many more such events, Josephine. Miami needs a theater where we can bring culture, such as myself, to the masses and showcase local talent, like my wonderful Zara. So if you don't mind, I'll be staying around a great deal longer."

Joy suffused her at his revelation. Rising on tiptoes, she kissed his cheek and said, "I won't mind at all, *Papi*. It will give us all a chance to get to know each other better."

As they broke apart, Ronaldo sniffled and dabbed a handkerchief to the corner of his eye. Then he held his arm out. "If you are ready, Josephine."

With a broad smile, she said, "I am."

"Ladies." Ronaldo directed her friends to the door of the rotunda and as they stood there, the chattering of the crowd was replaced by silence as an organist began to play. With that cue, Francesca took her first step down the aisle and, a few seconds later, Liana followed.

She was so excited, her heart was beating as if she'd run a race and her knees grew rubbery. Ronaldo offered support as they walked to the doorway together and watched her friends take the last few steps to the stage where Martin waited along with Father Juan from their local parish.

Martin, she thought, and though it hardly seemed possible, her heart beat even faster at the sight of him. He was dressed much like Ronaldo, every bit the gentleman, and so, so handsome. He'd cut his hair, and it was groomed back from his face with pomade, accenting the chiseled lines of his freshly shaven jaw. The black, silver, and lavender colors of his clothing made his eyes the color of the waters of Biscayne Bay in the early morning hours, just as a new day was about to begin.

Just as this is a new beginning for us, she thought, and as she peered down the aisle, it was as if the sun was rising where Martin stood, growing brighter and brighter. The light bathing him and Father Juan spilled down the aisle toward her, suffusing the entire room with its luminescence and calling her to start her new life.

With a subtle shift of his arm, Ronaldo urged her to take the first step down the aisle and the organist switched to the traditional wedding march.

As with everything Ronaldo, the march down the aisle was slow and theatrical, which was killing her since she was impatient to be with Martin and start their wedded lives together. But the almost imperial march with her father allowed her to see the many people gathered there to celebrate with them. Members of his troupe and a number of her coworkers, like Mr. Adams. Family, some of whom had come from as far as New Jersey for the wedding. Even one lone representative of the Venezuela contingent who had sailed in just a day earlier. Lucia, holding little Marcos. Rake beside Penelope, which made her wonder if a reconciliation was maybe possible for the two. Rake deserved to find his happily ever after as well.

Martin's parents, whom she'd only met for the first time a week earlier, sat at one side of the aisle along with a few of his other Ohio relatives, but not his brother who apparently wasn't one to do much for family.

Zara and Alberta sat in the front row opposite Martin's family. Her *mami* and *abuela*, tears gleaming in their eyes, looked so happy, and she was once again grateful that for family, for her, they would do anything.

Ronaldo stumbled a bit and when she looked at him, she realized that it was because all his attention had been on Zara, much as her mother's gaze had shifted to stare at him longingly. She smiled and thought that another wedding would not be all that far off in the future.

A second later, Ronaldo turned to kiss her cheek and then guided her to where Martin waited by the makeshift altar on the stage, still bathed in the light of the rising sun of a new beginning.

As Martin watched her, his crystal-blue eyes shone as bright as diamonds and twinkled with joy. He grinned that quirky, lopsided grin that made her heart skip a beat, and she walked toward him without hesitation, confident in his love.

Ronaldo clasped Martin's hand and then placed her hand in his. Her skin tingled and warmed as she twined her fingers with Martin's.

"Embrace your future, Josephine," her father whispered.

She smiled and kissed his cheek. "Thank you, *Papi*."

As Ronaldo stepped away and took a spot beside Zara, he slipped his hand into her mother's, offering support.

Josephine glanced up at Martin. "Are you ready?"

"More than you can ever know."

Together they took the final steps to the makeshift altar covered in pale lavender silk embroidered with Josephine's and Martin's initials. More flowers sat on either side of the altar, flanking Martin's family Bible where Father Juan would record their union and in the future, the children they would have.

Father Juan strolled around the altar, stood before them, and raised his hands in greeting. "We welcome you all to witness the wedding of Josephine Galena Valencia and Martin Joseph Cadden, Jr. Let us begin…"

The priest asked her and Martin about their intention to marry and whether they consented freely and without reservation to enter into marriage. At their affirmative answers, he continued. "Since it is your intention to enter into the covenant of holy matrimony, please join your right hands, and declare your consent before God and His church."

Josephine inhaled deeply before speaking her vows, wanting her voice to be sure and steady. "I, Josephine, take you, Martin, to be my husband. I promise to be true to you in good times and in bad, in sickness and in health. I will love you and honor you for all the days of my life or until death do us part."

Martin's hands shook in hers, and he heaved a huge sigh of relief. Then he recited his vows, his eyes shining wetly. *"Yo, Martin, te tomo a ti, Josephine, como mi esposa. Prometo serte fiel en lo próspero y en lo adverso, en la salud y en la enfermedad. Amarte y respetarte todos los días de mi vida."*

Overwhelmed, Josephine's heart clenched as he shot a sideways glance at Alberta, who was beaming from ear to ear. "Your *abuela* taught me," he said with a wink.

Smiling, Father Juan raised his hands heavenward. "O Heavenly Father, we ask you to bless and consecrate this couple in their love for each other. What God has joined together, let no man put asunder." After a pause, he asked, "Do you have the rings?"

Ronaldo popped up from his seat and rushed to the altar. "I, Ronaldo de la Sera, am the bearer of the rings." With a flourish, he handed one to her and one to Martin. "Please continue," he said with a bow and returned to his seat.

"Let us now exchange rings as a sign of your commitment to each other," Father Juan intoned.

Josephine clasped Martin's hand. "With this ring, I thee wed," she said, and with a slight tremor, she slipped the simple gold band onto his ring finger. It seemed to gleam and sparkle with light as she placed it there.

Martin raised her hand. "With this ring, I thee wed," he said and eased the ring onto her finger and, for good measure, lifted her hand to kiss the wedding band.

Oh my, oh my! Now comes the good part.

"Heavenly Father. Bless and consecrate this couple and the love they have for each other. It is my pleasure to now pronounce you man and wife. You may kiss the bride."

Martin wrapped his arm around her waist and drew her near, almost too slowly. Too patiently, and she was feeling anything but patient.

She met him halfway, kissing him. Opening her mouth on his as he deepened the kiss and dipped her—

He dipped her!

—pressing his body into hers as Ronaldo clapped loudly and shouted out happily, "I taught him that!"

They broke apart laughing and smiling, and kissed again, relishing the moment for which they'd been waiting for nearly three years.

As they walked down the aisle, the organist launched into a celebratory march and a choir made up of some of Ronaldo's troupe

began to sing, wishing them well. Urging them on to their new journey in life.

"Go, be blessed," they sang. "Go, be immodest. Inappropriate,"
she thought they sang as the hallelujahs in the chorus. She shook her
head to make sure she'd heard right, but as she listened, the chorus
of real hallelujahs resumed. Josephine smiled and walked toward her
new life with her new husband.

*Oh my gosh, it really happened! And now, just a little longer for
the important moment they've also been waiting for!*

Chapter Twenty-One

Dusk had started to fall by the time the reception was winding down, but Martin and Josephine were determined to spend their first night as husband and wife in their new home. Alone thankfully, since Rake, Lucia, and Penelope—yes, even Penelope—had agreed to watch Marcos with Zara, Alberta, and Ronaldo all staying in the hotel to offer support.

Luckily, their homestead was not far out of town, and the sun had just set when they turned down the lane to their new home. An immensely full harvest moon lit the way on the final quarter mile to where the large cottage sat amid the orange groves. The bright light beckoned them to the start of their new life together in their new home.

The main portion of the home with the kitchen, dining room, parlor, bathroom, and a bedroom was finished and partially furnished. In the next few months, as monies allowed, they would add on the other bedroom and nursery, as well as the room where she could write.

With help from some of his fellow Pinkertons and even Ronaldo—or rather, entertainment from Ronaldo, who had shown them how he had once played a carpenter in a skit—Martin had spent every spare moment working on their home. He'd had more time since the Sin Sombra case had gone cold with Sondra's disappearance. It was believed she'd left the country, and they had yet to find any trace of where she might have gone. The Woman with No Shadow was truly a fitting moniker.

But the only shadow on Josephine's mind right now was that of her new home glowing in welcome in the moonlight. "It's so lovely," she said as the carriage pulled up in front of their home.

"Not nearly as lovely as you," Martin said and drew her close for a kiss that went on and on until the horse pawed the ground impatiently.

"Give me just a few minutes, my darling," Martin said and quickly set about unhitching the horse and turning him loose in a nearby corral that he'd built. Being a farm boy at heart, he had also built a small barn and chicken coop.

Josephine had never pictured herself on a farm, but the idea of fresh eggs and milk held some appeal. But not as much appeal as the man swaggering toward her, a very sexy grin on his face and his gaze filled with the promise of what he planned for that night.

As he reached the carriage, he held out his hand to steady her as she rose and took the first step down, but then she found herself scooped up into his arms. She laughed as he whirled them around playfully before rushing to the door of their new home. He fumbled one-handedly for a moment with the lock, but then kicked the door open and strode over the threshold with her.

"Welcome to our new life, Mrs. Cadden," he said and kissed her again.

They stood there, kissing, until Martin gently released her and let her slide down his body. There was no doubt he was more than ready for their first very special night together.

As they broke apart, Josephine cradled his jaw and skimmed her thumb across his cheekbone. Meeting his gaze, she said, "It seems like we've waited for this forever."

Martin laid his forehead against hers and whispered, "I cannot wait any longer."

He shut the door and twined his fingers with hers, creating warmth with that simple gesture. With a gentle tug, he urged her to the narrow hallway that led to their bedroom in the rear of the cottage. They nearly ran there, laughing again until they reached the bed and time seemed to stand still.

The faced each other, expectant, hesitant, and Josephine took the first step. She eased her hands beneath the lapels of his frock coat and slipped them upward to ease the jacket from his shoulders.

Martin grabbed the jacket and tossed it to the side while she hastily undid the buttons on his vest, her hands trembling and seemingly uncoordinated on the last couple of closures until with a chuckle, Martin ripped the vest open. Buttons flew off and pinged on the wooden floor.

She jerked off his tie and tugged his trouser braces down while Martin's shirt met the same fate as the vest, fabric tearing and buttons flying until he stood before her bare-chested.

He is so beautiful, she thought and laid her hands on the broad swell of his pectoral muscles before skimming them down his lean washboard stomach to the fastening of his pants.

He grabbed her hands then, his touch commanding, but tender. "I don't know if I'll be able to wait once you do that," he said and the proof of his desire was greatly evident beneath the fabric of his pants.

"Then please hurry, and help me get undressed," she said, then whirled, presenting him with the long line of tiny buttons along the back of her gown.

"A gentleman never says no to a lady," he whispered.

He eased his hands beneath the satin and lace and slipped the gown from her body, leaving a trail of kisses along her shoulders and then down her spine as the dress fell to the ground, the soft, aged fabric puddling around her feet. Grasping her hips, he tenderly urged her to turn around and step from the pile on the floor.

As she did so, Martin worked free the ties of the corset she wore. "Please, Martin," she nearly keened.

"You are everything I've ever wanted," he said, continuing to undress her down to her thin cotton shift that left nothing to the imagination.

He bent and was drawing the hem of the shift upward when a loud creak came from down the hallway. They paused abruptly, but only silence could be heard. Returning to undressing her, Martin skimmed his hand up over her hip just as a louder thump echoed, the sound of a loose floorboard shifting.

Josephine started, her heart pounding with surprise instead of passion. *Was someone in the house?*

"Stay here," Martin said and turned to investigate, but then he cursed beneath his breath, and she immediately realized why. He had left his gun and badge in a kitchen drawer to avoid taking them to the wedding ceremony.

Fear gripped her hard, and she laid a hand on his arm. "Martin, don't go."

He put an index finger to his lips and whispered, "I will be fine. Please stay here."

Gingerly he grabbed a poker from the fireplace in their room and tiptoed into the hallway.

As the soft scuff of a footfall reached his ears, Martin no longer had any doubt that someone was in their home.

He inched closer and closer to the main rooms, gripped with fear. If he was lucky, whoever was out there wouldn't find his weapon. *Let me be lucky,* he thought, but as he heard the scrape of wood against wood signaling that a drawer was being opened, he realized this might not be his night to gamble.

Martin had been in his share of dangerous situations during his time as a Pinkerton, but he had never expected that one of the most dangerous times of his life would be in his own home.

The hackles rose on the back of his neck and his heart pumped so wildly, he worried the intruder might hear. Moonlight streamed in through the cottage's windows, casting the shadow of someone in a hooded cloak onto the wooden floor.

He took another step, wincing as a loose floorboard creaked beneath his foot this time. If he survived the night, he intended to remedy that.

Suddenly the light from a lantern flared to life in the living room and the intruder beckoned him with, "You can come out, Detective Cadden. There's no use hiding."

Sondra. Sin Sombra.

He stepped out of the mouth of the hallway, but stayed close as he realized that Sondra had located his gun and was pointing it in his direction. No matter what, she'd have to go through him to get to Josephine.

"What are you doing here, Sondra?" he asked, perplexed about why the crime boss would reappear after so many months of being virtually invisible.

"I was planning to leave for good, you know. Pin it all on Ernesto and start over somewhere else with Lu—" She stopped and growled with frustration. "Well it, doesn't matter now, does it? You've made that impossible. Now I just want plain old vengeance for the trouble you've put me through," she said.

"You may want vengeance, but I want justice, Sin Sombra," he said calmly and loudly, hoping that Josephine would hear the conversation and the name of their intruder. There were at least two windows in the bedroom through which she could make an escape, and he intended to keep Sondra talking so Josephine could do just that.

Sondra laughed that evil cackle that he'd heard the night of her escape on Rake's yacht. It sounded maniacal, especially as she said, "Justice, how sweet! Sadly, I think vengeance will be mine tonight. You and your newlywed wife. How tragic that your first day together will be your last."

No, no, no. This cannot be happening (although of course I knew that we hadn't heard the last of Sin Sombra). What will our intrepid detective do now?

Martin's mind raced as he tried to calculate if he could reach her before the bullet took him down, but the distance was too great. "Why, Sondra? Can you just tell me why?"

"Why?" she asked, and followed with that deranged laugh once again before she started talking, giving him the time to prepare for action.

"Do you have any idea what it has been like for me? Having to pretend to be the doting dutiful wife of Ernesto Solvino when I've been the real brains behind the Solvino empire? It was me—*me*—who convinced Ernesto to buy the Palm Beach property," she said, tapping her chest angrily, almost maniacally.

It let him take a small step toward her as she continued her rant. "It was *me* who knew Rake's little hotel and marina with its secret tunnels would be the perfect base from which to expand my reach to all of the Florida territory."

Keep her talking, he thought. "But all those deaths…those innocent people… Why did you kill Slayton?"

"Innocent? Hardly," she scoffed, still brandishing the gun in Martin's general direction. "Insignificant lowlifes and toadies keen for fast money. Unfortunately for them, they either got greedy or a little bit too close. Slayton saw me leaving the tunnel at the Regal Sol and followed me. I couldn't let him expose me as the real Sin Sombra."

With another tiny move, Martin edged out into the living room carefully, trying to draw Sondra farther from the back of the cottage. "So why did you take Marcos then? He's just an innocent infant!"

"I was this close to making my final move," she said, bringing her fingers together on her free hand. "But I had to make a clean escape. You were too close, always sniffing around the hotel. I knew that if I kidnapped the child, you would focus all your attention on rescuing the little brat."

"You guessed right," Martin said, creeping an inch closer.

Sondra huffed with annoyance. "But I didn't guess that you would put things together so quickly. I was certain that Rake would go to you to clear his name once I planted suspicion in him that his father might be Sin Sombra. Then I was going to kill Ernesto and leave the country. But you've been a little too clever, Detective. The other Pinkertons are no match for me. Once I take you out of the picture, I'll escape for good." A frown crossed her face suddenly and she cleared her throat before continuing. "Start again on my own this time." Sondra sniffed, but raised her pistol, her voice going steely once more. "So, now you have to die."

He realized that he had run out of time. Gripping the poker tightly, he took another larger step toward her.

"Stop right there, Detective," Sondra warned and waved the weapon around dangerously. "Drop the poker."

He wanted to resist but slowly bent to lay the weapon on the floor, wanting to eat up more time to allow Josephine to flee.

Sondra smiled, but it didn't reach up to her eyes which were as cold and flat as a snake's. Then, to Martin's horror, in a singsong voice, she called out, "Oh, Josephine! Dearest Josephine, come out, come out wherever you are!"

Oh dear. Remember before when we talked about Martin loving Josephine till he drew his very last breath? I sure hope that isn't happening anytime soon! Could fate really be that cruel to forever part these two lovebirds on their wedding night?

Josephine had pressed herself to the wall by the bedroom door where it was impossible to miss the entire exchange with Sondra Solvino.

She knew that Martin had been trying to keep Sin Sombra engaged so that she might escape through one of the bedroom windows, but she was not about to let Martin handle this alone. They had pledged to protect each other just hours earlier, and she intended to do just that.

But she didn't know how.

Martin had taken the only possible weapon in the room—the poker. There was nothing else with any weight except…

She reached out and grabbed her precious snow globe from the rosewood occasional table by the door. There was some heft to it.

Suddenly, her little devil popped onto her shoulder. "Think about Marcos, Josephine. He needs a mother, so don't do anything foolish!"

Her angel booted the devil off with a swift kick and said, "You're a fighter, Josephine. It's the only way to save Martin. You can do it."

I have *to do it,* she thought. She couldn't let the man she loved with all her heart die because of fear. She tucked that hand holding the snow globe into the fabric folds of her shift and inched down the hall, careful to keep to the shadows until she could see Sondra, holding a gun on Martin.

"Come out, come out," Sondra singsonged once more and angled her head to peer into the hallway.

With another step, Josephine moved closer and drew the attention of both Martin and Sondra even though she was still in the shadows.

"Now that's a good girl, Josephine. Step out here where I can see you before I have to hurt your dear Martin," Sondra said and gestured with the gun for Josephine to enter the room.

"Stay back," Martin urged and raised his hand to warn her, but she wasn't about to listen.

"I'll come out when snow falls in Miami."

At her words, Martin half turned and gazed at her quizzically. With the faintest movement, she drew the snow globe out slightly, and Martin nodded.

"Well, then snow might be falling right…" He paused for a moment, and she prepared for the shot of a lifetime. "Now!" he shouted, and she heaved the snow globe with all her might at Sondra.

It struck Sin Sombra smack in the middle of her upper chest and shattered, water and bits of glass and ceramic flying everywhere. The force of the blow had her reeling, but even before that, Martin launched himself at the woman.

He tackled her to the ground and the impact knocked the gun out of her hand and sent it skittering across the floor. With a quick roll, Martin pinned Sondra to the floor, but she kicked and flailed her arms, rocking from side to side to try to displace him.

Josephine raced for the gun and scooped it up just as Martin jammed his knee into Sondra's back, driving the air from her lungs. That slowed her and allowed him to grab one arm and then another, pinning them behind her back. But the woman continued to struggle until Josephine shouted, "Stop or I'll shoot, Sondra. And don't think for a moment that I won't." Sondra didn't need to know that she had no earthly idea of how to fire a revolver.

Sondra finally quieted and glared at her, giving Martin time to yank the braces off his trousers and use them to tie her hands together behind her back. Once she was secured, he hauled her to her feet and for good measure, used the other brace to secure her hands to the midrail and spindles on a nearby kitchen chair.

As he stepped away, the crunch of glass and porcelain beneath his feet drew their attention to the snow globe that lay in pieces on the wooden floor.

He picked up what remained of the base and walked over to her.

"I'm so sorry, Martin, but it was the only thing I could think to grab," she said and glanced at what was left of his wonderful gift.

He grabbed hold of her hand and ran his thumb along the gleaming gold band he'd placed there hours earlier. "Seems like a worthwhile sacrifice for a lifetime together, don't you think?"

She smiled, rose up on tiptoes, and whispered against his lips, "I most definitely do."

Can it be, my friends? Is Sin Sombra truly vanquished at long last? Will Martin and Josephine finally get their long-awaited happy ending?

Well, of course they will! Did you really think Martin was going to die? Come on, don't you people know this is a romance novel? Bring on the HEA!

Chapter Twenty-Two

It wasn't quite how she'd expected to spend her wedding night.

It had taken a couple of hours to deal with Sin Sombra. They'd bundled Sondra onto the back of their carriage and taken her to the Miami Pinkerton office. The agents on duty had been shocked to see who Martin had in custody, but had worked quickly to get Sondra in a cell and bring in Martin's boss to oversee all the details of her arrest.

"Amazing, Detective Cadden," the man had said and patted him on the back. "Outstanding job."

"Thank you, but if you don't mind, I'd like to get my wife back home since it's getting late," he said and glanced in her direction.

"Well, yes, especially since...well, it's your wedding night, so I understand," his boss said. "Take the day off tomorrow, Detective. We'll start working up a report based on what you've told us and you can fill in any blanks later."

"I appreciate that, sir," he said.

"Yes, we really do appreciate your thoughtfulness, sir," Josephine said, grabbing hold of Martin's hand and almost dragging him out of the Pinkerton office.

But when they got in the carriage, Martin surprised her by turning it in the direction of the Regal Sol instead of their home. At her questioning gaze, he said, "It's closer. I can't wait that long."

She laughed and leaned into him, kissing the side of his face. "I can't either."

The ride to the Regal Sol was blessedly short and in no time they were checked into a suite. Once inside, Martin pulled her close and kissed her while walking her at the same time toward the bed in the center of the room. At the edge of the bed, they faced each other, breathing heavily. Aware that they would no longer have to deny themselves what they had wanted for so long.

And I think it's time that we now close the door, only... Admit it! You want to see what happens next also!

As Martin shucked off his clothes and shoes, Josephine did the same, but with far less to remove he soon stood naked before her.

She sucked in a breath at the beauty of his body before her. "You... I... May I touch you, Martin?"

"Not yet. First I want to see you," he said and helped rid her of the last of her clothes until she stood naked before him. The heat of his gaze branded her as he passed it over her body, taking in the sight of her.

He laid his hand at her waist and drew her near, and Josephine trailed her hands up his abdomen to the muscles of his chest and laid her hand over his heart. A heart that beat unsteadily for her. And as her hand rested there, the heat of his love bathed her and spread throughout her body.

He bent his head and kissed her again while he caressed her, and she ran her hands along the powerful muscles of his shoulders, loving the feel of their strength and the restraint he was using for this first time together.

Time fell away as they continued to kiss and touch each other, but soon she needed more. She had waited too long to share her body and her heart with this very special man.

"I want you, Martin," she said and backed up to sit on the edge of the bed.

"I love you, Josephine. I will love you until I draw my last breath."

"And I love you, Martin. There is no man like you, my love."

At long last they joined together, moving in blissful synchronicity, soft cries of pleasure filling the night air as they rose higher and higher until her climax rushed over her.

"Martin," she screamed and dug her fingers into his strong muscles, needing his stability to keep her as the world spun crazily around her.

A moment later, he threw his head back and groaned as his release washed over his body. After he sucked in a deep breath, he braced his trembling arms on the bed at either side of her and gazed at her. "Are you all right?"

She smiled. "Better than all right, my husband."

Martin grinned and brushed back damp wisps of hair from her face. "I'm not sorry we waited, but now that we have… I'm not feeling very patient anymore. I'm not sure I'll ever be able to be patient again."

"Me either," she said with a chuckle and drew him down to her once more.

Well, well, well, since you've had your little thrill, now it's time to close the door so our Josephine and Martin can continue to make up for all that lost time, don't you think?

Epilogue

Two Months Later

Martin stood beside the mayor in the lobby of city hall. A journalist and photographer from *The Miami Metropolis* were at the front of the room along with Josephine's family, a contingent of politicians, and several Pinkerton staff including Martin's boss. Rake and his family had chosen to skip the event, trying to avoid any additional connection of the Solvino name with the infamous Sin Sombra.

Josephine watched with pride as the mayor raised the ribbon of the medal over Martin's head and her husband—*her husband!*—bent to make it easier for the shorter man. With the ribbon draped around his neck, the gold medal sat squarely in the center of his chest above his heart. A heart that she knew beat for her!

"The city of Miami owes you an immense debt of gratitude for your heroic actions in capturing the crime boss Sin Sombra and ridding our city of such evil," the mayor intoned ceremoniously.

"*That* is our hero up there," she said to baby Marcos and rocked him in her arms.

"And a wonderful man!" Alberta said with glee.

"Yes, he is. A wonderful man and my friend," Ronaldo said and clapped loudly before facing Zara. "Isn't he wonderful?" he said again.

"Yes, he is, Ronaldo, but so are you," Zara said and rose on tiptoes to kiss him.

Josephine's heart soared at their growing affection and hoped it would lead to more and soon.

Martin walked over to them a second later, slipped his arm around her waist, and drew her close for a kiss. "I missed you so, my darling."

Josephine laughed and playfully pushed him away. "We've only been apart for about an hour."

"Way too long," he teased and leaned down to brush a kiss on Marcos's forehead. "How are you doing, little one?" he said and took the baby from her arms with the ease of a man who had been doing it his whole life.

She wasn't sure if there was anything more touching—and enticing—than a powerful man holding an innocent baby so tenderly.

"We should get going," she said. With winter having arrived, night came earlier, but on top of that, she wanted to be alone with Martin and savor the freedom that the long winter night provided to be together. And although they'd been careful after their wedding night, it might be time to soon discuss adding to their family.

"Before you go," Zara said and reached into her purse. She drew out an envelope and handed it to her. "The postman delivered it this morning to the cottage."

Josephine peered at the envelope emblazoned with the name Crimson Romance, the publisher to whom she had sent her story so many months earlier.

"What is it, my darling?" Martin asked, peering over her shoulder at the envelope.

"I don't know," she said, not daring to guess at what it might say. Hands trembling, she tore open the envelope and pulled out the letter. The words jumped at her, and she had to read it several times to make sure she had not misunderstood. Glancing first at Martin and then at the rest of her family, she softly said, "They want to publish my story."

As her family reacted with jubilee, Martin hugged her and twirled her around, and she threw back her head and shouted this time, "They want to publish my story!"

Even after the congratulations were over and Martin, the baby, and she were in the carriage and heading home, she kept on repeating it. "They want to publish my story!"

"They most certainly do." Martin smiled happily and tucked the blanket tighter around her and the baby. It was an unseasonably cold winter day and the sky hung heavy with dark gray clouds that promised a storm was on the way.

Martin pushed the horses as fast as he could to avoid being caught in bad weather. The wind that whipped into the carriage had a bite to it, and Josephine huddled tight against him, tucking Marcos between them. Drawing comfort from Martin's presence and the heat of his body.

They arrived at their homestead in less than half an hour, and Josephine smiled as she took note of all the progress that had been made in the last few months. Catching Sin Sombra had come with an unexpected blessing—a monetary reward from the city that had allowed them to accelerate the work on their house. In another week or so, the rooms for Alberta and Zara, as well as a separate nursery for Marcos and her writing room, would soon be ready.

She sighed with happiness and with the peace that being with Martin had brought her the last few months. Peace and passion, an unexpected mix. Even now her body awoke with desire as Martin pulled the carriage up to the door of the cottage.

He helped her down and as she set foot on the ground, she noticed the fat, white flake that settled on the dark brown of Martin's sack suit. Peering upward, the cold kiss of another snowflake landed on her cheek and was quickly followed by several more.

Snow falling in Miami? She laughed, wrapped an arm around Martin's waist, and faced him. "Do you remember what you told me once?"

From the lopsided grin on Martin's lips, it was obvious he did. "I said I would love you until snow falls in Miami. Only I hate to disappoint you, Josephine."

He pulled her close, mindful of the baby caught between them. Tenderly cupping her cheek, he said, "I'm not going anywhere."

They came together, laughing and kissing. Grateful for the miracle they'd been given… Each other.

Ta-da! Now that's a happily ever after, my friends. What started so well and got so complicated has ended much as we all wanted… Well, except possibly Rake. But while one story is complete, there are still so many others waiting to be told. You just must be patient—always patient—and see what will happen next.

Acknowledgments

This book would not be possible without the help of my wonderful editor, Jeremy Howe, and everyone at Lorden + Gregor and Simon & Schuster. Big thanks to the city of Miami for giving me a rich history to draw from! Thank you to my oldest friend, Lina, who read multiple drafts of this book, even though she hates reading. Thank you to Marlene Donaldson, my mentor, for constantly pushing my limits. Thanks especially to my mom, dad, and *abuela*, and my son, Mateo: I love you and could never have done this without you.

And finally, my deepest gratitude to Rafael Solano, without whom this book wouldn't have been written. Thank you for being the first person who believed in me as a writer. Thank you for teaching me how to be brave.